Veil of Secrets

– KATHLEEN STEELE –

FASTPRINT PUBLISHING
PETERBOROUGH, ENGLAND

VEIL OF SECRETS

ISBN 978-184426-817-7

First published 2010 by
FASTPRINT PUBLISHING
Peterborough, England.

Printed by
www.printondemand-worldwide.com

My sincere thanks t all those who have helped to inspire this story as well as the places and events that provided the required stepping stones in its sequence

Chapter One

The dark tendrils of the night were already looming when that rowing boat left it's mooring and ventured out onto the Lake. Stacey Kershaw knew only too well that no mooring was allowed on the Island of Lady-Holme even if in truth one or two rowing boats had often taken advantage of picnicking there during the balmy weather, that indeed was the reason why she had persevered until nightfall before she had ventured out, for the visits of the tourists were casual and therefore quite different to her own intentions on that day. Besides with dusk now falling she firmly believed that those figures from the Hall would remain oblivious to her actions, a factor which could only be for the good! Therefore Stacey made to approach the Island silently and under cover of darkness when any warden of the Lake would also be otherwise occupied.

"An apt name for it I suppose!" The thought now of the Island's name ran through her head in a jingle like fashion as she allowed herself to be guided by those strategically placed buoys but then after all she was and never had been a lady, despite what the Island was called!

Still during her efforts to steer the boat across she mused upon the fact that she had found it remarkably easy to borrow the same from the Marina itself and because the craft was dependent upon oars there was no engine noise to disturb the tranquillity of the night air and there was nobody present to query her own presence down by the Lake at this God forsaken hour.

Ahead of her the trees had not yet reached their first full plumage of the year, a factor that had made it necessary for Steven to occupy the more central part of the Island where he could remain hidden and where he stood less chance of being spotted. And once again her thoughts turned upon his mission that he had explained was basically to get the information he held, as well as a wealth of other information to the relevant authorities whilst all the time those people who were currently imposing themselves upon a Management Course right here at the Hall were apparently determined to stop him!

Glancing back yet again as her craft nudged the shore, and still feeling the anxiety in case her own absence had been discovered, it was perhaps with a sense of relief that she noted that the Hall she had left behind was now in complete darkness, for now no lights served the place to indicate to anyone that the girl had gone missing. Yet even so Steven, it appeared, had been anxiously watching out for her arrival and even before she had a chance to moor the craft he had indicated that he was ready to try and make a break for it! Stacey swallowed hard as she now feverishly tried to remember whether she had completed all the relevant detail and the onward arrangements they had spoken of,

She supposed in one sense it was hardly surprising that the man wanted to get off an Island that was inhabited only by wild fowl and without such things as modern conveniences. Indeed there was not even some remote shelter from the elements at this place, and what was more, to have supplied such could have been easily spotted, and therefore the man had been lying low in the undergrowth towards the centre of that Island and simply praying that during this enforced respite the elements would not play foul upon him.

"Ready?" The word formulated upon her lips without a sound being uttered, She needed no sound for having guessed the question, even though it had not been uttered in so many words, he merely nodded as he emerged from that undergrowth and clambered into the vessel. At the time she could not see his features clearly but the stench of body odour indicated that the man had slept rough for the last few days. Indeed the stench attested her nostrils even as the craft was moving again, but this time it was moving around the other side of the Island and crossing the Lake now to the far side whilst still sheltered from view by the Lea of the hunted man's abode!

Well strange situations often attract strange bedfellows, she mused. But then she had not been rowing on the day she had first met Steve. In actuality she had been out walking the dog along the pathway that bordered the Lune valley. It was this peaceful setting that had been vandalised by having its peace rudely disturbed with the noise made by two crazy canoeists who appeared to be out in the river at the time more out of sheer enjoyment than with any serious intentions behind their activities. One of the two she had the misfortune to recognise for it so happened to be Pete her brother, currently on vacation from the cloisters of his University.

Noting the presence of his sister on the shoreline Pete had decided to leave the temptations of the river and pull up alongside of the banking close to where she was, whilst the person he was with had decided that he might just as well follow suit.

"Oh --a friend of mine, His real name is Gareth Futton, but we prefer to call him Steve!" Her brother had nodded in an almost matter of fact way in the other man's direction more out of politeness than anything else, or so she had deemed. And the stranger, after first acknowledging her had himself turned away, his mind obviously on other matters!

Yet the same man was now on board and Stacey sighed with relief as she began to pull away again from the Island, this time dutifully carrying the load she had been destined to collect. It was now the Island itself that served to disguise the craft's presence should anyone be looking out towards them at this time. Although to her mind why they should be doing this at this unearthly hour, unless of course they were involved in actively looking for them she had no idea!

Even so it was not to Ferry House that Stacey was now heading for that destination would have been far too obvious. She already knew where the car was waiting to whisk Steve and his precious documentation away anyway. She knew this for it was a matter that she had organised herself. But there again if Steve was expecting to see anything other than an old banger waiting for him or if indeed he had possibly thought he was going to be chauffeur driven, then he was in for quite a surprise! The thought amused her as she landed the craft after negotiating around the back of Belle Island where a clearing had been made in the shrubbery. The area had most probably been initially made by children who were still keen to act out their Swallows and Amazons roles from the stories they had been bred upon. But the clearing was now to be put to good use by herself, for the road was not too far distant and a car could be discretely left concealed for some considerable time in that amount of overgrowth!

He said noting when he finally realised that she was the one intent upon driving the clapped out vehicle, he merely looked at it almost disdainfully but at least she supposed it made a distraction to the hollow expression that he had conveyed after being cooped up for some days on the Island. At the time of the change over neither of them gave a second thought to the boat, perhaps Stacey had previously considered where to place it, but again she believed that once it was found then the warden would probably be the one to return it back to the jetty convinced that some youngsters had initially taken it and then conveniently forgotten all about returning it when something else had taken their fancy.

There was however one muffled squawk and flapping of wings as Steve inadvertently stumbled across and disturbed some nesting birds as he attempted to get into the vehicle. Creatures who upon having their rest disturbed were rightfully annoyed and because they deplored many of man's actions they could hardly be expected to appreciate the fact that one of these creatures had inadvertently stumbled over them!

She watched as he fingered the document case before finally depositing it on the back seat of the vehicle. It was almost indeed as if the man was undecided whether he ought to be parted from it even for this short duration and Stacey inwardly cursed him for now to her eyes it appeared that he thought more about his precious documentation than what he had ever felt for her! She immediately scolded herself for being so childish for she knew of course that the contents provided a valuable mission for him and that it was moreover imperative for him to get this information through to the Authorities he had spoken about in London.

"Are you all right?" She suddenly realised that the man besides her had become unusually quiet and she actually wondered for a moment whether he had fallen asleep! After all she could hardly be surprised if he had for he must have slept little on that Island in such uncomfortable conditions

"I will be perfectly all right once I have had the opportunity to get some of this muck off. But I hope that you are not anticipating driving this contraption all the way to London!"

Stacey shook her head not a little annoyed with his attitude after all that she had done for him and the way she had stuck her neck out. Somehow the thought hurt that he had disregarded the vehicle she cherished as her personal property. Not only that but this vehicle, old as it might be, she still regarded as her friend.

"I understood you said that you wanted to clean up first. Anyway I would be missed if I came with you!"

"Perhaps that is just as well for I doubt this contraption would have got us that far!" His tone seemed almost embittered as if he was now looking for someone to blame for his previous discomfort. "Where is it that you are taking me now then?"

"I took the liberty of renting a cottage for the week with this venture in mind. It's situated just on the outskirts of Sawrey so you soon will be able to clean up there, I have taken the liberty also of bringing you a change of clothes, the others that you are currently wearing can be destroyed afterwards!"

"You mean that you will actually wait for me to get them off my back before you start to tear them up? My God you've changed Stacey!"

She found that she couldn't help but blush at his remark. The reason she had been motivated into trying to help him now had nothing at all to do with the past. "Perhaps at the moment there are other things to consider!" She attempted to produce an icy tone in her response, whether this was to keep him at bay or disguise her true feelings, was difficult to differentiate.

"Touche! Still I suppose I ought to thank you for currently sticking your neck out for me!"

"You can thank me best by getting yourself showered and changed. Oh yes, a shave wouldn't go amiss either unless you are considering making a beard a permanent feature! And when you have finished doing that you can then get the hell out of here!"

She had pulled up quietly outside of the remote cottage she had hired for the week potentially for relatives of hers or so she had said who were into walking. Because the place was so isolated there was little chance of anyone spotting them at that time of the night. Steve left the car with almost a lurch and Stacey bore the fact in mind that she must remember to clear up any mud or slutch that had been left inside the vehicle from off his clothing as well as that on the outside of the vehicle by first light and before she herself went to catch the ferry to take her back to the camp for her work the following morning. She had also let the owners believe that she had relatives staying in the area for the week and therefore with a little bit of luck they wouldn't be too surprised when they saw her arriving at the camp by car so early on in the day. Taking a last look back at the vehicle it was then that she noticed he had left the document on the back seat after all and so swearing that the man must be tired she called him back.

Looking at the anxiety showing in her face Steve mused that in some ways it would have been good to spend the night right here with Stacey even for old times sake, yet now the realisation that unfortunately he had to keep going hit home! From here, he supposed that it would probably involve one tedious bus ride after another to finally make civilisation but this he insisted, was a price well worth paying in order to get the evidence back to London. He was also fully aware that others would be prepared to risk everything in order to stop him from doing that!

Finally washed and changed and now provided with a little sustenance Stacey watched him as he made to leave the cottage. At the time her heart appeared to be doing queer things to her especially as she saw his figure beginning to disappear over the top of that hill. But then life itself never worked out to be all that simple. That was something she had realised some time ago when their hay days had finally come to a close, for both men after qualifying as engineers had finally left University to take up positions in different parts of the country even though they had kept in touch. Pete, she knew had been based for a time at one of the oil terminals in the North Eastern region. Finding himself involved with a new engineering project in that area he had been absolutely full of it until the unexpected explosion had taken him from them and after that Stacey had lost touch with the man who preferred to be called Steve because others in his young adult life had ribbed him unmercifully that Gareth was an apt name for a pimp! To all intents and purposes Steve had become a changed man, his boyish dreams now pushed to one side and with them the girl he had become more than a little friendly towards during those long summer vacations!

It was perhaps now thinking of the past that made her take the decision to call him back before he was out of earshot completely. "Here, take the car!" She jangled the keys in front of him even as he still looked hesitant. "I know it will probably not get you all that far, certainly not as far as London before she decides to pack up on you, I even know what you think about it, but at least it will save you from these initial bus journeys that will take simply ages to get from A to B!"

He still looked dubious. "But what about you, how will you get to your work from here? No Stacey you have done enough for me already!"

"I will act like the other locals and catch the ferry. After all I can easily walk to the camp from Ferry Nab, it isn't all that far from there. Now get going, I understood that you were in a hurry!" With that she practically forced the keys at him and he was left to pause and look at her before he finally took them.

"I guess I owe you one for this Stacey!"

"Only one? Don't worry I shall be along to claim my reward in a very short space of time. Now go, before I change my mind!"

He took one long last lingering look at her almost as if he wished to say more and then finally he was gone!

It was only as she finally arrived at the camp later that morning that Stacey called back to mind the point when she had actually heard from Steve again after such a long absence. She knew of course that he was still involved in some engineering project in the North East but unlike her brother Steve was employed on shore and not on the rigs as Pete had been. Apparently however he had been able to trace her current whereabouts by cajoling one of their mutual friends but that was only when he thought the need arose and most certainly not on the strength of their past encounters.

She remembered that when he had first spoken to her over the telephone it had sounded, at least to her ears, that he was uttering forth a load of mumbled gibberish that quite frankly didn't appear to make sense. She knew of course that the second of those helicopters had tragically come down, killing all the oil workers on board at the time, who hadn't, for the news had been broadcast far and wide about some technical failure that had caused the copters to fall from out of the sky on those short journeys and had resulted in such a loss of life of those currently working on the oil rigs as Pete had been, but she had no idea that Steve was involved with them, not that was until he had contacted her rhyming on about this evidence that he needed to get to someone in the London region who could be trusted. At first she had believed the whole scenario to be ridiculous for London in her eyes at the time conjured up a picture of politicians embroiled in the expenses scandal and it certainly didn't give the impression that any of them could be trusted! Perhaps what had finally persuaded her to accede to his demands for secrecy however was when he had added the rejoinder "Otherwise Pete's death will have been in vain!"

At the time, and most conveniently to her mind, she had become aware of the pending boat regatta on the Lake itself, something that was held on Windermere each year at this time and that was when she had hit upon the idea of hiring a boat like so many others. Yet unlike other folk this was not for the sole purpose of dressing the ship up but rather as a means to dropping Steve off on that Island in the middle of the Lake. Neither had she gone about this in the correct manner for Stacey knew full well that at the present time those boats were left out all night. The answer therefore had been simple. Of course he had been forced to remain in that place until certain criteria had been put into position in order for her to get this man away but now finally all of that had been accomplished!

It was as she was walking from Ferry Nab that she now realised that there was now some sort of trouble at this side of the Lake. This was to manifest itself however as she attempted to negotiate the camp gates and found the entrance partially blocked by police vehicles. What was more as she tried to ascertain what exactly was happening, she suddenly found herself in the company of a tall sombre looking individual who tapped with his cane on the ground almost as if he believed that this would give him the same sort of comfort as a baby's dummy!

"Stacey Kershaw?" He finally posed the question, yet for a moment Stacey looked around as if she was trying to find out who was using her name before she eventually found that the person now in front of her had no intention of moving his own position.

"Yes, that is my name but who wants to know?" Still puzzled Stacey made to answer the person who appeared to have piercing blue eyes, which she now felt sure tried their best to pry into her head. "What happens to be the trouble?"

"Maybe I ought to introduce myself. My name is Detective Inspector Forsyth Miss Kershaw. To the best of my knowledge you have not been on the site all last night. Might I enquire as to why?"

Idly she wondered whether the man would now produce a notebook and pen for her response or whether the man had a Dictaphone at his disposal. "Well as I am not required to commence my employ until nine am, I can't for the life of me see any reason why I should not have pleased myself!"

"There has been a reported incident and as such it is out duty to look into the matter!" She was now convinced that this man had now resorted to clicking his teeth in irritation, an action, the thought of which, in spite of her tiredness and the other things of her mind was now in danger of making her chuckle. "Therefore under the circumstances I believe that it is right for me to try to establish your own whereabouts from eleven thirty last night until the present time!"

"You mentioned an incident Inspector, what sort of an incident are we now talking about?" A hand full of icy fingers had by this time clutched at her heart.

"A man who is currently wanted by us for questioning was seen in this area Miss Kershaw. Furthermore we also believe that you have some prior knowledge of this person. But I believe you have not yet answered my own question and yet you proceed to ask your own Miss Kershaw!" The police officer looked disdainfully down his nose at her almost indeed as if he was now accusing her of trying to obstruct the law in some way.

"Me -----? Oh I stayed overnight with some relatives who are currently in the area. As they happen to be into the craze of walking like many others who visit the Lakes, they had rented a cottage on the other side of Windermere!"

"Interesting!" His tone conveyed to Stacey the distinct impression that the man did not believe a single word of her story.

"Well I was under the impression that we were all expected to do our bit in promoting the Lake District especially in the current economic clime with the global recession and all that!"

"If I may be so bold as to say so Madam your speech sounds very much as if it has been well rehearsed!"

"That is absolute nonsense Officer. You are always at liberty to check my story out, as no doubt I presume you will Inspector. In the meantime I now consider that it is high time that I reported into work if you don't mind!" She glanced at her watch for effect for already she was aware that it was already past quarter to the hour and she knew one thing that the owners of the site deplored and that was lack of punctuality.

"That will not be necessary Miss Kershaw. Your employer is already aware that you have arrived. Before you go however we will require the address of this cottage that you say that you have rented, the place where you say your relatives are currently staying!"

By this time Stacey could feel herself beginning to shake a little at the thought of the police descending upon the cottage and finding it totally empty and with no sign of any of her supposed relatives. She also began to wonder if she had tidied up sufficiently well, not withstanding destroying those discarded clothes after Steve had left. What she really needed to find first of all, she supposed, was a couple of relatives who were keen on walking! But at this time she had no alternative but to supply the address of the place to the Inspector and simply pray that Steve had left nothing behind!

---------They finally allowed her to go with the briefest of nods of dismissal and with the promise of getting back to her in the future should the need arise but from first stepping across the threshold of the place Stacey became conscious that everyone in the office was looking expectantly in her direction. It was not that anybody actually said anything at least not until one of the men who ran the Management courses up at the Hall decided to pop his head round the office door.

"Queer goings on around the place or so I am told! As a matter of fact one of the lads up at the Hall said he thought he noticed something moving in the early hours of this morning. He said that he couldn't sleep or something although in my opinion he had been out on the town last night and he's had more than sufficient which resulted in frequent walks during the night!" The man half laughed at what he considered to be a joke to lighten the current mood. "Anyway we just heard the story on the local news about the scientist who has apparently done a runner from off those oil rigs with some important documentation that it is rumoured he has a market for! Still I never thought anyone would resort to coming round here with the loot. Who for example I ask you, is going to buy that sort of stuff off him around here?"

"I suppose it is always possible that he had arranged for a contact to meet him here!" The Manager entering the office at the time decided it was time for him to put forward his own theory.

"What meet up with him in the middle of Lake Windermere for example? Have a heart man. I know my mate claimed he saw a boat heading out towards Lady-Holme in the early hours but I don't really think that is the ideal spot for some pre-arranged clandestine meeting!"

"Well the authorities obviously think that there is something in it anyway!"

"So that is why they were here? Were there any boats missing from off your jetties this morning then?"

"No, we have already checked that out. The police have now the theory that whoever it was actually took one of the boats from the jetty on the promenade. Well they are not actually locked up at night when they are being used in the season, but then no one is expected to steal one of them on Windermere, for in truth where could one really escape to with it? Anyway apparently the warden found this boat left at the other side of the lake, pulled up carefully onto the banking there. I believe they are checking for finger prints but it is rather dubious that they will find any with all the water about!"

"But why would anyone want to go over to the other side of the Lake in those circumstances? What have they got there anyway?"

"Well I suppose one could think about Sawrey and Beatrix Potter's place for starters!"

"Not to mention the fact that our Stacey has hired a cottage there for the week! I understand it is for some relative the girl has only just realised that she has got!" Another voice had now joined into the conversation and glancing up Stacey noticed the stance of Avril Togas currently looking rather smug and self satisfied with herself especially as she was now able to impart this information to the gathering. In truth Stacey had never cared for the girl much, what it was about her she previously could not have said, she only knew that the female was now thoroughly enjoying her own discomfort. There was another thing too; how on earth did this girl know that she had rented that cottage?

She knew of course that in rural communities gossip often travelled faster than the truth and in these isolated pockets of habitation someone usually knew someone else who lived in a neighbouring community. To some of these folk gossip was like the bread of life especially if it concerned unusual happenings. Perhaps indeed the surprise at having her business so disclosed nevertheless showed on

Stacey's face for she became conscious of the muted laughter now circulating about, upon which Avril Togas gloated, behaving now almost as if she had scored some major victory

Perhaps more than a little discouraged Stacey moved herself in the direction of the kitchen area deciding that she might just as well make herself a brew and to leave the rest to prattle on about her in her absence. She suddenly realised that in her effort to get Steve away she had not had the time to either eat or drink that morning and so the promise of some liquid nectar helped to raise her spirits. At least she presumed that this would help to take her mind away from the rat race for a little while. Still it appeared that this was not to be for she had no sooner got herself installed when Dick Soper, the young management consultant whom she had left currently behind in the office decided to follow her.

"Please don't take all this talk to heart so much Stacey. You ought to know what that lot are like when they think that they have something they can prattle on about. I expect it's the result of living a life of hermits! But you my girl look tired!" For once the face of this individual had changed to show some concern. "Don't tell me that you have had to burn the midnight oil with your entertaining?"

"No I guess I didn't sleep very well last night. Probably the result of not sleeping in my own bed!" She smiled feignly back at him.

"Now that I consider is a great pity because I had been wondering if there was any chance of me inviting you up to the Hall tonight. We have a meal laid on, outside caterers of course, it's actually being put on as a thank you to out of town dignitaries and the like. Sort of a gesture of good will if you like!"

Stacey felt very tempted to refuse. At any other time that is exactly what she would have done for it really wasn't her scene to go around making idle chatter to pass the time away, but the fact that her name was currently being banded around the office made her decide to give them something to talk about for a change.

"Well I suppose if you wouldn't mind if I fall asleep during the speeches!"

The young man smiled taking her answer to be in the affirmative. " Good, then shall I say that I'll see you at the front door to the Hall around sevenish? Oh yes smart casual dress will do, nothing formal!"

She was forced to raise a smile upon these words. The thought of wearing evening attire even up at the Hall simply for a meal seemed to her to be totally ludicrous anyway and that even if those largely puffin heads up there did have notions of grandeur!

Perhaps her first impression of Meredith Drew, whom Dick had introduced as being their visiting Supremo who had also promised to stay for a while because he had some new activity in mind, was that the man appeared suave, pleasant and attentive. Such impressions however can quickly change when conditions so dictate. For his part Dick had been ready and eager to meet her that evening at the designated meeting place and had admired her dress, her appearance and had generally made Stacey feel good, for the girl had spent ages trying her best to perfect the ravishes of the sleepless night with care, knowing full well that one could hardly look at one's best otherwise. Thus his words upon greeting her had done much to waylay the fear that her appearance that evening was in any way letting him down.

Continuing in this vein Dick had then appeared almost anxious to introduce Stacey to the rest of the grouping, almost it appeared to her mind, as if he considered he had himself won some surprise trophy at being able to persuade her to come. These introductions had naturally included this visiting head of the company and although there were other women present it soon became obvious to her however that Meredith Drew sought to monopolise her for himself for reasons he had obviously perfected beforehand. Therefore once the meal was over the man sought her out to first of all to begin with the niceties of the day, naturally enough, before proceeding to questions that were obviously more to his liking and which had obviously been well prepared.

"Tell me Miss Kershaw, do you know someone by the name of Gareth Futton?" Upon this Stacey was stunned, shocked even that anybody should refer to Steve by this name for it had long been a forgotten entity to him after professing that he disliked being called by that name.

She shook her head feeling that this must be a truth, for after all the person she had known and fallen in love with all those years ago had been called Steve! "Only in so far as I believe that my brother Pete was at University at the same time as someone of that name!"

"Ah yes I believe your brother was killed when that helicopter exploded. Such an awful waste of life!" Glancing at the man's expression as he spoke she doubted that these words were sincere.

"And now apparently there has been another crash!" She surprised even herself by now being able to face up to this person.

"Yes –yes---I did hear something about it!"

"One would have thought that after the first crash such means of conveyance would have been grounded until the fault had been discovered!" She didn't know what possessed her to suddenly argue in this manner. It was simply that this man, polite as he might be, appeared to rub her up the wrong way.

"Pilot error or so I am led to believe! And one can hardly ground a whole fleet of aircraft for pilot error, now can one Miss Kershaw?"

She had no wish to argue with the man further. In fact she just wished that Dick would come back and rescue her from this impasse. Still the man appeared to now wish to change the subject.

"Perhaps in truth I do not come often enough to fully appreciate your beautiful Lake District and the surrounding countryside!" Now he even applied his tone to sound a little sad indeed that his visits had to be so infrequent. Not that Stacey could appreciate any reason for this. "I suppose that working here at the camp you must see a great many visitors Miss Kershaw?"

"Naturally, we do have quite a frequent turn over of guests!"

"Which I presume like all rented accommodation must present its own problems!"

Now Stacey began to wonder exactly what this man was intimating, for having already figured out Meredith Drew as being nothing if not devious she had also suspected that the man had something additional on his mind. Perhaps his following words did something to illuminate the matter.

"As a matter of fact some relatives of mine are currently planning a visit to these parts. Apparently they have heard quite a lot about Conniston. In fact I believe their fascination for the place dates from the raising of

Campbell's Bluebird the other year. I was wondering if you could recommend somewhere for them to stay in that region; they are not exactly hotel minded therefore perhaps they would appreciate a rented cottage more!"

Stacey was mindful of the hairs on the back of her neck beginning to bristle as she wondered now exactly what this man was getting at. As the situation was quite familiar she began now to try to access how much the man knew or at least thought he knew of her own ventures.

"Well there are many cottages for rent in that area Mr Drew!" She at least managed with a struggle to keep her voice on an even keel. "The Lake District is not exactly devoid of such accommodation to rent, it is simply short of homes for first time buyers! Still perhaps the best thing for you to do is to contact the tourist office at Conniston for I feel sure that they will be able to help far more than what I can!"

"I wasn't actually contemplating them staying as far away as Conniston for that would be quite a trail for me if I wanted to visit. Perhaps something more this side of that place would prove better for that but on the other hand it would also provide easy access for them to visit the places they have read and heard about. What for instance is there at Sawrey Miss Kershaw?"

So that was it; the man was finally getting around to the crunch question and saying what he really wanted to know. She braced herself before making her response even as she thankfully spotted Dick Soper now heading in their direction.

"Well I guess there is Peter Rabbit for starters there not to mention Jemina Puddle Duck, always providing of course Mr Drew that you are familiar with those characters!"

She could have laughed at the expression on Meredith Drew's face as Dick Soper thankfully escorted her away claiming that she was there as his guest and yet he had seen little of her that evening. For once in her life she no longer cared what these people thought of her, whether or not they believed with half a mind that she was some local wit immersed in romanticism or anything else!

"I really am going to have to call it a day Dick. It has been lovely really and thank you for asking me to come but honestly after last night and my consequent lack of sleep I am feeling absolutely wrecked and I am afraid if I don't make my excuses now and go and get my head down very soon then you are in danger of finding me fast asleep here!"

He appeared to be a little disappointed with her words but then Dick Soper considered he had done his duty by bringing her here in the first place at the request of Meredith Drew for reasons quite unknown to him; although having said that, it proved always to be the case that when this man snapped his fingers then everybody jumped to attention. Still Dick now obliged by fetching Stacey's wrap for her but true to form the girl stayed him when they eventually got to the front door of the Hall when he was about to follow her.

"No you stay here please with your associates and then I won't feel quite so bad. After all I can hardly get myself lost going back to my own apartment from here! And you cannot risk offending your boss by doing the disappearing act on him as well!"

He looked a little dubious at first but no doubt upon reflection saw the merit in her words. Whatever anybody else said about her this was one hell of a girl. "Then I will see you again. Perhaps when you have fully recovered it would be nice for us to arrange to go somewhere on our own?"

"Of course!" She attempted a smile yet it was one that was only surface deep. There was no way she wished to be involved with this person whatever he had to say!

Consequently Stacey let herself back into her apartment on her own and totally glad at the thought of finally being able to kick her shoes off and crawl beneath her duvet at least for a few hours. With this factor paramount in her mind she ignored the telephone and her computer for she declared that should there be any messages on either of them they would have to wait until the following morning. She was just coming out of the bathroom finally ready to make herself a nighttime drink when she became conscious that someone was currently moving about outside of the place. Frowning a little at this intrusion she drew back the curtain of the ground floor flat in time to witness a shadow now disappearing back along the road in the direction of the gates to the camp. Stacey shrugged her shoulders, it was probably only some joker but there again what was the security guard doing? She stopped as she noticed the envelope that had been roughly forced underneath the door.

In spite of her tiredness curiosity mow overcame her as she stooped to pick up the inoffensive looking article. Yet the contents of this envelope served to give even Stacey Kershaw food for thought as she sunk down in perplexion upon that sofa, leaving the kettle to sing away at its merry tune for nothing! For what it was worth, the note was signed by a person who called himself Bob Eldon and the contents moreover were requesting her to ask Steve if he would get in touch.

Who this person was Stacey had no idea whatsoever and what was more puzzling was how he knew that she had been in any sort of contact. The fact that someone else must be aware of this fact made for an uncomfortable feeling now in the pit of her stomach, and this was something that would not easily go away!

★ ★ ★ ★

Chapter Two

Stacey took a deep breath of fresh Lakeland air as she made her way along the shale beach that would ultimately lead her to the park and finally onto the car ferry road, the ferry that plied the lake and saved its users miles of travel if one had to go all the way around the lake by road. This she informed herself was the way that she liked it, the fresh morning air that still had the hint of a nip to it before the sun got a firm hold of the land mass and her only companions at that time of the day the ducks, swans and geese who had already risen from their slumbers at first light in an effort to catch the morning worm before it chose to retire below the surface. The geese that were now rapidly growing in numbers in the area had been but passing visitors at one time but had found how exceedingly pleasant life was here and they had therefore stayed on to honk their greeting, especially to the human whom they associated with the frequent titbits supplied. She mused too upon the fact that perhaps her mother had been more than a little surprised to receive the phone call, but upon due reflection and especially after last night's occurrence Stacey had decided that perhaps it was opportune to call the woman for it might indeed prove better if the cottage she had rented was indeed occupied for the week and not standing empty now that Steve had gone. And Mrs Kershaw now bereft of both husband and son had been glad to oblige her daughter, even if she did consider such a request to be rather odd!

It was with something that resembled relief therefore when Stacey noted that the ferry was ready to begin its morning run, mainly for the benefit of commuters at this hour that wished to cross the lake in order to get to their employ, but as yet the vessel had not yet left its berth. She glanced anxiously at her watch, with a fair wind her mother should not be long before she arrived for the main roads, so often thronged with traffic, would still be relatively quiet at this time of the day.

Even so the expression on her face altered as she finally spotted her mother's car edging its way down the ferry road and the woman, after catching sight of her, paused as she drew near to the boatyards so that Stacey could get in herself, for now her look of acceptance of the natural world and the creatures that inhabited it had been replaced by one of sheer determination. Because they were anxious to catch the ferry that was now just about to leave Ferry Nab, no words were spoken at the time even though Stacey knew full well that a barrage of questions were already being stored and were bound to descend upon her in the near future, and therefore she spent the intervening period trying to strain her mind as to the manner in which she could reveal certain things and yet at the same time keep much of what had happened to herself, for that would have been Steve's choice if he had been here.

"So then what is all this about?" The boat had hardly moved away from the side before her mother decided she could keep quiet no longer and had decided that perhaps the time was opportune during the minutes it took to travel across. "You know of course that I am always willing to help out in any way that I can, but you are saying that you have rented out a cottage at the other side of the Lake, whatever for? I admit the whole idea sounds quite bizarre to me when you already live not more than a stone's throw away!"

"Because I thought that it might be an opportunity for us to spend more time together!" Stacey failed to look at her mother when she spoke but at least, she preened herself, that part was not actually a lie for surely it was time that the two of them did spend more time together. She guessed that her mother had taken Pete's untimely death badly, but then she had just reason for feeling like that for didn't she, Stacey, show many of the same emotions. It seemed to be nigh on impossible that her brother was no longer with them, but the time for tears had passed and now it was action that was required so that his death had not totally been in vain. Still her mother chose to elaborate on the point she had already put across.

"But I don't live all that far away as it is. If as you say you want to spend more time with me then why didn't you save your money and come back home? Sometimes our Stacey you remain a complete mystery to me. For starters you had the brains to go to University itself but instead you decide to leave school as soon as it was possible, you don't go on to find yourself a worthwhile career by taking your degree, but instead choose to leave home and bury yourself away in this neck of the woods!"

"I actually thought that you could probably do with a break!" Stacey ignored the reference to past choices she had made. "Surely there is nothing wrong in that!"

"And so for that reason you have chosen to incarcerate me in splendid isolation over here? If you wanted to see more of me then why couldn't you have found me somewhere to stay closer to where you work?"

"Mainly because it is peaceful and quiet over this side of the Lake. Over in Bowness it is getting the time of the year when we will have throngs of visitors and folk will scarce find space to move in. And you know how you have always maintained that you hated crowded places!"

The older woman fell silent. Admitting that her daughter's words held some truth in them, however reluctant she felt to do so, she nevertheless felt that there was something more in Stacey's reasoning. "So will you be staying at this cottage with me then whilst I am here?"

Stacey shook her head feigning a reluctance that she did not actually feel. "No, I'm afraid that I can't because of my work. But I promise that I will come over when I am not on duty. Why we can even go on walks together!"

"Walks!" Now Mrs Kershaw definitely had her suspicions for this impromptu get together, for her daughter had never been into the walking game, sailing perhaps in a loose sort of way, but most certainly not walking! Still the woman decided that perhaps it was not opportune to pursue the matter further at this point for she knew that the Stacey of old would reveal her true motivations when she was good and ready and not a moment before

Still it took only a few minutes to motor the short distance to Sawrey once the gates of the ferryboat had opened to let them ashore at Ferry House and at least Agnes Kershaw had to concede that their arrival at this cottage had been much as Stacey had previously predicted.

"Sawrey isn't that the place where Beatrix Potter used to live?" A sudden thought crossed the older woman's mind as she tried to break through the silence that had crept upon them.

"The same, yes she had a farm here, Hill Top Farm as a matter of fact, so if you do occasionally see coach parties passing, pay no heed for that is where they are making to!" Still the smile her daughter wore on her face at the remembrance of this was suddenly to alter as she cast her eyes upon a sight that wiped the presence of her mother clean out of her head. "Hell fire, they've already been, just take a look at the place!"

Casting her eyes in the direction Stacey was now pointing it seemed obvious even to Agnes Kershaw that there had been a break in of some description. Still not knowing properly what she was supposed to be looking for all that the woman noticed at first was the mess that these vandals had left behind. Yet as she followed Stacey into the place something else caught Agnes' eye and stooping she held these aloft.

"And what the hell are these, don't tell me that your visitors left these behind?" Following the voice Stacey almost moaned at her own lack in failing to remove them like the rest of Steve's gear.

"They're a pair of underpants!" The answer she knew was absolute trite, everybody could see exactly what they were.

"I know what they are, I am familiar with a gentleman's under garment. The question is what the hell are they doing here? Surely your burglar didn't feel the necessity to have to change himself did he?"

"No, they're Steve's!" Stacey had looked long and hard at the other woman's features. This was the one who had given her birth and she knew she could trust implicitly.

"Steve's?" The woman appeared to be no wiser for she was still searching in her mind as to the meaning of this.

"Yes surely you remember Steven. He was Pete's friend at University. They were both doing an engineering degree at the same time!"

"Oh that Steven, the one who was christened Gareth and then changed it to Steve because he didn't like it. A pretentious young man I would say. But of course, wasn't it the case that the two of you were as thick as a facsimile of the terrible twins at one time, that was of course once you stopped hating him for treating you like a child. But if I remember correctly didn't he go to work once he had finished University in the gas field in Morecambe Bay?"

"When he first left University yes whilst Pete went to work on the opposing coastline!"

"Then if it isn't too difficult a question what are his underpants doing here?" One look at her mother's face made Stacey realise which way the woman's mind was working.

"If you are thinking what I now surmise you are, then you can forget it Mum. But the truth is a long story to reveal to you especially at the moment when I am due back at my work! Perhaps for now therefore it is sufficient for me to say that Steve was required to take some documentation up to London and he needed to change before embarking upon that journey!"

"And because of that I suppose he took your car, I presume that is where it has got to? I thought I hadn't seen it around here when we came in. But surely you don't anticipate he will get as far as London in that clapped out old banger. Let's face it Stacey I've been on at you for simply ages to have a change in your mode of transport!"

Stacey's face flushed. The old jalopy as her mother termed her mode of transport was sufficient to suit her own limited activities and to her mind that was all that mattered.

"He might not get as far as London in it but at least it will help him to get away from here and from those who seem to be hell bent on stopping him!"

"And who might they be?" Agnes Kershaw received no response to her question this time around and therefore her curiosity went unabated, for Stacey considered she had said quite enough on the matter already. Therefore the woman decided that perhaps the time had come for her to change tacks. "So I presume this was the reason why you rented this cottage in such an isolated spot. It was for Steve and not with your mother in mind at all?"

"Make no mistake my mother so happens to have a very important role to play in all of this. I mentioned walking to you if you remember? Well I actually rented the cottage on behalf of some relatives who were well into that sort of thing. And now, not to place too fine a point on it, at least for appearance sake, you just happen to be the relative of whom I was referring!"

"Well thank you so much for that vote of confidence!" The woman pulled a face again at the very idea of such an activity. "But I can assure you that will not be taking place until you have made it worth my while by filling me in with a few more details!"

"Later Mum, I promise!" Stacey glanced at her watch. "But now I really do have to get going for I dare not be late again or they will truly begin to suspect something!"

"Not exactly your style being late is it Stacey?"

"No it was just that something cropped up yesterday that made me late in arriving for work!"

"Then before you dart off tell me one thing. Why the break in. Obviously the would be burglar didn't choose to come back for his underpants?"

"I should have destroyed them like the rest of his clothes and I suppose it was careless of me to have disregarded them. No I believe that the break in was an attempt to find the documentation that Steve had with him. I'm sure about that!"

"Is anything missing then that you can see?"

"No things appear to be intact!"

"Then I can take it that you have no intentions of calling in the police?"

"No!" The girl shook her head rather determinedly for by this time she realised that her mother was delaying her even further by wanting to continue their conversation. "If I did call them I doubt whether they could help in the matter and the result could easily be for me to draw even more attention to our own position!"

"Well I suppose as a child you always did enjoy a good mystery. Not at all like your brother, for he believed that there was an explanation for everything that happened. Oh all right I know you want to be off ----I will run you if you like, after all I still have my car!"

"No thanks Mum. I can easily get to the car ferry from here and go across as a pedestrian. On the other hand with a little bit of luck I should be finished today at two o'clock so why not spend your time until then unpacking and making yourself feel at home here?"

"And when you do finish then I take it that you will reveal more of this story of yours?" The words appeared now to be issued more like a command more than anything else.

"In all probability whilst we are out on our first walk together!"

The older woman sighed. "And no doubt you will have one or two surprises in store for me on that as well. But just remember one thing, at my age I have certainly no intention of going in for the coast to coast, at least not until I have got some training in first!"

In spite of herself Stacey felt a smile curving her lips. At least her mother now appeared to be showing a little of the sense of humour that Stacey had previously credited her with, and which she remembered from the past when the woman had shown great amusement after the boys had inevitably fell into that river and returned home wet through, but only after their kid sister had made a bee line to get home first in order to inform on them. Perhaps upon reflection these had indeed been the golden days.

"No I was actually thinking in terms of a slow amble to Esthwaite Water to begin with!" The response was however somewhat muted as she finally took her leave. She had offered to help to tidy up the place but her mother naturally enough had waved her away.

"I thought you said that you were late for that boss of yours?" The woman had fixed her with her eyes, the same as she had done after Pete's death in that explosion, the cause of which had never been properly explained to them! Maybe the powers that be had considered the technical jargon far too complicated for two mere women. But her mother was right on one thing, it was now time that she was getting back for she certainly did not want a repetition of yesterday!

-----------Perhaps by the time she arrived back it was most fortunate that her boss himself was currently tied up with a client and therefore did not notice Stacey's untimely arrival. In truth once the man was entertaining a potential customer it was quite usual for all other bodies to be ignored.

"So how was the party up at the Hall last night?" Others of her colleagues however tended to be more inquisitive and were not bashful in voicing what they required to know.

"All right I suppose if you are in to that sort of thing. But in my opinion it was a great deal of talk with very little substance to go with it!" She really hadn't the patience to go into any more detail and all she wanted to do now was to bury herself away at her own desk.

"Give me half a chance to find out for myself! I honestly don't think you appreciate the fact of how lucky you were to be invited. As a matter of fact I don't really think you appreciate the fact that we had to cover for you this morning either. It's a good job for you that Mr Warner was busy and didn't notice that you were late again!"

"That was because I had to walk. I haven't got my car at the moment, it is still in the garage!" She had no idea why she was bothering to lie to this junior, why not ignore the infernal woman instead? Still her decision made she turned to immerse herself into the pile of files that were awaiting her attention and ignore all of this outside intervention.

Funnily enough she supposed that was exactly what Steve had done following that first helicopter crash in Morecambe Bay in which many lives had perished. Steve, she remembered, had been quite adamant that there was far more to it than simply pilot error. At the time he had travelled back to see Peter for although the two of them had qualified together and more or less in the same profession, the width of the country now separated them. She supposed too that it was round about this time that Steve had suddenly stopped regarding her as Pete's kid sister and a nuisance factor always there at their every meeting, usually to make her own impact and thus prevent the two of them sharing personal confidences! Yet in truth all it had taken was one quizzical look from those large brown eyes that had possibly been enough to kindle a spark in their relationship. Not so much for Stacey for she had been dotty about this man for absolutely ages before this time but rather because perhaps for the first time Steve had regarded her as less of a kid and more as a desirable young woman! Matters between them seemed to have taken off after this; she remembered she had gone with him to Tyneside to visit her brother that was the last time however that she had seen Pete alive. For it was not long following on from that occasion that they had received the tragic news of Pete's death and whilst both she and her mother had been devastated it was as nothing when compared to the effect that this news had on Steve. That was the time when he had suddenly and uncharacteristically become silent about his work and the next thing she knew was that he had requested a transfer to the area himself.

"Stacey, do me a favour please!" A voice brought her thoughts back again to reality and looking up she noticed that her boss had poked his head through the office door into the reception area. Feeling rather guilty for first of all being late that morning and secondly for now spending her time day dreaming about the past, Stacey looked up almost expectantly. Yet far from having any intention of finding a few chosen words to reprimand her, Clive Warner looked rather harassed at the time. "Take this message and deliver it to the Lakeside timber lodge for me will you? Apparently someone needs to get in touch with the owners there who for some apparent reason have their mobile switched off. I would go myself but just at the moment I am just about up to my neck in it!"

Well considering his appearance his words certainly did not appear to be any falsehood and she wondered just what the potential customer had been rabbitting on about to leave him in such a state. Still she supposed that it was occasions such as these that hallmarked one of the restrictions of management.

"Of course!" She had forced a smile to her lips as she switched off her computer and locked her drawer before taking hold of the slip of paper he was now offering to her.

"Thanks Stacey, you're a pal. I shan't forget I owe you a favour for this!"

Not until the next time, she breathed to herself, but still getting out of that office for ten minutes or so especially on such a lovely day couldn't really be considered to be all that bad! In fact she found she had a new spring to her step as she passed by the caravans on the site and then down towards the lake. Tom Smethurst, one of the handymen belonging to the site had at the time parked his jalopy down on the slipway, his current job being that of attending to the new wooden poles that now hallmarked the new Marina there and to move several of the boats into their new berthing positions. For this he was using his ancient craft that at one time had probably undertaken every job on that lake. At this time it appeared that he was waiting for two of his colleagues to arrive to give him a hand, one to steer the boats whilst the other applied the rope that Tom could pass to them from the water thus dealing with any awkward vessels in a methodological manner. As he was currently at a loose end waiting for them to arrive, upon seeing Stacey he immediately attempted to draw her into some form of conversation. For her part Stacey stopped to speak to him first of all because he was a pleasing character and secondly because in fact she appreciated that this man knew more about the local area than anyone else and the facts he could impart were often well worth listening to.

It was whilst she was in this position that she heard the engine noise of the 4x4, a vehicle currently towing a trailer carrying a boat and the owner of the same wished to use the slipway in order to launch his vessel. Not that there was anything unusual in this activity for after all that was what the slipway was for even if the grunting engine noise that the vehicle made on its approach did jar a little on her ears and serve to halt the conversation she had been enjoying with Tom. Yet the driver of this vehicle who alighted from it with something that resembled an air of pomposity as well as with eyes that reflected scorn upon those whom he considered to be his inferiors was something she regarded as quite different. For glancing in the man's direction Stacey recognised the features of Meredith Drew.

Immediately upon recognition Stacey drew herself back against some nearby bushes hoping that these would shield her presence for there was literally no way in which she desired to be in this man's company. Yet the interloper had obviously reserved much of his spleen for Tom and the fact that Tom's own car and boat were in his words blocking his path and thus preventing him from continuing with his own launch.

The fact that at the time Meredith Drew could see little beyond himself and his own desires caused her to sigh with relief but at the same time to feel a little sorry for Tom for in all honesty there would have been ample room for this man to have passed him by. Meredith Drew however demanded all the room as of his right and hinted as much as he turned upon the fellow he considered was an underdog

"Won't be more than five minutes mate!" Tom kept his cool, no doubt remembering the pledge he had made to be as nice as possible to the paying guests although Stacey guessed that in his heart at the time he would dearly have loved to have given this impertinent fellow a mouthful. Still he didn't need to give vent to any such feelings for just at that precise moment his two colleagues arrived ready to carry out their allotted task, thus leaving Meredith Drew to stand watching them, hands on hip, and with a look that indicated that he considered that the world owed him something. As at the time the man then appeared to have another occupation that involved gazing out across the lake, Stacey seized the opportunity to walk further down the path and out of earshot.

Even so as her eyes flittered across towards Lady-Holme perhaps even she was surprised to realise the reason for his action. For coming from the direction of Bowness a further boat with four different individuals on board chugged its way across the Lake. Currently this craft appeared to be heading in the direction of that Island but what appeared even more significant to her eyes was that Drew appeared to know who they were for he offered them a solitary salute as they passed close by, even if his feet now upon the jetty frightened one particular teenager who was currently sunbathing so that she almost fell off the jetty completely to receive an unexpected bath.

Because it was a weekday as opposed to weekend there was not all that great amount of traffic cluttering up the Lake at the time Stacey could see the action clearly and was left in little doubt that the boat was going to and indeed had finally landed on Lady-Holme. It was then that she finally remembered the message she had been entrusted to convey and therefore needed to leave the scene altogether. It was a little later as she returned from completing this task that she noticed that Tom Smethurst had finally shifted his barge and that Meredith Drew was currently in the act of mooring off the Island where the others had landed.

Still fascinated, possibly because it was Lady-Holme that they had chosen she decided to wait for a little while and after several minutes she was rewarded for her efforts by the sight of Meredith Drew standing on the shoreline, the only place that was in fact debarred of trees and other foliage and now he was obviously barking out his orders to the other four characters, who by this time had lost themselves in the dense greenery. The sight of these characters currently on Lady-Holme filled her with a feeling of gall, for this Island she considered was her own and Steven's special place and in her terms she hated to see it tarnished in this manner. It had been their special place long before Steve had been compelled to spend those miserable few days there. This was the place where, on such a summer's day as it was today, even though outsiders always deemed that it rained in the Lakes, they had exchanged their first passionate kiss. It had been quite unexpected for just a few moments before she had been tormenting him on his rowing prowess, and he had pulled the boat alongside of the Island and moved to kiss her confessing that this was something he had wanted to do for some time.

"Heard of hike-swim?" He had referred to the latest fad that was just taking off in the district where hikers chose to complete their trail by swimming back across the lake to avoid having to retrace their steps. "Well if there is any more cheek from you young lady it will be a swim-hike in your case!" Now she remembered how he had tormented her yet again as they had climbed through the bracken to catch a better view of the Northern shoreline and the fells that lay beyond. They had in fact stayed on that Island for some considerable time, content simply to be in each other's company, and now this despicable character was out there sullying their own place by his very presence! She remembered that was the first time she had made reference to Steve's name for it had always puzzled her why he had been content to be called that when he had been christened Gareth.

"Tell me something that I have been dying to ask you for simply ages. Why do people call you Steve when your true name is Gareth?"

His nose had crinkled up into something that gave the impression of someone who had stood in something quite distasteful. "I suppose it started off at school. Well you know what boys are like when it comes to nicknames? Anyway after that who in their right mind would have wanted to refer to such a name as Gareth?"

"It's a very nice name!"

"But not I think in the midst of a group of boys and anyway I much preferred being called by my other name!"

Her mind turned back to the present situation! What Drew was actually doing there she began to realise as he barked his orders to the henchmen to now comb the interior of that place. They must be looking for any sort of clues that Steve had left behind and therefore if they were now aware that this place had featured on the man's escape route then it was also possible that they had gleaned more. She thought now of the break in at the cottage, the one that had never been explained and shook her head in quiet disbelief for as much as she detested the sight of this man it still seemed hard to believe of other underlying tendencies attached to his purpose!

Tom was back at the launching slipway as she made to pass by. "Guess your companion back there was a nice friendly individual!" She nodded to where the 4x4 and boat trailer now stood.

"Well I suppose one could say that it takes all sorts Miss. Not, I must admit, that I was in any rush to move for the likes of him. In fact he was damned well pouting when I finally moved my jeep and craft away from that area, and I have to admit it was the first time in my life that I have been content to see a man in such a state for I have always deplored such tricks! Still I don't know why he bothered to go to all the trouble of launching the damned thing when all he has done since is to sail it over to that Island. Why he could have jumped practically as far as that!"

"Perhaps he didn't want to risk getting his feet wet!" She tried to pass over the conversation as best she could. "Anyway just to remind you don't get sunburnt out here today will you?" She referred to the fact that the workman had now all stripped to his waist in the heat of the day. At least her words seemed to have some effect on him for the man quickly slipped his tee shirt on again. Even so Stacey had still to appreciate the fact that the man was as brown as a berry with constantly working outside and with the weather as it was at the time his position could only be envied!

At least her mother seemed to be in a better humour when she returned to the cottage later that afternoon. Indeed the woman appeared to have spent her time in putting her own stamp upon the place and seemingly had thoroughly enjoyed herself doing it. She also seemed now to appreciate the idea of the proposed walk to Esthwaite Water although there were still certain things that the woman was nevertheless determined to clear that were obviously lingering on in her mind.

"How did you happen to run into him again then?" This time around it was Agnes who made the play determined as she was that she would be the one to ask the questions instead of waiting for her daughter to drip feed her on the situation when she felt in such a mood.

For a moment Stacey watched the rabbit as it chose to scamper across the track where they were currently walking thinking at the time what a vulnerable position the creature was currently in. A simile came to mind of her own position at the time.

"As a matter of fact Steve contacted me!" She thought back to the telephone call she had received. At the time she hadn't heard anything from Steve since the stupid tiff they had, mainly when he had told her that he had decided to go in for a transfer from the Morecambe bay field to the North Sea. Of course she hadn't wanted him to go not only because it was further away and thus made it less easy for him to get back to see her when he was off duty, but perhaps more importantly because this was the same place where Pete her brother had been killed!

"Look there happens to be a team of us and we're in the process of developing something that we consider to be rather special and in order to continue it is necessary for the whole team to transfer for both better facilities over there and as well as these facilities we will also have access to the University!"

"But why have you never mentioned any of this before?"

"Perhaps because the whole of the project is rather hush-hush at the moment!"

"And therefore because of that I am not considered to be trustworthy enough to be taken into your confidence I suppose!"

"I can assure you that it is nothing like that Stacey!"

"Well I am afraid it sounds to me that is exactly what it is like!" She had been petulant at the time and she had realised that at a later stage but by that time in was too late for Steve had already gone. At the time he had simply shrugged his shoulders and walked away. She knew then she should have gone after him and apologised but pride proudly stood in her way. After that his visits had become less frequent and something of the feeling that they had once shared seemed to gradually drift away.

All that was however until out of the blue she had received the phone call begging for her assistance and that was something that Stacey never could have refused Steve. At the time he had told her of the necessity for him to get some documentation through to London and Stacey, still in the throes of learning how to use the web and with this currently uppermost in her mind had wondered then why he had not sent the information by E mail or something like that. Even so she had gone along with his suggestion of finding a place where he could hide out for a time for apparently other interested parties were after grasping the same documentation with their greasy palms. The suggestion he had come out with was the Island and after she had been convinced Stacey supposed that it made poetic justice for them to use it for this purpose. Even so it was with something of a shock that his appearance gave her when she finally set her eyes on him again. For the boyish looks she had remembered had now all but disappeared and she had been faced with a man who now wore something of a haunted expression in his eyes.

"So can I take it that it is back on between you two now?" Her mother's voice brought her quickly back to reality. "After all I always considered that the two of you made a fine looking couple!" Perhaps it was only natural that her mother had managed to get hold of the wrong end of the stick for Agnes Kershaw usually saw things in black and white. "Well I'm sure our Peter would have been pleased!"

"Mother at the moment Steve has been charged with passing some important information to someone in authority who resides in the London area. The reason why he was here was simply that certain people sought to stop him from doing exactly that and they also thought nothing of spending their time in chasing from one place to the next in search of him!" She just hoped with all of her heart that this explanation would suffice and at least for the time being this appeared to be the case.

"Isn't that Hill Top Farm we can catch a glimpse of over there?"

"Yes that's it. Apparently from all accounts Miss Potter loved the view of Esthwaite, the same as you are seeing today!"

"Then I consider the woman had good choice. In fact if I myself was inspired with the creative mode I also could wax lyrical!" And that decided Stacey was praise indeed from her mother who had been brought up to appreciate the beauty of the Crook of Lune. Still returning in the direction of the cottage feeling at least some things were all right in the world she almost succeeded in pushing the woman into the hedgerow when she noticed the very same 4x4 approaching in their direction from round the next bend in the road.

"So what was all that in aid of then?" Quite rightly the other woman now showed more than a little indignation at her treatment.

"Just someone for whom I have recently developed an avid dislike and who I want to avoid!"

Her mother looked at her in a somewhat perplexed manner. "But I don't understand our Stacey. Wasn't that the nice Mr Drew who actually called at the cottage earlier on today looking for you? I think I told him at the time that I expected you to be home by teatime today!"

Stacey groaned. How on earth could she explain this away? Not only was this Meredith Drew onto her, but now it appeared that her own mother seemed to be unwittingly helping him.

A black cat darted across the road carrying its prey. In fact the creature was travelling at a galloping pace for one of the gulls that had previously claimed this prey as its own was currently after him. "Guess I've never seen that before!" Now she was attempting to change the subject but her mind, whilst looking at the wild life not with too an antagonist attitude, was just wishing that real life could be half as simple!

⋆ ⋆ ⋆ ⋆

Chapter Three

The effect of now being fully aware of what he had to do even though at the same time he was still baulking at the very idea became increasingly prevalent and uppermost in his thoughts as Steve finally neared the metropolis of the capital city. Initially this act was something that Steve never in his wildest dreams had ever visualised especially when he was first employed as a design and development engineer to a private firm that was attached to the off shore gas and oil exploration in Morecambe Bay. Yet now he had to remember that he was not here for himself or for personal aggrandisement but to represent the small team that had been employed to monitor the findings of the C.I.A. and to look for possible solutions following that first fatal crash.

In truth his journey from the North of the country had been much as he had anticipated. Of course as expected Stacey's car had not been able to complete the journey and he had almost reached the service station just north of Birmingham when that vehicle finally decided that it had suffered enough and thus it was finally left standing rather forlornly on some garage car park perhaps even feeling as frustrated as what he was at the time that it could not complete the journey.

Now however after a series of bus and train journeys he finally stood in front of the man attired in shirt, tie and formal suit, who was about to make an assessment of the teams work.

"So by this you are trying to prove that the initial helicopter crash into Morecambe Bay was not so much pilot error but was due instead to a fault on the aircraft?" The man tapped his pen against his neck as he spoke. Whether this was done through incredulity at what this young upstart was now suggesting or because the man was trying to think Steve had no idea.

"Yes Sir, from our findings we actually believe that it could have been metal fatigue!" Steve at least attempted to go some way to assist the other man's reasoning.

"But I have already got it on good authority that this was not the cause!" Now the conversation appeared to be developing the talons of a legal argument.

"Initially I accept that pilot error was the official reason given for this crash. Yet after considering the more recent disaster in the North Sea where fortunately all the passengers and crew were rescued, it would appear that further suggestions of metal fatigue have now been put forward. Indeed it was even suggested by one independent source that such metal fatigue occurred in the shaft that led to the gear box!"

The other man now tutted, an action that now suggested to Steve that he had made his point, not that the other individual was to pleased with the suggestion even so! "So now I presume you have come here with some so called solution to this problem?" The man looked at the folder that Steve was still clutching as if his life depended upon it. The look however was fringed with a certain amount of scepticism that questioned what he considered that it was that gave Steve the right to monopolise his time on a matter of some trivia.

"I cannot claim complete credit for our findings Sir. Indeed a group of us who are likeminded over the matter and also currently working together were granted permission by our employers to monitor the findings of the C.I.A. and afterwards we were also transferred to the Tyneside region in order to continue with our investigations!"

The man still regarded him rather clinically as Steve then made to open the file he was holding and place the relevant pages down on the table. "But this-----," the man claimed after a brief perusal, "this documentation relates to some completely new type of Air Craft Transporter?"

"Yes Sir, that is correct. After working for some time in this field we now feel that such a craft if adopted would not be subjected to the same mechanical demands that is made upon some of the key components in the helicopter ferry service!"

"But surely man you must agree that the helicopter has more than proved its worth over the years in this sort of handling?"

"The helicopter has indeed been a willing work horse in this field Sir. But time passes and maybe after such a lapse of time it is now opportune to consider making a change, especially if the new adaptation should prove in the long run to be more reliable?"

"I am sorry but I am afraid that I cannot accept your premise young man. Think of all the costs that would be involved in setting up such a project of which we would have no guarantee would prove to be successful? Who are you people anyway? What gives you the right to believe that you could be more successful than our recognised designers in this field?"

"To begin with we are all qualified engineers. In addition to that two of the members of the group have already been employed in the designing of such craft and moreover they can provide excellent references to that effect!"

The other man still shook his head. "I'm sorry, you can if you wish of course leave your plans here on the table and I will get someone to take a cursory glance at them. One thing is definite however we cannot afford to have our system sullied by a group of mavericks however well intentioned they may be!"

Steve picked up his papers and returned them to the folder. "I'm sorry Sir, but if you are not interested in becoming involved with this project then I think it is a pointless exercise in leaving these here with you. I feel I owe at least that much to my colleagues!"

The man who was conducting the interview swung back on his chair obviously now taken completely by surprise at this young man's attitude. Yet even before Steve reached the door he stayed him. "I have been thinking however. Maybe it is possible for you and your team to broach this matter further. You will of course have heard of Tim Greatorex, the aircraft designer?"

Steve nodded for who indeed had not heard of this man who was the foremost aircraft designer that this country had so far produced.

"I would like him to take a look at your idea. If you are in agreement I could arrange a meeting and then perhaps always providing he is in agreement, your theory could be put through some clinical testing?"

Steve paused as he thought of the group back on Tyneside who no doubt would urge him to accept the offer. More than that he also thought of Pete who had lost his life because of one of those prehistoric relics.

"So if I agree, what would this involve?"

"As far as you are concerned I will ask him to contact you. I happen to know that he visits the North East on a regular basis so I now suggest that you put your ideas concerning this new type of craft to him. I presume you have a contact number that you can leave me?"

Steve watched as the man methodically recorded the same. He supposed that in a way he was sticking his neck out by doing this but then the others expected it of him and in any eventuality there would be nothing lost by calling this man in. The other watched as Steve now carefully refolded his papers ready to replace them in the document case he still held. In some senses Steve now felt it had perhaps been a waste of time in coming all this way and in such adverse circumstances just to receive a refusal, but it had been a necessary step if the group ever wanted to see their plans mature and moreover that much he also owed to Pete.

In his endeavours however Steve never noticed the tightening of the other man's lips as he took his leave of him. He might have been even more surprised however if he had been party to the man's actions after he had left. For the phone call that this individual made was to someone themselves currently in the North of the country and there most certainly appeared to be no expression of understanding on the face of this man as he spoke down the telephone to the person he was calling!

Stacey cringed as the slimy character approached closer to them wearing upon his lips a beaming smile of falsehood that was aimed in her mother's direction.

"I called round earlier today to see you Stacey. I guess I forgot that you were working until after lunch, but my journey was not entirely in vain for then I had the privilege of meeting with this charming lady at the time, which I considered to be my good fortune!" Even as the words issued from out of his lips Stacey was convinced she could spot the venom escaping with them.

"Perhaps it would have proved easier to find me back at the Hall!" Her reply was clipped in its tonality with the words issued almost in a machine like fashion.

"As it happened I was currently employed over this side of the lake. It is all part of the new management training course we are currently developing for our young people. Obviously we try to change their activities from time to time so that one cannot become too complacent, in fact not to put too finer a point on it helps to keep the tutors as well as our students on their toes. Perhaps though you are not yet familiar with the latest fad that is currently taking off and might well in the future make it through to the pentathlon. It's actually called swim hiking?"

"I have heard of it of course!" She thought back to what Steve had told her about the sport. Well there was no way that this fellow was going to consider that she was stupid as well as vulnerable.

"You have?" Meredith Drew sounded surprised and she relished the thought of having this advantage over him.

"Yes as a matter of fact I spotted some of your inmates exercising themselves out in the Bay between the Islands there!"

"That is because of course the activity as such is still in its embryonic stage. But now we are required to develop this exercise further especially as far as swimming to and from the Islands is concerned and also more especially as far as the hike part is involved. Personally I believe that having to climb the hill from the Ferry House up towards Sawrey after swimming the lake with a full pack on their back will prove to be a tremendous test of character and help to further develop a team spirit more especially if the students have to rely upon one another to supply some of their basic needs. Wouldn't you agree with me on that?" So this, she presumed was what he was using as an excuse for having his henchmen combing Lady-Holme earlier on that day. It was almost as if he had indeed spotted her and now wanted to justify his position. Apart from that she began to wonder if this really was her mother currently standing open mouthed as she listened to every word the man uttered. "But of course that was not the main reason for my visit to see you. I felt in fact that I needed to apologise for the other night Stacey. Maybe in truth my behaviour towards you was totally out of order!"

It was then that she remembered this man's attitude towards Tom earlier on and there was no doubt in her mind that this devil could most certainly put on the act of a charmer when he wanted something, which to her mind meant that employing his henchmen to search that Island for any clues left by Steve had yielded him nothing!

Still the mention of a previous encounter between her daughter and this man had her mother now raising her eyebrows a little. In fact the older woman was now beginning to feel that she would never understand this girl even if she was her daughter. The fact that the girl was clever had of course been made obvious by the glowing reports she had received from her teachers at school as well as by her exam results. But instead of listening to and going along with the advice that had been proffered to her from numerous sources along with the active encouragement provided by herself and the girl's father before he had died, Stacey had defiantly chosen to bury herself away in a rather mundane nondescript job. At first they had not believed that she would settle there in the long term but Stacey had proved them wrong. And now it appeared she had met this rather distinguished looking gentleman who appeared to cultivate both etiquette and good manners as well as a large bank balance and had declared him as being the devil incarnate!

"There is really no need for you to apologise Mr Drew!" Once again the girl appeared to have adopted a different guise. "As a matter of fact I was rather tired after a busy day!"

"Touche!" Her mother mouthed the words without sound.

"In that case you must allow me to make amends. Your sister here has been telling me that you are into walking in your spare time?"

Her sister! The man was at it again. "I think you mean my mother Mr Drew!"

"Good gracious I never would have thought ----!" No doubt by this time her mother would be purring and ready to lap the cream from out of this fellow's hand! "Anyway I wondered if these magazines on Cumbria that includes a variety of walks available might possibly be of some use to you!"

"Well providing the walks are all at low level!" Her mother had now taken up the challenge by portraying an almost worried expression as she surveyed the surrounding fells.

"I can assure you that there are quite a variety of different walks on offer both at high and at low level Mrs Kershaw. No doubt you will be able to make a better assessment once you have browsed through them. After all it is a great pity to come on a visit to this part of the country without partaking in a variety of experiences!"

He took his leave of them giving a quaint little bow that to Stacey's mind reminded her of something out of a Dracula movie and her mother watched his retreating figure almost rapturously.

"That is such a nice man our Stacey, and you are saying that he works at the Hall?"

"He is affiliated to dealing with the organisation of courses that they set up and run from there yes and he also manages to impart a feeling of fear and trepidation amongst those whom he considers to be his underlings. But personally I see the man as something rather different. He reminds me of some dark satanic force that is surrounded by a veil of secrecy!"

"That is hardly like you to say that of anyone Stacey. Sometimes I really don't know what has got into you!"

"Possibly I don't speak of anyone like that in general terms. But then remember he was the one who was trying to prevent Steven from taking that documentation to London, and I doubt very much that his visit here was made as a courtesy call. I rather believe that he was using it as an excuse to use his guile to find out exactly who was currently staying in this cottage and whether indeed Steve had left any evidence behind!"

Her mother made a sound that possibly indicated that she found it very difficult to accept this story and immediately turned her attention back onto the magazines.

"What do you say to Tarn Hows? It has a good write up here as well as being listed in the most impressive low walks as well, why they say that it is even suitable for children. That means I should be all right, I think!"

The breeze had managed to blow up during the afternoon that was more than welcome for it certainly helped to cool the heat of the day a little. All of which Stacey found to be delightfully refreshing as she paused to watch some of the sails on the boats move gently backwards and forwards as if they were in harmony with nature's elements.

The morning had started out quite differently, with a veil of mist that had practically shrouded the lake from view and hidden the secrets it kept from any watchful eye, but now, through the kind heart of those gusts that set out to prove who indeed was the true master of the elements, such mist had all been dispersed giving yet another refrain of the summer weather they were currently experiencing. Now the colours also showed their vibrant best determined that all who had eyes should see the splendour of the foliage before the summer eventually gave way to the turning of the year and a hue of a different kind.

Even so, unlike most afternoons the local fowl population had not yet retired for their afternoon siesta, which was often taken under the same forms where folk often sat, whilst in all probability they blissfully wondered whether these same people would find it in their hearts to leave behind some tasty morsels

Stacey nevertheless presumed that she must have been dreaming when the shrill tones of her mobile chose that exact moment to rouse her. She had previously been aware that her mother had decided to spend the afternoon shopping in Kendal, "to make a bit of a change I think Stacey!" and therefore she had felt this afternoon that there was nothing for her to rush back to the cottage for, at least not until later on in the day. Therefore that was why she had obeyed her own inclinations to act out the part of a holidaymaker, at least for a short time! Wondering now who it could be that sought to destroy her pleasures of that afternoon she made to answer it, all the time wondering as she pressed that O.K. button whether or not she was in the process of making more work for herself.

"Stacey, I need to see you! There is something that I need you to do for me!" The voice she heard was not that of her mothers however for it came from the very last person she had expected to hear from at this time.

"Steve -----? Where on earth are you?" Her question showed genuine surprise but she knew his voice well enough to realise who it was.

"I'm heading back to the cottage!"

"No!" A thousand thoughts percolated around her mind at the very suggestion. The place was now far too dangerous to chance such a meeting, especially with all the recent interest that had been shown in it.

"Then I will come to your flat. I'm not fooling Stacey, I really do need your help!"

"Then we will have to find an alternative venue. The places you have mentioned are currently far too dangerous if you need to keep out of sight!" Her mind began to race quickly for it seemed that everywhere the girl normally frequented now appeared to have Meredith Drew's markings on them. They obviously needed somewhere they could talk in private but on the other hand somewhere that appeared to be so open that they could possibly be passed by without folk paying attention. "Look the men are currently here beginning to set up part of the fair on the Glebe ready for next weekend's air show. As there are presently dozens of bodies around the place I don't think that two more will be noticed. I will explain then why I think the cottage and my flat are bad ideas. What time can you make it for?" Even as she spoke she wondered why she had never questioned him further on what he wanted to see her about, but then that was Steve for if he said that he had something he felt necessary to inform her of this must indeed be the case.

"I'm currently at Burton in Kendal Service Station so give me half a hour. Is that O.K. with you?"

She never asked in her reply how he had managed to get there, surely her old banger could never have lasted that long, a simple yes to his question was enough before he switched off. In fact she was stood by the site of the big wheel that was being erected a good ten minutes or so before he finally arrived waving his hand to her from the inside of a red fiesta as he made to park it.

"A hire car!" He answered her question before she even put voice to it. "You see I needed something to get back to the North East in!"

"The North East?" Of course she knew that he worked there, that he had initially brought the documentation from that place, but then the Lake District was hardly in that direction.

"I made a slight deviation mainly to ask a favour off you!" His eyes softened to an almost pleading look that suggested that he knew that this girl had already done enough for him without asking her to commit herself further.

"Which is?" She looked at him quite coquettishly now. In point of fact it had almost been on her lips to ask him what it was worth. A collar dove perched overhead in one of the trees chose that moment to interrupt their discourse with a throaty call.

"I was going to ask you if you would keep these papers safe for me?" He held out the file and Stacey's first reaction was to think of the search attempt on the cottage not to mention Meredith Drew's own attempts to seek out something belonging to Steve.

"Perhaps it would be safer for you to keep them for things have not been quite so plain sailing here since you left. Indeed a variety of folk seem to be rather anxious to redeem anything like that you may have left behind the last time you were here. But I understood that the general idea was for you to take them to some person in London?"

"To put it in a nutshell I found it extremely difficult to convince my contact of their worth although almost as an afterthought he did put me on to another person even if I still question whether I could trust him!"

"But surely if you are intending to go back to the North East it would make more sense to take them there?"

"That is one thing that I do not relish for I still believe they will be safer here with you. But you mentioned that after I left people had been asking for me?"

"Does the name Meredith Drew mean anything to you?"

Steve thought for a moment before shaking his head. "Nope, sorry I guess it doesn't. Why who is he?"

"In his official role he is one of the big cheeses up at the Management training Centre at the Hall. Even so he has managed to devise a scheme whereby he can search Lady-Holme. In the first place by using his henchmen and after that his students, claiming that he was trying to incorporate that crackpot idea you once talked about, swim- hiking was it, into his assessment role!"

"That's strange for now it rings a bell. The second day I was cooped up there on the Island I actually spotted some of the young ones. At the time I confess the idea of an organised activity never occurred to me for I thought quite frankly the lot of them were crackers. Young men in their prime of life with nothing better to do than to swim to the Island, strip out of their wetsuits, then partake in some physical activity before donning their gear again, hoisting their packs on their backs and then taking off back into the water!"

"Then did they spot you? Was that the reason why Meredith Drew was so adamant about having the Island searched later?"

"I don't think that they did. In fact the only thing they appeared to have eyes for was their own stopwatch almost as if they were checking just how long it was taking them to carry out a particular task! I told you at the time, I thought they were quite crackers!"

"But someone must have spotted you for the very next day after you had left the cottage was broken into. Yet it was no ordinary theft, nothing was taken to my knowledge!"

"So did you notify the police about it?"

"No, because by that time I had notified my mother! Well initially I did hire the place for a relative so I persuaded her very much against her will to come and stay. Not only that but follow the party patter of going for walks!"

"You mean you actually got your mother into walking?"

"I could only get her to attempt the easy ones of that I assure you!"

"So I suppose she is still at the cottage?"

"For the rest of the week yes!"

"Then perhaps she could prove to be the perfect custodian for us. Nobody, but nobody would ever dare to remove anything from your mother's clasp, especially if she never realises that she has got the papers in the first place!"

"And this is all you came back to see me about; just somewhere to hide these?" She took hold of the file dubiously as one rankling question still sought to disturb her.

"Perhaps not exactly all. Is this was you were inferring by any chance?" Quite suddenly he bent and kissed her in full view of all those who were passing, and the kiss was certainly not of a platonic nature. But then all the world is supposed to love to see a lover and therefore such an action was accepted and remained unchallenged. Indeed even the men occupied in the erection of the big wheel passed the occasion with mere wolf whistles, but then they were strangers themselves to this place who were interested in completing their own task that day and they certainly posed no threat.

"But you mentioned someone else I believe who had been enquiring about me?" His mind had returned to what she had said earlier and consequently he now broke away from their entanglement.

"Well yes, the day after you left I had a visitor. Well at least a note was dropped into my apartment. It was signed by someone who called himself Bob Eldon and he said he needed to contact you!"

"Bob Eldon you say is here?" Incredulity now showed up in his eyes.

"Presuming that it was this person who pushed the note under my door then yes. But who is he Steve?"

"Bob? Why he is one of the group with whom I am currently working. But I guess I have no idea how he found out where I was or rather had been!"

"He didn't for I never actually saw him!"

Still it appeared that Steve remained a little disconcerted with the news. Then pulling his mood around he endeavoured to speak to her in a natural sounding voice. "We have much to talk about Stacey once all of this has been cleared up successfully. But this, I am afraid is something that I am determined to go through with if only for your brother's memory. That is why these documents are so important and why I must now beg to leave then here with you instead of taking them back to a place where I am already known!"

"By that I suppose you mean that you stopping no longer than what is necessary. You came simply to deposit these and we have thus no opportunity to spend any time together at all?"

"I'm sorry but the answer must be not this time around Stacey. Believe me I wish with all my heart that things could be different. But if we remain together for any length of time this could result in dire consequences. That is why I asked to meet you secretly and that is the reason why you chose this place above all others, remember?"

She studied the man whom in one sense she felt she knew well but yet in another found the veil of secrecy he chose to adopt difficult to penetrate. "What exactly does that file contain Steve?"

At first he seemed reluctant to say anything and then possibly realising that if he refused to speak the girl was quite likely to open the file for herself in an attempt to find out. "If you must know it is a design for a new type of Transporter. One that we believe will save lives even though vested interests seem to be hell bent on stopping us to realise our objective. Does that satisfy your curiosity?"

"Not totally but I suppose I must accept it!"

"Then all I can say is to thank you from the bottom of my heart for I know that you will not let me down. You needn't look so worried about the issue, I promise that I will be in touch shortly!"

She watched him leave still not fully understanding the man but simply following her instincts, and a few moments later he was back in that red fiesta speeding away.

-----------"Well have you had a good day out then Mum?" Stacey finally returned to the cottage to find that the woman was already installed and was sipping at a cup of tea as if this gave her time for contemplation.

"I suppose so, anyway where have you been until this time?"

From her appearance Stacey discerned that the woman had not been long in the cottage herself. "I delayed coming back for I didn't expect to see you so soon!" She said nothing of her meeting with Steve and what had transpired between them just a short time before.

"Well I came back because I expect it will rain shortly for I can feel it in my bones that the weather is about to change for the worse without any weather forecaster going on about it with his weather charts. Funny really how such a change always effects my rheumatics before they even get around to thinking about it!"

"Well there are theories abound that it is something to do with an alteration in the air pressure!"

"Well maybe they would find an excuse for it now that so many of us are suffering the pangs of restless nights. After all arthritis is the poor relation of the National Health Service. I guess if they spent more of their finances in trying to find some drug to alleviate it then there would be less for that tier of Management who have to find funds to pocket their own pet issues. Still what is that in your hand you have brought back with you?"

"This? Oh nothing, merely some nighttime reading for myself. It's not an Agatha Christie Mum so I doubt very much that you would enjoy reading it."

"Hmm I suppose chance would be a fine thing on that score!" Still having established that these alien papers were full of theories and the like the woman quickly realised that they were not of the remotest interest to her. Still perhaps after all it was her mother's belligerent attitude that gave Stacey her first clue as to where to place those papers, for up until that moment she really had not much of a idea, everywhere she had initially thought about being up for question. As a child part of Mrs Kershaw's mannerisms had dictated an atmosphere of tidiness around the house and upon viewing the condition of Stacey's bedroom as a young teenager, the woman had clucked initially most disapprovingly before resorted to buying her a nightdress case fashioned in the form of some alien from out of space, and insisted that was where her night attire would in future be kept and not left draped across the first piece of furniture Stacey had come across. And because her mother had a habit of insisting that her will was carried out, Stacey had at the time reluctantly adopted this creature she had named Jason for that story was surely where a creature of this type could be found.

Strangely enough she had grown accustomed to having Jason around, so much so that when she had left home Jason had gone with her. Not only that but Jason developed a habit of following her around wherever she was. Consequently Jason was right here in the cottage with her at the time, only now Stacey believed she had a slightly different role for this hero of Greek Mythology for the creature seemed to be an ideal choice for the deposition of hose papers. In the daytime wrapped up in her pyjamas it was extremely doubtful that anyone should suspect their existence! And furthermore when darkness fell she herself should be in charge to be custodian to them.

"Have you seen any more of that nice Mr Drew then?" Now the woman decided to exert her curiosity and for once Stacey didn't know whether to cringe or laugh. Meredith Drew was one person she most definitely didn't want to see and on the other hand her mother must never know whom her daughter had actually seen that afternoon. It was the dichotomy of characters between those two men that made her want to smile for to her mind who on earth would want to entertain Meredith Drew when Steven Futton was available?

Avril Togas was posed wearing a smirk on her face when Stacey arrived at work the following morning. Quite obviously the woman gave the impression that she was coveting an audience eager to impart some good fortune of her own, news that had already left the rest of the staff in the office with deaf ears.

"You will never guess what has happened!" She hardly gave Stacey a chance to pass through the door before she started upon her rhetoric now that she felt she had achieved yet another listener and true to form the rest of the office staff sighed with relief and got their heads down to complete their own individual tasks.

"Go on then, tell all!" This, decided Stacey, was the least point of resistance for she had realised that whether she had agreed to listen or otherwise she was most certainly going to be treated to this oration.

"Mr Drew has been to see me this morning!" The girl puffed out her chest rather resembling one of those geese on the lake. "What is more he asked me if I would type up his new programme that he has now devised for the Management Course up at the Hall! Of course as it will all be completed in my own time he has promised to pay handsomely for my services plus he has invited me to take it to him at the Hall when I have completed it. Such a nice man he is too, but then you have met him Stacey, do you think he is married?"

"I have really no idea!" The idea that Meredith Drew had decided to now spend his time soliciting Avril's favours pleased her for to her mind this meant he would not have the same amount of time to devote in searching for either Steve or his papers!

"I do hope that he isn't, but there again nowadays one never knows I suppose!" Avril was still too full of herself to be aware of Stacey's lack of interest in the matter; perhaps indeed the girl was still naïve enough to believe in personal aggrandisement.

"I noticed that they were starting to erect the fair for next weekend's festival!" Stacey decided that perhaps it might be easier to change the subject!

"Oh that -------It's so noisy with all those aircraft zooming about. Personally I don't consider that the Lake District is a suitable place to hold such a venue as it serves to ruin all the peace and tranquillity around these parts!

Guess what, when I was coming to work this morning I actually saw a rabbit, a baby one I think, do they call them leverets? Anyway the little mite was sitting down by the lake amongst all the ducks there as if it thought it was one of them! I don't suppose for one minute you will see anything like that with all the noise and pollution that festival brings with it about!" Avril at least looked pleased with herself for she considered she had got her point across quite well.

"Well I suppose the festival does attract visitors to the place and after all we do need to keep attracting them especially in the current economic climate!"

"Speaking of visitors how is you visitor enjoying her holiday then? I thought initially that you said that you had rented the cottage for a party of walkers but Meredith told me it was for your mother!"

"Well I suppose you could class my mother as a visitor as she normally lives outside of the area, but as a matter of fact she also enjoys a little peace and quiet as well!" Stacey now almost snapped the words out and was rewarded for her effort by a look of positive delight on the other girl's face, as she believed she had finally succeeded in getting under Stacey's skin!

"Meredith's schemes involve peace and tranquillity anyway. His latest scheme involves all three of the Islands out there in the Lake. On the course the students have to visit all three of them and then also get to Low wood by a system of swim- hiking. I must say this swim-hiking sounds exciting Stacey, have you heard of it before?"

"Have you ever tried swimming the lake with a pack on your back Avril? So the big man has now altered his initial plans a little?"

The other girl looked surprised that Stacey should even know anything of this and Stacey could not resist attempting to take her down a peg or two. "Initially you see he suggested that the young men should attempt jogging up the hill towards Sawrey from Ferry House after they had swum from the Islands. But perhaps at the time he considered that we might be persuaded to set out a table with bottled water on for them on the way!" A note of sarcasm tinged her tones even as she spoke for Stacey had already decided that it wasn't bottled water the man wanted his students hanging around that cottage for.

"I never realised that you were so familiar!" Now the girl was trying to save face.

"Not me Avril, it is my mother that Mr Drew appears to be familiar with. In fact you would think that they were a couple of conspirators if you saw them with their heads together! But there again they are probably of similar age to be able to share a confidence!"

⋆ ⋆ ⋆ ⋆

Chapter Four

Although she knew that the Air Show was imminent, there was no one who was more surprised than Stacey when she received a call on her mobile from Steve. Naturally enough she already knew that as an engineer he had a particular leaning towards new designs, but perhaps because this air show was completely land ridden, and Steve's work mainly concerned transport to the oil rigs in the North Sea, perhaps the last thing she expected to hear at the time was that for some apparent reason he was to be drafted in along with a team on that particular weekend.

But that was only her first surprise however, the second one came in the form of her mother, who after the initial barrage of moans and groans as to why Stacey had inflicted this stay upon her, now decided that she was enjoying the peace and tranquillity as well as the place where she was staying and pleaded with Stacey to obtain another week for her at the cottage if this was at all possible. Well it was possible just about for the owners had decided to extend their own holiday but all this meant that Stacey found herself with a great deal more running about to do than she had ever anticipated. Not that upon due reflection she considered that this was a bad idea for after all the documentation was still concealed in that nightdress case and if her mother stayed put then Stacey would not be forced to find a new home for it.

Still to add to her frustration as she set out to work that day it was to find that the apparent good spell of weather had come to a rather rapid conclusion for she was met with a typical Lakeland drizzle that morning that she considered was enough to even persuade the white lady of the Lake to appear out of her lair in order to make an appearance and portend gloom and doom upon all of her surroundings, not withstanding the folk who chose to inhabit them at the time! Thus such climatic conditions did little to lift her spirits that day plus the fact there were still so many things that she had to think about before Steve finally arrived. One of these things was of course Meredith Drew! Maybe on the surface it could be said that the man resembled some puffed up chicken with the scheme he had devised now attracting some attention and admiration, but Stacey could not forget the other side of this man's nature; the way that those dark calculating eyes seldom appeared to miss a thing and the way in which he seemingly looked through a person as he attempted to discover secrets that they held sacrosanct. Indeed with Steve arriving shortly she dreaded to think of the outcome should these two men meet and therefore an additional charge on her mind was to try to make sure that the two didn't!

"You are day dreaming again!" It was Dick Soper, looking somewhat concerned but a man who for all that had never really been able to fathom Stacey out.

"Oh me---? I was just thinking of what to do next. My mother has now decided to stop in the area for another week!" The lie sprang to her lips with little effort on her part for after all what she had said was partially true.

"In that case you have my deepest sympathy!" He looked serious for a moment before his eyes started to sparkle. "I suppose you could always take her to Castle Craig, tell her that Wainwright says that it is a must for all visitors! Not that she will ever attempt to climb the fell but the tales of stone crags, solitary hermits and Viking sheep should give her something to think about. Besides the Borrowdale Valley is well known for being the wettest place in England so after sampling a little of it she might possibly decide to cut short her visit after all and head towards more pleasant climes!" She knew he was joking but nevertheless he had at least said enough to project a sort of smile on her face. "Now I consider that suits you a great deal better my girl. All of which brings me back to discuss the night out we promised ourselves before the boss took one look at you and decided he would steal you for himself! Anyway hopefully this time around he should be fully occupied. I have just heard that he is expecting a close friend of his to come over for the air show, some aircraft designer he's been friendly with ever since his University days!"

Stacey glanced through the office window. The drizzle of the early hours seemed to have now abated but instead of the promised sunshine dark clouds still hung in ominous patches overhead. Dick she knew meant well but this sort of jollying it up was not for her, not whilst Steven's impending visit still remained uppermost in her mind.

"I'm sorry Dick, I really am, but I'm afraid it is all hell let loose at the moment, what with everybody phoning up and seeming to want accommodation for this weekend. Just pray for nice weather will you? Otherwise we will hardly be able to cover the cost of bringing in all these outsiders to the affair. But thanks for the offer anyway and I'll certainly bear in mind your suggestion for my mother!"

"What's that?" Neither of them had noticed Avril Togas entering the place. Of course because no one had taken any immediate notice of her she had decided to interrupt the on going conversation and to put it in a nutshell to find out if she was missing out on anything. Stacey was determined to ignore the woman for she had plenty of other matters to chew over but Dick was possibly naïve enough to be taken in by the woman.

"Oh we were just discussing taking Stacey's Mum to Claife Fell and seeing what she made out of it!"

"Surely you can't be serious?"

"Why not after all Wainwright considered it to be a must?"

Stacey waited to hear no more for as far as the other two were concerned they could chat away with her blessing. It might even prove profitable to get rid of two birds with just one stone and therefore she seized the opportunity to leave.

Perhaps however the ides had not decreed that she should be able to leave quite so easily for as she was taking a walk through the park grounds before she finished work that afternoon in order to complete a favour for her employer, whilst at the same time enjoying the fact that the weather, behaving as its usual unpredictable self, had now turned out to be fine and warm, she decided to take her time in order to savour the day. In addition a family of swans had attracted her attention, swimming majestic and proud as mother and father shepherded their six cygnets almost as if they demanded royal attention for this freak of nature. This was something that they had obviously achieved for folk had gathered to marvel at this sight and to use their cameras to their full advantage. Fascinated in watching the no longer camera shy babes she did not immediately see him approach for his movements were sleek comparable to those of a big cat who was metering its prey, until she finally sensed his presence standing behind her on the pathway where she would have passed.

"So this is how the charming Miss Kershaw enjoys spending her afternoon when others might suspect she is working, is it?" How this man could develop such a flippant tone to his voice whilst it still remained chilling she vowed she would never know. What she did know however was that at the time his body was successfully blocking her own path back to the office buildings.

"I was just admiring the swan family like so many others!" Her excuse slipped off the edge of her tongue.

"And there was I really believing that you had become enthralled in watching my new activity project in action!" Again he allowed just enough false pathos to saturate his tones. To be absolutely truthful Stacey had not noticed the young men out on the lake involving all three Islands in their activities. "Why don't you take a fresh look my dear? You will see that I have more than six cygnets swimming in the water at the moment. Whilst you are here I must tell you what a splendid job your friend Avril has done for me in the co-ordination of this activity and all in her own time as well. Talking of which I believe I have heard that your mother is planning to stay on with you for a while longer. A splendid woman, your mother, if I might be forgiven for saying so!"

"She has muted the idea yes!" Did this man miss nothing, or perhaps his mind was so little that everyday occurrences became prevalent to him. Somehow she thought not and she awaited his next crunch line with not a little trepidation. Of course it was not long in coming after he had paused to wait for this feeling of expectation on her part. "A friend of mine has been telling me that a group from the North East are expected to be attending the sir show this year. Will your Steve be with them by any chance?"

How could she answer this question without issuing forth a tissue of deliberate lies? As it was she skirted close to the truth in her response. "I suppose a great deal will depend upon whether he is included in that grouping! At the moment I have no idea!"

"I was merely thinking that if he was then we might be able to clear up one or two issues!" Again she sensed his mood change as his eyes momentarily lost their more friendly approach. Yet this lasted for only a brief moment. "Anyway onto other things. I have half promised to take your mother over Kirkstone to Glenridding. I believe she has mentioned a preference to visit Aria Force. I must confess I have been rather guilty in tormenting her over it previously when we were talking so I think it only right that I make just retribution for my sins by now taking her there! But tell me how would you like to come as well?"

Stacey started a little for her mother had mentioned nothing of this to her and she had no idea that the two of them appeared to be on such friendly terms. Her mind now revolved around that nightdress case where she had placed Steve's documentation. Thank goodness she had mentioned nothing about it at the time to the other woman for it was extremely doubtful that person would touch it of her own volition, she merely considered her daughter to be over sentimental to have kept it for all of this time. Now however it hurt her more than a little to think that Agnes had chosen to confide in this man instead of herself about where she wanted to go! Still perhaps she could imagine her mother's reply if she challenged her on this.

"Oh but you are far too busy dear to take me all that distance! But anyway why shouldn't I enjoy myself with a good-looking escort for a change? After all he is the one who offered. Perhaps our Stacey you could do far worse for yourself than to cast your eye in his direction. The man is eligible and obviously he thinks a great deal about you!"

Perish the thought, she almost cringed, but at least she managed to keep a servile expression on her face as she responded to the creature in question. "I would love to have come Mr Drew but unfortunately I believe that I am tied up here especially at the moment as we are getting far busier with the summer now being upon us!"

"That I consider is a great shame Stacey. By the way the name is Meredith you know!"

That was something she knew all right; nevertheless she still managed to smile sweetly in his direction. "Perhaps another time then when conditions are more favourable. But do enjoy the trip both of you!" Maybe the best issue out of this would come with her mother succeeding in removing him from the vicinity even if this was only for a short period of time!

Even so Stacey's peace of mind was not destined to last for very long, for returning from that trip out with Meredith Drew, Agnes, as well as extolling the man's praises presented her with an envelope.

"What's this?" For a moment Stacey was nonplus.

"It's an invitation for you my dear from Meredith. He was very upset that you were unable to accompany us this afternoon otherwise no doubt he would have given it to you himself, but apparently he wants you to accompany him to a civic dinner that is being given for prominent townsfolk as a sort of thank you for their assistance in the planning of this forthcoming air show and the effort they are putting in to its organisation!"

Stacey tore open the envelope in a rather disgruntled fashion undetermined whether to dispatch the card within it in a similar manner. Granted the occasion was at a rather prestigious hotel, she had to grant them that much, but this was the last thing she felt that she wanted at the moment especially with that toad as her escort! In any event her mind was currently filled with Steve's own potential visit. She had no idea yet exactly when he would arrive or how long he would be staying for, or even for that matter where he would stay whilst he was here. Why then had Meredith chosen her for surely he had recently been extolling the virtues of Avril Togas, therefore why on earth hadn't he invited that girl as a sort of thank you for all the work she was supposed to have put into the project on his behalf?

"I don't really think this is for me! For starters it's not even my style!" She used the invitation card to fan herself for the day appeared to have suddenly got warm.

"Oh but Meredith was most insistent. He said that he would have stayed and mentioned it to you himself but that there were certain matters he had to get back to the Hall to see to. And I must say Stacey that I don't know what you can possibly have against the man for he is the most charming person to be with. After all he has only invited you out to a dinner as his escort, not a long time engagement and considering it, I do believe it is quite an honour for you to be invited anyway so surely you could spare the time to go with the fellow if only to say thank you for his generosity in spending his time in taking me out?"

So that was it! His reason for offering to take her mother to see Aria Force was to persuade her to go out with him, was it? Well if that was the case the man could think again!

Even so Stacey had perhaps underestimated the guile of the man for she had no sooner arrived at the office the next morning when she was met by the site manager who also was aware of this invite and was now himself practically bending over backwards to offer her the time off work if she needed time to prepare for this banquet.

"It is indeed an honour for us all that we will be represented at this function!" Behind him even as he spoke Avril Togas clicked her teeth furiously. Little did she realise that at the time Stacey would have done anything to change places with her and allow her to go in her place.

Moreover Stacey still felt that her hands were being tied over this issue now especially on the job front for a buzz now ran around the office at her so-called stroke of good fortune. It was a feeling that persisted even as she got herself ready reluctantly for this extravaganza. On the other hand Meredith's eyes flashed with pleasure as he picked her up in his Jaguar later that evening, obviously anxious to prove that he was in possession of more than one vehicle, one she presumed for work and the other for occasions such as this; pleasure no doubt that he had managed to get his own way on the issue! O.K. maybe she looked all right from the outside but inside she currently felt as if a cauldron was in imminent danger of boiling over. Yet the pleasure that was obvious in her mother's face as she came to the door to see them off was probably the factor that persuaded her to hold her tongue.

To be honest she was forced to admit that initially it was rather pleasant to sit at that lounge window overlooking the gardens that led down to the lake with its private moorings as she was served champagne during the reception. But then at the time Meredith had disappeared choosing now to mingle with the dignitaries currently arriving and therefore for a time she was left alone. She only wished with all of her heart that he would simply leave her there and find someone else who found his attention flattering. But that scenario was obviously not in the main scheme of things for a few moments later he arrived back at her side beaming a false smile of seduction upon his lips and accompanied this time by another man whom he had obviously been on the look out for.

"Ah Stacey, this is an old friend of mine I would like you to meet Tim Greatorex. The two of us were at University together but now Tim has aspired to greater things for he is now quite a prominent aircraft designer, which of course is the real reason for him being here. –Tim this is a friend of mine Stacey Kershaw. I have recently had the good fortune to get to know her family quite well!"

What a load of cobblers. The man had taken her mother out on one occasion, crossed swords with her daughter and now claimed that they were all good friends. "Oh do excuse me for one moment will you because I have just spotted the Mayor coming in and I must extend an invitation to him to the launching of my latest outdoor pursuits project!"

Well she supposed the blessing of that was that he had at least left the scene and Stacey found the stranger's presence a great deal more satisfying than her escort's! It was the usual mode of small talk nothing more profound but at least the time appeared to pass quickly until the D.C announced that it was time for them to all adjourn to the dining room at which point Meredith instantly reappeared grabbing hold of her arm as she made an effort to stand up almost behaving as if she as one of his prize possessions.

The hotel she had to admit was a definite mixture of the old and the new, for now passing from the luxurious comfy but otherwise dated lounge area and stepping into the Restaurant was like stepping through the centuries but as if this wasn't enough Stacey found that in this place they were destined to be stationed far too close to the top table for comfort and also a long way from any exit where she could perhaps have sought to escape from!

The ethos of the affair was that of a general welcome to all those fortunate enough to be invited not forgetting to extol all that they had done to ensure the forthcoming air show would be a complete success. And although Meredith appeared polite and attentive she had still no idea as to why he had invited her for his mind certainly appeared to be in other places. This was a tendency that was to remain even after the excellent meal had been served immaculately and the speeches of mutual admiration had commenced. She was conscious that Meredith had plied her glass with wine but now she sipped at it slowly less he would take the opportunity to refill her glass. There was literally no way she was going to drop her guard even if her escort did appear to be pre-occupied in casting his eyes around the assembly for someone who was obviously not there!

"You must come to my own presentation tomorrow Stacey!" He had finally turned his attention back onto her now obviously having given up his search. Not that she desired it for indeed she much preferred to remain in the background and simply pray for the evening to draw to a conclusion. But then she supposed once she arrived back home her mother would be waiting up for her prompting her in what to say!

"But you know that I will be working Meredith. Let's face it Dick has been very good in allowing me the time off today especially when we are so busy. I really cannot impinge on his good nature any further!"

"But Dick is coming up to the Hall himself to find out what it is all about. Tomorrow is a good day for us to start the ball rolling for we have an influx of new students and the Management team have already got everything in place!"

"It is very kind of you Meredith. But on the other hand I understand that Avril has done a lot of the work for you therefore surely it would be more courteous of you to have invited her instead?"

"Oh Avril!" He didn't seem to be at all impressed. "But then I wanted to invite you my dear so that you could learn that we have finally found a use for those Islands in the lake. Not Belle island of course, well at least not at this time, for I consider that Island already gets its fair share of visitors, but maybe, just maybe, we will now be able to open up some of the others!"

He deftly picked up her wrap and moved to place it around her shoulders a motion that caused her to shiver apprehensively. She felt his fingers beginning to burn through the material. "By the way did I tell you how delightfully elegant you look tonight my dear?"

She blushed and opened her mouth to say something in return but no sound issued forth from her lips. Fortunately his attention appeared once more to have become diverted. "I must just say good night to Tim my dear. I have no doubt that you will be seeing him again very shortly when the air show commences. I do believe that at the moment he is staying in Ambleside!"

She nodded feeling relieved that the moment had passed and stood patiently awaiting for his return. It was whilst she was there that one of the waiters caught her eye and moved towards her. "Miss Kershaw, I am right I hope?" She nodded haphazardly as she watched her escort's progress across that room. "There is a gentleman in the reception area who wishes to speak to you Miss!"

Stacey frowned. Surely there must be some mistake. No one knew that she was here tonight outside of her immediate circle and surely no one from the office would have taken it upon themselves to follow her here. Still because it appeared to be expected of her she nodded in reply before making her way back up those stairs. The man who apparently had been waiting for her turned and it was with something like shock when she recognised the features of Detective Inspector Forsyth.

"Ah please forgive this untimely intrusion Miss Kershaw. I called at your cottage earlier this evening and your mother informed me where you were!"

"But how can I help you Inspector?" She glanced around her wondering if the others about had noticed; but if they had indeed recognised the man out of uniform the hotel staff were far too polite to let any emotion show on their faces.

"We have heard from one of our sources that Gareth alias Steven Futton is heading in this direction Miss Kershaw and there are still some matters that we wish to clear with him. The question is have you seen him, has he contacted you or do you know of his whereabouts at this time?"

She shook her head not a little perplexed. She knew of course that Steve had planned on coming to the air show but as to why the police wanted to speak to him was something that was very different. Warning bells started to ring in crescendo like fashion within her head. "I'm sorry Inspector but I am afraid that I cannot help you. This indeed is the first that I have heard about it. But if the man is here why do you believe that he will contact me?"

"We do believe Miss Kershaw that at one time the two of you were very close!"

"As a matter of fact Steve was my brother's friend and yes he spent many summer vacations with us when they were at University together. But I am afraid that is the end of the story!"

"I see!" The inspector inferred that he did not see at all. "Well if he should contact you perhaps you will ask him if he will call us on this number!" The policeman handed her a card "I must insist that it is a rather important matter Miss Kershaw!"

"Of course -----!" She was interrupted from saying anymore with the arrival of Meredith.

"Now I wondered where you had got to!" Then noticing the Detective he frowned. "Is everything all right Stacey?"

"Perfectly all right!" Never before had she ever imagined that she would ever be glad to see this one's face. But now quite suddenly she had begun to feel as if she was stepping into some sort of a trap. "Actually I am ready for home if that is all right with you Meredith?"

He looked pleased with her delivery and slipped his arm around her shoulders as they made to leave the hotel together. Outside, it being the summer months it was not yet completely dark and crowds beginning to arrive for the forthcoming air show were now milling around in the streets. But there was one face in that crowd that drew Stacey's attention, for at the time this face was looking somewhat puzzled at the sight of her leaving the hotel with Meredith Drew and now as he was possibly thinking that his eyes were deceiving him, there could be no mistaking the face of Steven Futton in amongst that crowd.

Still conscious of the fact that the detective was not far behind them Stacey could do little more than look hard in his direction and hope that she could convey some sort of a message to him, but again it was Meredith's arm that was still around her shoulders and she had to wonder what hope she had of succeeding.

As it was she realised that her mobile would be shrilling its head off any second. In fact her only surprise was that it didn't actually ring before she seized the opportunity to turn it off before Meredith noticed her move!

Still she endeavoured to be polite to that satanic devil on the way back to the cottage even if at the same time she was wishing the man to be far away. And for once in her life she was almost pleased to see that her mother had not retired when they arrived back for at least the woman's presence there had the effect of swiftly dispatching him even if he did wear a slightly hurt expression on his face at the time.

"But of course you will come to my presentation tomorrow won't you Stacey?" He had finally changed his tactics to portray an almost beseeching side to his nature.

"Of course she will be glad to come!" It was Agnes who was the one to respond to that for Stacey's own mind was currently tied up thinking about Steve and what exactly he was doing at the time. Therefore she made her own response by mumbling something which Meredith was happy to take as being the affirmative and Stacey realising perhaps this was obviously a little late strove to add an after phrase.

"It will of course all depend upon Clive and whether he agrees of course!" She crossed her fingers behind her back even as she spoke and hoped with all of her heart that the boss after huffing and puffing and probably stroking the beard on his chin rather thoughtfully, would declare that he didn't consider that she could be spared.

Still at least this half promise seemed to satisfy Meredith and it also succeeded in persuading him into saying goodnight for which she was truly thankful although even after he had gone, as she had fully anticipated, her mother persisted in going on about the evening, asking her who was there and what happened etcetera until finally Stacey felt that she could stand no more of the tittle-tattle and begged to make her excuses.

"Look Mum I really am dog tired and I do have to work in the morning so if you don't mind I'll turn in!"

"But you have remembered that tomorrow after work you did promise to take me on that shorter walk, the one you said was around the beck and past Elter Water to Skelwith Force Waterfall. Weather permitting you do want to keep up the pretence of having a relative who is interested in walking I suppose?"

"No, I haven't forgotten. I promise you that is exactly what we will do providing it stays fine, but before then I really do need to catch up on some sleep. Anyway you can do me a favour by reading up about it in the guidebooks and then tomorrow you will be in a position to tell me all about it on route!"

She left her mother who was still feeling a little disgruntled as if she had missed out on something and now practically made a bee line for her own room. Once inside with the door securely fastened behind her she finally retrieved her mobile.

"Tell me woman what the hell is going on? I've been trying to ring you for simply ages!" The person she called now sounded genuinely irate. "And who, if I might enquire was that dandy who was holding onto you as if he possessed you when you came out of that place earlier on, whilst you were practically begging me with that look of yours not to speak to you?"

"Steve it's a long story and something that I will eventually tell you about when I see you. But if I tell you now that Detective Inspector Forsyth was only two steps behind us when we came through those doors and that the man's one desire is apparently to speak to you perhaps you will begin to understand my reasoning. The fact is you might not recognise it as the truth but you are in danger around here!"

"I am in danger, so what exactly are you inferring by that?"

"I am trying to say that there are too many people around these parts who appear anxious to know your whereabouts for starters for it to be considered a healthy situation. In my opinion for what it is worth you need to keep a low profile!"

"Look I need to see you and talk this through, shall I come out to the cottage? Are you still there?"

"No because I have my mother still here with me at the moment and she had already been charmed by the good looks of Meredith Drew who is also either after you or your documentation for some reason!

"Then where can I see you? You do have the documentation safe I hope?"

"Of course I do, can't you trust me? But as to where I can see you----well perhaps Sawrey village is our best option, at least it is over this side of the lake and I presume you have got your car?"

"I will be there in less than half an hour!"

"Then please promise me that you will be careful. Shall I bring your package with me when I come to meet you?"

"No, not if it is in a safe place, just leave it be for the moment. I still don't really know whether I am au fait about this cat and mouse game though!"

"Please Steve, just trust in what I have already told you. For some apparent reason there are folk around who will literally stop at nothing to be able to wrest those papers from out of your grasp. I'll sneak out of here and meet you in half an hours time then!"

She took a good look at herself as she climbed out through that open bedroom window thanking her stars that the cottage only had a single floor, hoping that at least her mother would be none the wiser for this impromptu exit, and Stacey finally decided that perhaps a streak of lunacy had taken over her brain acting like some wayward teenage rebel. But this seemed to be the easiest way of getting out of that house and she decided that she would just have to think up something very quickly to tell her mother if the woman protested she had missed her when she made her return.

He was there promptly on the half hour as he had promised even though he still looked almost suspiciously in her direction. Still the first words to be spoken were her own.

"First of all Steve what exactly is in those papers that makes everyone from the police down seem to want to get their hands on them?"

He shrugged his shoulders perhaps inferring she should know. "Perhaps you are the one who ought to start by telling me all about your escort tonight?"

She glanced up at his face and noted he was speaking now in all seriousness. A sudden thought crossed her mind. Surely Steve wasn't jealous, not at a time like this and certainly not jealous of Meredith Drew!

"If you must know his name is Meredith Drew and he just happens to be the chief Indian of the Management group up at the Hall. Initially he came there on a visit and then he decided to stay, much to many folk's disgust. I myself was cajoled into going with him tonight to a civic dinner that was given in honour for all the organisers and sponsors of the forthcoming air show. It was an engagement that try as I would I couldn't for various reasons, get out of going to. Does that satisfy you?"

"You could have tried saying a simple no to him I suppose!"

"Under the circumstances that was not an option so perhaps now you will consider getting down from your high horse and tell me what the hell is going on? What for instance is in those papers that you appear to treasure so much?"

"If I said that they contained the design for a new prototype flying machine that has been devised by a team of us who are currently working in the North East as a means of safer transportation, would you understand any better?"

For a moment Stacey felt devoid of something to say but then after a momentary lapse a thousand thoughts crammed themselves into her head. "But if this idea was initially refuted by your contact in London why on earth do others now seek to get their hands on them?"

He shook his head. "That I am afraid is something I cannot tell you for I do not know the answer for certain. I can only suspect that now someone desires to get his or her hands on them far more than I first anticipated. The only conclusion I can draw from this is perhaps the team were right after all and the plans are worthy of someone's houseroom. One of the reasons why I managed to inveigle myself a visit to this air show is that it was suggested by the contact in London that I should make myself available to meet with a certain person, an aircraft designer who will actually be present here at the air show this weekend!"

"You are talking about Tim Greatorex? I think that I have already met him!"

"You have, but how?"

"Because I was introduced to him at the dinner. But as he also happens to be a friend of Meredith Drew my advice to you is to be careful. All the way round I am beginning to suspect that your presence here spells danger!"

"And who do you presume that might come from? Could this be a way of you trying to get rid of me? Is this why you've decided to play this game of cloak and dagger, meeting by moonlight and so forth?"

"Steve now you are talking absolute rubbish!" She silenced him with a kiss. "Does this answer your question, has it never occurred to you that I happen to care what happens to you?" There was a catch now in her voice that almost made her words sound like a plea. It was something that the other did not miss for before any more time elapsed she found herself in that man's arms his lips exploring her own whilst his body moulded against her own setting it now burning with desire to get even closer to this man.

"Why is your mother still at the cottage?" He almost moaned as he realised that the place was so close.

"To cover for you in the beginning although she does not know it. You see I hired the cottage initially for relatives who were supposed to be walkers and therefore I needed someone to fill that role in order to keep the lie. The only trouble is that after a slow start she found that she liked it and stayed on!"

"But surely that will not stop us from going back there now?"

Stacey shook her head. "I'm afraid to confess that sadly my mother has now fallen under the spell of Meredith Drew, therefore I am afraid that place is a non starter!"

"Then what about your flat then?"

She shook her head yet again. "I'm afraid that I also am in the position of being watched. I realised that much when I called to collect some items of clothing for the dinner tonight!"

"Then where do you suggest that we can go to spend some time together?"

For a moment she did not respond until quite suddenly a smile curved around her lips. "Well I suppose there is always one place if you are game ----our Island!"

Maybe his initial look suggested that he considered her to be completely mad but then came the imperative question. "And if I might enquire, how do you propose we get there at this time of the night?"

"Well remember we have done it before and there are definite ways. You have the car and I just happen to know that there are some rowing boats left near to Ferry House, meant to serve as tenders for the yachts moored close by along that stretch of parkland. I suppose it would be feasible for us to borrow one of them for a few hours providing a) we find something that we can use as a paddle as unfortunately they didn't leave the oars alongside of them and b) we put it back afterwards and I am also back at the cottage before Agnes rises in the morning!"

The look he gave her provided the answer and they made their way back to the car together.

She feigned the excuse of a cold coming on the following morning, enough to persuade Clive to allow Avril Togas to go to that damned presentation instead of herself, for there was now no way she craved to see Meredith Drew's face that morning, especially as by this time she was totally convinced that for some reason he was conspiring against Steve. The latter had now gone back to be with his own team but the time they had spent together on that Island still stayed at the forefront of her mind so much so that earlier on she had found herself saying yes to Agnes even without realising what the other was asking of her.

Maybe though Stacey might not have felt so complacent in her mind if she had realised what the outcome of that meeting was, and Avril Togas for one was certainly in no hurry to inform her!

⋆ ⋆ ⋆ ⋆

Chapter Five

It was Jonathan Brownhills who was the first to break the news to Steve upon his return to the group. During the time they had worked together and following their transfer from the Morecambe Bay area to the North Sea, the group of four had become firm friends. Now however there was something that was sadly amiss, a point that Steve realised when he spotted the other waving a piece of paper about like someone demented and in perhaps the most undignified of manner, almost indeed as if the man cared little whether the breeze that had recently blown up out of seemingly nowhere, wrenched it from his grasp or not!

"There's one of these come for you as well!" The other's first words held a tenet of gloom within them that appeared to be echoed in his tones just as soon as he beheld Steve's figure returning to the bed and breakfast accommodation where the quartet were currently residing. "Apparently due to the current economic climate it now appears that our services are no longer required on Tyneside!"

"But that can't be true for we are all employed on the project, which was the reason we were transferred there in the first place!"

"Afraid you'd better believe it Buster. The other two have received their notice as well. Strange as it might sound the damned things were delivered here by hand, although who the devil's advocate was to be employed on such a task and how the devil managed to find out just where we were staying, I'm sure is beyond me! But the letters are clear enough, to put it in a nutshell our services are no longer required, or to say it a little more bluntly we've been sacked mate!"

Steve's lips tightened as he moved to collect his own envelope typed out ever so professionally. Even so at the bottom of this formal thank you but no thank you dictation there was also a request; that is providing one was prepared to review it in that light. Basically this read that all the research that had been developed up until the present time should now be handed back to the firm immediately as their one time masters claimed all such property rightfully belonged to them and therefore they could not consider it to be their own.

"Over my dead body!" The other responded with an explosion through gritted teeth. "Damn it, what gives them the infernal right to consider our findings as belonging to them? Some of the material we already had with us when we left the Morecambe Bay area; other items we have often worked upon in our spare time!"

"Maybe today's news has something to do with it. I'm afraid that there has been another crash in the North Sea. No survivors! I've also received a text from one of our loyal supporters back there that there was after all a suspect gear box, something about sheared metal in it and what was more the damned machine had only just been in for a service!"

Steve visibly swore. "Then it is no wonder that they want our bloody plans now. Perhaps they believe they will solve the mystery for them and they will then be able to claim complete innocence. Well as far as I am concerned they can damned well wait!"

"There's more to follow!" Jonathan Brownhills cleared his throat. "Whilst you have been away we have also had another visitor; a gentleman from the constabulary asking for you Steve. How the hell they knew we were here goodness only knows but fortunately you were out at the time, a matter that did not appear to please the Police Inspector one little bit! Talking of which, where the hell have you been anyway?"

"I prefer to say that is my own business. On the other hand I can assure you that it is nothing that need concern any of you!"

"There was a news flash on the tele earlier!" Jonathan continued now ignoring Steve's statement. "It appears that the general public are now demanding that all such flights should now be banned and the copters grounded until declared completely safe. I suppose this could go some way in explaining why we have currently received our own marching orders. But if they do ground all the craft, what about those poor devils still out on the rigs? Don't tell me that they have ideas of sending the lifeboat out to bring them back! You've gone pensive again?"

"Actually I was just thinking that under the circumstances it is as well I went back and collected our tabulations before we left!"

"Hell fire man, no wonder we had the cops round then!"

"You forget –it was me you said they wanted to see!"

"Perhaps it might be as well if we all scarpered mighty quick. What the hell did you do with the documentation anyway? I thought you said that London wasn't interested?"

"I was hoping to see one certain aircraft designer, a person whom it was suggested I should see by London, and who also happens to be here this weekend. The trouble is that the man never came to the North East as was first intimated. Then when I heard that he would be present here at the Air Show this weekend that was when I managed to wangle us an invite to the affair!"

"So it wasn't our prowess with the copters that brought us here? But this fellow ----where've you got the damned things anyway?"

"Maybe it is enough for you to know that at the moment they are in safe hands. Even so I feel that I have to say that after coming here to see this man in the first place I am now not quite so sure that we are doing the right thing!"

"So you think that it could be a set up then?"

"Yes there well could be I'm simply not sure. One thing is certain however they have nothing at all on you three. I however am in a slightly different position because I happen to know where the plans are. That is the reason why I now propose to get out of this place today before they catch up with me for it's not fair for me to implicate the three of you in this!"

"Where the hell do you think you're going then?"

"Certainly not far!" Steve tapped his nose. "Other than me moving out we will carry on as usual and attend this air show as we previously planned. There hopefully we ought to be able to seize the opportunity to grab the attention of this character, whoever he happens to be, and also if it is possible without giving too much away before we decide what the man has to offer if anything!"

"So where do you think you are going now then?" Jonathan frowned as he persisted with this question upon noticing that Steve had moved to collect his gear.

"From what you have just told me I can no longer consider this place to be a safe haven. I'm going not merely for my own sake however for it is a fact that if I stay I could easily be placing the rest of you in possible jeopardy!"

"But where will you go? Accommodation is not so easy to find this weekend. Secondly how will your absence assist in this job we are supposed to be carrying out at this show?"

"You know full well you needn't worry on that score for I have said that I will be there at the appropriate time. As to where I intend to go, well apart from the fact that at this moment in time I can't really say that I know for sure, even if I did I wouldn't dream of telling you. Why should the three of you have to carry the burden of always having to watch what you have to say?"

Something at the back of Steve's mind rang a bell. It was something someone had told him. Yes that was it, Stacey had mentioned receiving a note from Bob Eldon. "By the way, was Bob trying to contact me about something before?"

"Not to my knowledge!" Jonathan shook his head thoughtfully. "But why don't you ask him if he did?"

"Oh it doesn't really matter. I don't really think it was of any importance. In fact I think my informant was mistaken anyway. We can well do without stirring the mud between us at the moment!"

"I still can't say that I like this idea Steve and I'm afraid I still don't follow your reasoning!" Jonathan had now reverted back to his original topic.

"As far as you not liking the idea, well none of us are intended to. As far as my reasoning, well I thought I had already made it perfectly clear, I cannot in all fairness accept the jeopardy my staying would place you under!"

"Then this aircraft designer you were on about. The one you decided to come here to meet?"

"I will see the person in my own time and at a place of my own choosing because for starters I now have my own suspicions in this individual's direction!"

"Perhaps you are now showing your own susceptibility Steve. After all I understood that you inferred that the person in question had a respected name!"

"It's not the chap's name I am worried about, shall we say, rather more his tendency to have certain friends that I call into question!"

"Now you really are talking in riddles man!"

"Perhaps in all truth I am. At least I only hope it will remain that way although I cannot help my own suspicions on the matter!"

John watched as Steve left the bed and breakfast accommodation with a thoughtful look in his eye. He knew Steve Futton far too well to ever doubt that the motives for his action were genuine enough and he also knew from past experience that Steve was and had always been loyal to the group.

In all truth however when he left the place Steve did not have a single clue as to which direction it would serve him best to travel in. Indeed there was only one such place that came to mind as being reasonably secure and well away from those who demanded too many questions of him. He shrugged his shoulders resignedly and supposed that it was quite possible that the boat they had used earlier would still be where they had left it upon their return to shore and by the look of this vessel when he arrived at the place he hazarded a guess that this craft did not appear to be currently in use by its owners. Not that he fancied adopting the hermit life style again for one single moment but then he supposed that needs must when the devil drives!

Avril Togas' eyes brimmed with extreme confidence as she took her place in that assembly room up at the Hall knowing full well that the eyes of a score or more young persons were upon her as they obviously wondered what this female was doing here and why the man they held in such high esteem had smiled profusely in her direction as she took her seat. Of course the students who had recently commenced upon this course had failed to notice the tinge of disappointment that Meredith Drew had shown when he had realised that it was Avril and not Stacey who had arrived in answer to his invitation to hear his presentation this morning.

"Oh Stacey feels that she could have a cold coming on and in the current climate with all this flu knocking about I suppose one cannot be too careful for she would hate to think that she passed any infection on if she happens to be carrying the virus at this time!" Avril had of course smiled sweetly as she had made the other woman's excuse, for she had still no idea why Clive had suddenly decided she should come here today in Stacey's place! Still the switch had suited her purpose and to give him credit Meredith had rapidly recovered from his initial surprise at this move and had acted as the perfect escort. Therefore Avril now savoured the questioning expressions in the eyes of those who were present before finally turning her eyes back onto the man who had just mounted the podium handling the sheaf of papers with dexterity as he cleared his throat and looked around the place casting an almost benevolent eye upon those selected to be the guinea pigs in his new trials. In all truth however Avril had little interest in any message this man who now peered over the top of his rimless spectacles was about to deliver, for she was merely interested in the figure of the man himself, especially after conceding that as he was living this lifestyle this person must have money! Indeed sitting there she could almost hear the tinkle of the cash as it trickled down from some generously proportioned waterfall.

"Ladies and Gentlemen, first of all I would like to extend a very warm welcome to you all on the Management course that we run from the Hall here. I suspect that by this time you will have taken the opportunity to browse through the literature that you received upon your arrival and no doubt some of you may have heard rumours of certain trials we have been completing here of late. We are of course always eager to incorporate different activities in our itinerary and the one I am now referring to involves one of the new extreme sports that has recently been evolved and is rapidly growing in popularity. No doubt you will already be familiar with other extreme activities such as ghyll scrambling and mountain boarding currently in operation. Well this is a completely new activity to be added to that list! As the pros and cons of this activity are well presented in the documentation you received upon your arrival I will come straight to the point. Tomorrow at 6 am prompt one of your number will be selected to be the first to commence this test intended to develop initiative within you. For you will be embarking upon the new method of outdoor pursuits, namely the one known of as hike and swim!

Using the Windermere Lake print outs you will find within your welcome pack I will be expecting you to plan your own route in this. Initially you will leave this place by the jetty in the Marina here, hike across the three uninhabited Islands situated in the Lake before making your way to the Low Moor Hotel where light refreshments will be served before you recommence your hike back to the Hall here. Upon your return I will be expecting a short report including your experiences and observations whilst you have been so occupied!

Because these are of an individual nature you will travel individually initially leaving this place at twenty-minute intervals to ensure that your opinion will not be influenced either by the person who is just ahead of you or the one who is coming behind you on this trek! The order you which you will attempt this course will be drawn by lots to keep the onus completely fair.

I am now going to ask Mr Soper here if he will demonstrate the right way for you to pack your knapsacks so that they will both hopefully keep your clothes dry whilst you are in the water and also act as a buoyancy aid during your swim. Once Mr Soper has demonstrated the technique for this then I suggest you try it out during the rest of the morning and possibly get the feel of the water!"

Upon this Meredith Drew smiled almost expectantly in Dick's direction and then leaving the other man to complete this mission and also the draw to allocate the student's start times, he left the podium and sidled back to where Avril was sitting.

"So what did you think of all that my dear?"

If the man was coveting praise he had obviously come to the right person and Meredith Drew began to forget his initial disappointment that Stacey was not here after all, for to his eyes it seemed to be quite obvious that this one was both ready and willing.

"Perhaps we should take this opportunity to adjourn my dear. I'm sure that we can safely leave the task now in Dick Soper's capable hands!"

Avril did not argue. Indeed the perfume from the masculine hormones he was now giving off practically intoxicated her as she stood to leave allowing him to take her arm.

---------------At 6 am prompt the following morning Rowland Smethurst swallowed hard before he leapt off the jetty into the icy water of the Lake. Momentarily the guy was definitely wishing he was somewhere else, but then to let the side down he supposed would be to send a curt note of failure to his employers and therefore choosing the nearest Island to his current position he made his way towards the Island of Lady-Holme!

Naturally when he arrived he had no idea whatsoever that someone could just be sleeping on that Island and Steve had passed a rather miserable night dozing only fitfully as he toyed with the notions of what had been happening recently. He was in fact just in the process of finally drifting back into a slumber like state when he was positive he heard the crackling of twigs close by. Immediately the man was wide awake and on his guard wondering if by some means he had been traced. Securing a more permanent cover he spotted his disturber trying his best to hurriedly push his way through bush and trees banging and scratching himself for his trouble. "I must be bloody mad; six o'clock in the morning and prancing about like this!" Whereupon the annoyed traveller after passing within feet of Steve's hideaway appeared to speed off into the distance.

"Well I suppose it takes all sorts!" Steve tried to settle himself once more in order to complete his slumbers yet barely twenty minutes had passed by when he was similarly disturbed by one irate female, scurrying and scraping as she attempted in her turn to speed past the place where he was hidden. Still in the girl's case Steve felt convinced that things were not quite the same for he could have sworn he caught the glimpse of a camera flash.

Steve was to find he was disturbed fourteen times in all in those early hours, and yet every time one of the females passed by there was a camera flash.

Of course what Steve was not party to the conversation amongst the female sex once they compared notes back at the Hall.

"Out there on that Island------I had the strangest notion that someone was watching me when I was on that Island!"

"Funny you should say that but I got the same impression. In fact I'll go as far as to say that I'm sure I saw a camera flash just when I was getting changed!"

"In that case I think we ought to report it. Personally I object to anyone taking photographs, however innocent they might be, especially if they depict me in the throes of my suffering. What about the boys? Did they see anything?"

"Apparently not, although knowing the male sex they would probably never see anything peculiar even if they were likely to fall over it. Even so perhaps we are duty bound to compare notes with them and glean ideas as to our next step in this matter!"

The conversation drifted away as the two girls went about their daily business awaiting the right opportunity to return to the matter in order to get some answers that would satisfy them!

In truth no one could have been more surprised than Stacey when her car was finally returned to her at the camp looking more in pristine condition than it had done when she last set her eyes upon it. It arrived quite ignominiously on the back of a car transporter along with several other vehicles still bearing signs of the coating of grease placed upon them for their protection during transit and which were destined to be delivered to the nearby garage.

"If you don't mind signing here for it Miss. I have been told to inform you that the car can now be considered to be road worthy again although it might be rather foolhardy to attempt any more long distances in a car of this age ------- No Miss!" The fellow was obviously embarrassed as Stacey searched for her wallet ready to pay her dues. "Everything has already been paid for. All that we require from you is a signature to say that you have received it all right!" He held out a clipboard for her to sign in a space opposite to the car registration number.

Still feeling a little bemused at the vehicle's sudden re-appearance Stacey decided to play the matter low key. Obviously she would get on to Steve at the first available opportunity for he was the only one that knew about the incident when it had broken down. Not that it was of any consequence to the others for hadn't she previously told them of her dilemma at having the vehicle rescinded to some repair shop? Even so these good intentions were not to be kept secret for very long for she had not had the car in her possession for long at all before Detective Inspector Forsyth had arrived on the scene accompanied with two of his colleagues from the local constabulary

"You car Miss Kershaw. We have just been led to believe that it has finally been returned to you this morning-------" Stacey with all her intentions of keeping the status quo now had the distinct impression that the man who was currently speaking was also regarding her with an attitude of some disdain. She wondered if the reason for this was because he found the idea of Stacey's car being locked away in some garage undergoing repairs to be quite fanciful.

"Yes as a matter of fact that is correct Inspector!" Her voice portrayed a coolness that she certainly did not feel but after all there appeared to be little point in arguing upon the issue, as he had most probably been witness to the delivery. Still what this matter had to do with him she quite frankly had no idea. "I believe I remarked previously that my car was in the garage undergoing some repair work!"

"Tell me something then that still puzzles me Miss Kershaw. Do you normally seek the facilities of some garage located in the Midlands then?" She did not reply to this. Instead she merely stood with a look of perplexion upon her face at this man's line of questioning. "I happened to notice that the transporter that brought the vehicles here came from that area!"

"Sometimes the parts appertaining to an older vehicle are difficult to find in this area!" She finally found her voice. It was the truth of course even if the parts in question could possible be ordered through some local dealer.

"I see!" The Inspector now gave the impression that he really did not see at all. "Would you mind Miss Kershaw if we took a look at the vehicle in question then?"

For a single moment Stacey actually imagined that the Inspector and his entourage were interested in examining the car's lines, yet it soon became apparent that the Inspector had a different task in mind for his men for they took this opportunity to start the examination within the car itself. She supposed that she could have objected most strongly to this action if Clive Warner's hand suddenly steadied her as if in warning to bite her tongue to keep her silence.

"Maybe it would prove better for you if you consider letting them have their own way Stacey!"

She hadn't heard his step approaching from the office door. Perhaps in all truth Clive was wondering how this latest intrusion would reflect upon his own business. Yet he was probably right in stopping her from objecting and after ten minutes or so the two accompanying police constables emerged from the vehicle shaking their heads.

"Nothing Sir! The car is clean!" Stacey now felt sure that the Inspector was showing signs of some irritation at this news and yet she still failed to see the significance in their statement.

"Of course the car is clean. It was valeted both inside and out whilst it was at the garage and that in addition to the engine being repaired! Anyway what did you expect to find there Inspector?"

"Somehow I don't believe that the Inspector was referring to the appearance of the vehicle Stacey-----!" Again it was Clive Warner who chipped in.

"Then what exactly were you looking for in my car?" Stacey drew herself up to her full height. In actuality she thought no further than the immediate at the time.

"We have reason to believe Miss Kershaw that there is a strong possibility that we could find something that appertains to one of our current cases!" The Inspector now presented a stern face but seemed determined to say little more on the subject. Perhaps it was Clive who again read into the situation better than Stacey for now he seemed determined to drag her away from the scene.

"I suggest then that we leave the Inspector to carry on with this inspection Stacey for after all our time could be more fruitfully occupied. If as you have already said that there is nothing to be found in the vehicle then there is little point in you standing here worrying about it. I am sure if the Inspector needs us for anything he will shout for us!"

Somewhat reluctantly Stacey allowed Clive to persuade her to follow him. Even so deep within the recesses of her mind she could not help but wonder whether there was the slightest chance that Steve had left something behind inadvertently. But Clive was right, she would just have to bide her time and wait for the final outcome!

"We are sorry Mr Drew but we have had reports that this has happened to several of our members on the course, something that was discovered when we compared notes upon our return!" Meredith Drew now faced the bulk of enquiring faces when the students presented their reports on their findings for that day. In this the girls, who had been subjected to the flash photography had most assuredly received the full backing of their male counterparts for in their eyes competition was one thing but this matter was something that was entirely different.

Still portraying tight lips Meredith Drew responded by pacing several digital images in front of them on the long table that had been set up for this purpose. "I claim full responsibility of course but the idea was most certainly not intended to embarrass any of you but rather to monitor this new activity to see if there was any way in which it could be improved! After all one can hardly publicise the findings of any new activity without the evidence to back up ones theory. Nevertheless if I have unwittingly offended anyone by my actions I do apologise. But please take a look at these photographs for yourselves before making any further judgement and then if anyone still feels that I have placed them in an uncompromising position then I promise you that all such evidence will be immediately destroyed!"

On the surface at least the prints appeared to be much as Meredith Drew had stipulated and therefore the students felt duty bound at least openly to withdraw any previous allegations for perhaps even they realised the significance that any such claims could have upon the future of the Centre itself. Even so, whilst on the outside Meredith Drew portrayed an amicable expression, inside this man was now positively seething that these nincompoops had shown the audacity to stumble across his actions. He turned and left the group with hardly a smile but rather drumming his fingers instead upon a nearby ledge. Well he supposed he would just have to take more care in the future with his form of art. He didn't know why his thoughts suddenly turned upon Stacey Kershaw at the time. Of course he supposed the girl would make an excellent model for his purposes if he could but use his persuasive power. Looking out through the long window as he left he spotted her with Clive Warner currently speaking to that policeman and his eyes widened somewhat.

Meredith Drew was nothing if not quick witted. Indeed it could be said that it had been his wit rather than his brain power that had succeeded in establishing him in his current position, and it was his current wit upon observing the two of them together after the policeman had taken his leave that finally brought to mind an idea that he now felt duty bound to act upon.

The initial invitation to Clive Warner to come up to the Hall to share a coffee with him came by way of a telephone call rendered in the friendliest of terms. It was a call that no doubt had its recipient initially puzzled for in truth the two of them had little that they had in common but even so Clive Warner felt that he could not ignore without appearing to be rather churlish.

Therefore taking him up on this invitation he found his host in the long dining hall that overlooked the lake, which was itself magnifying its splendour after finally shrugging off the veil of mist of the early morning that had at one time threatened to spoil the day. Moreover he was treated for having taking the opportunity to trudge up to the hall with an atmosphere that the uninitiated might have declared spelled out the words bon ami! This very situation ought to have signalled to Clive Warner that there was obviously more afoot than the seemingly obvious, but in his excuse it can be said that at the time the manager of the camp site found his mind still fully occupied by that visit from the police.

"I need to beg a special favour from you Clive!" Again the words that greeted him ought to have promoted a further warning that something was afoot, but if the camp manager bore any inkling of this he let the matter pass for a certain curiosity had now taken hold of him. Meredith Drew was a person who seldom asked for favours for this after all was a man who usually took what he wanted without asking and then left it to others to raise their objections at a later stage.

"You do?" The site manager did not sit as requested for he merely stood as he tried to gauge the other person's mind even before any words were spoken.

"Yes!" Meredith Drew puffed himself up like some prize cockerel as he worded his next phrase of verbiage. "I have no doubt that by this time you will have heard of the new outdoor pursuits activity that we have recently put into operation. We have had some degree of success also even if I say so myself!"

Clive Warner nodded for this was a matter the man could hardly deny especially as he had suffered the whole of the procedure rammed down his throat on more than one occasion.

"The only trouble is that I now feel we need to seek some publicity for our little venture!"

Clive remained silent as he still wondered how this statement was going to affect him, as it surely must considering Drew's words issuing forth. "I thought that you might be able to help me in this Clove!"

So that was the crunch line, was it? "You say you thought I might be able to help but in what manner do you mean?"

"The fact is that I require a model to demonstrate the techniques that can be photographed to satisfy the media interest!"

"But surely you must admit that this well outside of my jurisdiction?"

"Shall we simply say that you do have some rather attractive girls currently working for you Clive in that office of yours. I was sort of wondering if I could lean on you just a little to persuade one of your girls in particular to act out this role for me?"

Clive pulled a thoughtful face. "I don't know about that for such a suggestion goes well beyond my brief!"

"Perhaps there is also another point to consider. In return for your efforts I do not think you will find that I am ungenerous. If I remember correctly you were talking some time ago of a certain portion of land that you were keen to develop. A plot that I claimed at the time would if developed spoil part of the view from the Hall's position. Well after consideration I feel sure that I will be able to persuade the board that the loss of this plot, especially if such a development is landscaped and surrounded by the trees, which are after all its natural setting, would not compromise the Hall's own interest. I do know for a fact that your own directors have been pushing for some means of expansion, more especially now, if the trend of people choosing to spend their holiday time at home continues and I have no reason not to suspect that it will for some time yet. So tell me what are your own feelings on this matter?"

Clive opened and closed his mouth several time as he tried to recall his thoughts. He knew full well that his own Board would be quite keen to acquire such an offering and for him to now be able to negotiate this for them would surely provide some degree of security for his own position within the firm. "I believe you mentioned a girl that you would like to pose as a model for you? Who did you have in mind then?"

"That is correct. I must confess that I had Stacey Kershaw in mind to fulfil this role for she appears to epitomise the outdoor type far more than what your other girls do, as charming as they might be. The filming will not take her away from her duties for too long and during that time I can assure you that a sense of propriety will be observed at all times!"

"But what if this particular girl refuses to take part? If that was the case would you consider one of the others?"

"I do not really think so. You see to my mind Clive if the girl shows any reluctance to participate I would expect you to then try to persuade her. After all just think of the reward you can expect for such a simple task!"

"But the fact remains I will still have to ask her. Supposing that she is adamant in her refusal, surely there must be another girl on site who could take her place?"

Meredith Drew shook his head. "Now I wonder why you have suddenly adopted an air of timidity in this case? The fact remains however that I have set my mind on Stacey Kershaw fulfilling the role and I do believe that with a little perseverance on your part you will be able to exert your charm to extract an affirmative from her lips, more especially I would suggest if it so happened that her job depended upon her answer! Once we have overcome that obstacle perhaps you will then send the girl in question to the hall to enable me to discuss the project further with her and then we can arrive at an understanding?"

Clive Warner nodded. In his heart however he did not feel too happy about that current situation, but then the aspirations of pleasing his Board by acquiring for them the land he had been promised possibly overruled any of these initial sentiments.

Stacey posed on the jetty at the Marina within the site in the early hours of the following morning still feeling unsure as to what she was doing here with the man she had grown to quite despise clicking his camera lens at her.

Her first reaction to Clive's request had been to claim to Meredith that she could in no way claim to be a swimmer. That was when the other had simply smiled in her direction exerting the charm of a rattlesnake and had told her that the intention was not for her to actually get wet during this filming but merely to pose as if she was going through the routine. After that his boat was moored close by to transport her to Lady-Holme for the second phase of filming. Still even at this initial stage it had meant her donning a wet suit for authenticity, which was something she had never done before and also something that she had found to be extremely difficult especially when she considered that this garment revealed far too much of the contours of her body than she considered to be appropriate. In truth her initial reaction had been to refuse to carry on with this exploit but by this time Clive Warner had been persuaded that his job depended upon their co-operation and therefore he had exerted a firmer hand than was usual in her making the ultimate decision.

She had also been subject to the look on her mother's face when she had told the person why she had to leave so early that morning, for there was no doubt that Agnes Kershaw strongly disapproved of the whole idea. Even if she did concede that she supposed Mr Drew was after all a gentleman and therefore her daughter would come to little harm in this endeavour.

"Still I suppose that if you are starting so early this will mean that you will get home at a respectable time today, which is just as well for with the advent of that blasted Air Show that is due to start tomorrow, I am seriously considering returning home tonight. The whole area is bound to be crowded out this weekend and all that noise is not really conducive to my well being!"

Now Stacey found she was having rather mixed feelings over her mother's departure. Even so by this time Stacey had also been led to believe that her own job lay in the balance of her completing this bizarre expedition.

"Splendid!" The man with the camera finally seemed to be satisfied with his results. "Now the next stage is for us to travel across to the Island. No, you must leave the wet suit on for the time being my dear for when we arrive there I want to make it appear that you have already completed your first swim. To this effect we will splash a little water over your costume to apply a little subterfuge. And now my motorboat awaits you!"

Stacey remained silent during the short crossing to the Island. Indeed it was only after they had arrived there and she had been splashed with water to give the sense of more realism in the further photographs that were then taken, that Meredith Drew intimated the time had now come for her to get out of her wet suit and into the hiking gear she had so far carried in her knapsack. That was the point when Stacey felt truly justified in voicing her objections.

"But it is all part of the sequence of the activity!" Now he was pouting. "Anyway there is no one here to see you change!" The man changed his pouting expression to accompany the whining note in his voice.

"But you are here!" The girl still persisted. "If you weren't here then you would be unable to take these pictures you keep on about. Perhaps it might be an idea if you put your camera down and left off filming whilst I get changed. After that you can take your pictures quite openly!"

"But if I do that it will not give the full story of the activity and I should not need to remind you of what is at stake on the job front especially as far as you are concerned if you refuse to co-operate!"

"Never! You can sod the job!" She faced him with a defiant streak in her eyes after first dismissing the idea of jumping back into his motorboat and leaving Meredith stranded here on the Island.

Peuse with anger Meredith Drew raised an arm almost as if he was ready to strike her for her effrontery and for what he saw as sheer insolence on the part of this girl. Yet before he could bring his fist down to take his spite out of the girl another figure suddenly appeared like an apparition from out of the surrounding foliage. The figure resembled something of a wild man now in a rage and almost before she could draw breath the form of Meredith Drew lay motionless at her feet.

"Steve! What on earth -----?" The shock of seeing him here must have been obvious in her eyes yet the response from the other person was decidedly cold.

"I have no idea what the hell you think you are playing at Stacey or why you are dressed up in that ridiculous manner. All I do know is that by putting yourself in the position to come here alone with that toad you must have been well aware of exactly what you were letting yourself in for!"

"But that is wrong, I had no idea!" She tried failingly to object and to try to explain the circumstances to the other, but that person had no intentions of listening. Picking up the camera from where it had landed on the ground he pocketed it quite deliberately.

"Your escort appears to be now coming round therefore I advise the pair of you to get back into that boat of yours and go back where you came from! What is more go back quickly as well before I get tired of seeing that pleading expression on your face!"

★ ★ ★ ★

Chapter Six

Perhaps the stirring form of Meredith Drew would still have objected most strongly had it not been that just at that precise moment the warden's boat could be spotted approaching the Island and moreover this craft just so happened to be carrying the form of Detective Inspector Forsyth on board.

"This creature has attacked me!" Now a long whimper could be heard issuing forth from Meredith Drew even before the craft had chance to draw alongside of them, as he pointed an almost shaking fist in Steve's direction.

"Under the circumstances Mr Drew I would advise you to return back to the Marina and take Miss Kershaw with you. It should be sufficient enough at this stage to warn you that I have already received one complaint against you that has been made by one of your students. If therefore you do not wish me to pursue the matter further then I would advise you both to go now. My own business here at the moment concerns only Mr Futton!"

Stacey immediately looked towards Steve. Yet she got little joy from those brown eyes of steel as she was motioned back towards the boat she had come to the Island on. The expression he portrayed at that time was most certainly far removed from anything that resembled concern in her direction. Indeed it could be said that it was more damning than anything else in its projection and to her mind he was willing her to get back on that boat and return back to the mainland along with the man she abhorred. Still Stacey was now in no hurry to move.

"I believe that you have some documents in your possession Mr Futton that do not rightfully belong to you!" The Inspector having now dismissed the pair, deliberately ignored the other two, and Meredith having had his initial wails ignored seemed now anxious to take his leave. To Stacey's mind the man almost resembled a cat that had suffered the trauma of having its tail docked! "I would therefore be obliged if you would hand such papers over to me so that I might return them to their rightful owner!"

"There is nothing in my possession that does not rightfully belong to me Inspector!" Steve's jaw was set in a determined fashion and Stacey knew that once that look was set Steve would be persuaded to do nothing that was against his will.

"I must advise you that my instructions from the firm where you were until recently employed, appear to disagree with that statement Mr Futton and I am therefore persuaded that what you say is not the case!"

"I can assure you Inspector that it is most certainly the case. I must also say that despite the task that has been set for you I find it rather strange to find you out here at this time of the day!" Steve frowned as he still determined that he would stand his ground. Yet to his own mind the issue relayed itself around the notion that if the police had come out to the Island in order to track him down then it would appear that someone had given his whereabouts away. Yet who could that be? For nobody, not even Stacey was aware that he was here on this Island before this moment in time.

"I am afraid that if you are going to be disruptive in your answer Mr Futton I shall have to ask you to accompany me to the police station where we can pursue this matter further."

"In that case I am sorry but I am afraid that I must decline your offer for you see I find myself far too busy for such niceties at the moment!" Then before the other had chance to respond Steve was away and even before the policeman had regained the initiative and recovered from his surprise the runaway had already reached the boat that he had previously left on the other side of the Island, thus leaving the Inspector to huff and puff until the man he wished to apprehend had disappeared out of sight.

"Well are you going to get in or not?" She was still gazing back to the point where they had left Steve or rather been ordered to leave, when she heard the words issuing forth, hissing noisily and with something of a bad grace from the lips of the person who now eyed her almost suspiciously as he motioned to where his boat was currently moored. In truth Meredith Drew's face was peuse with anger. For one thing he objected most strongly to being ordered about by a person he considered to be a lesser being and for another he could have kicked himself that he had underestimated the girl whom he had previously considered to be fair game.

"Certainly not!" Her face was set, more interested now in ascertaining as to whether Steve had managed to get away than she was in obeying the commands of this toad. She knew full well that the Detective Inspector had focussed all his attention onto what he considered to be this runaway, thus now completely ignoring the other two in a similar way as he did the previous complaint made against Meredith Drew. Thus to Stacey's mind although she may have been left to her fate, come hell or high water she determined that she was going no place with this smarmy devil she did not trust one inch!

"Then you can suit yourself. As far as I am concerned you can stay here and rot or even try out your new wet suit. That should make interesting viewing considering you cannot swim and therefore you would be totally dependant on the buoyancy aids. Who knows with luck maybe they might even work!" If that was the way this female wanted to play it then damn it, she could take the medicine she had self-prescribed. Once she had come to her senses and swallowed her stupid pride then perhaps she would be willing to accept his approaches and with something that resembled humility at that!

Perhaps he expected her even at this late stage to grovel to his wishes as she feared the unexpected, but then after all he had grossly under rated the mind of this by now belligerent female.

"Do me a favour will you; get back in your boat and go to hell!" The words were issued through gritted teeth even if she did realise that with this man's departure her own escape route from the Island would subsequently disappear.

"Then have it your own way then!" Meredith Drew certainly did not appear in the mood for either arguing or cajoling, for he turned and simply made his way onto his craft and set the engine going to take him back across the Lake. It was only when he had finally disappeared that Stacey began to realised the full extent of her own predicament and she looked around the Island almost as if she expected it to show some form of support in its foliage.

But now this place seemed to do little to inspire her. Indeed it appeared is if now the place was exuding an air of disappointment in her, almost scolding her that she should have been so foolish as to land herself in such a position in the first place and thus feeling utterly dejected she finally sank back against the trunk of a tree. Perhaps, she thought, if she waited long enough, some well meaning tourist who was out sailing on the Lake would decided to land on the Island and could be persuaded to take her back to shore with them, although surely one look at the wet suit she was still wearing would possibly be enough to convince them that the woman it currently adorned obviously didn't really know what she wanted!

Yet even such half conceived plans were unlikely to come to fruition when in typical Lakeland style, the mist that had earlier hovered in the heavens decided that the time was ripe for it to shed its precipitation upon the earth. Now no right-minded individual would choose to venture forth out onto the Lake in this! She considered shouting to try to attract attention, but that thought could be regarded as stupidity in itself for who from this distance could possibly hear her even if they were listening?

It was then that Stacey thought about Steve and the long hours he had spent here without complaint, but such thoughts in turn led her to remember the way in which he himself had raced off and more importantly perhaps the expression he had cast in her direction before he had disappeared. Thus whilst it was understandable that he wanted to escape from the presence of the policeman, the look he had cast her way had been something else and she consequently wiped away the tears that were now rapidly forming with a total lack of patience. She never even noticed the departure of the warden's boat with one frustrated Inspector on board. But then if she had noticed it, then it was dubious whether she would have called out to him, for to her mind the character on board the vessel was yet another devil whom she intended to avoid at all costs even if the alternative made for an unpleasant sojourn on that place!

She supposed that she must have slumped down in a semi-stupefied state against that tree, and the wild fowl, having had their resting place so rudely disturbed came out to view what they considered to be the cause of this. Of course they never pretended that they would ever understand the human mind. Why indeed had that breed of livestock with all that promenade placed at their disposal along with its various outlets to sustain them such as picnic tables and an endless supply of bread that they regarded as their own staple diet, to come here and park themselves on this Island. The fact that they were here invading their own territory gave these creatures a feeling of agitation and thus they shook their feathers almost disconsolately.

Stacey never noticed these natural inhabitants or even the insects who found a different aroma upon which to land and subsequently explore, whilst the trees, not to be outdone by this spate of natural activity shook down some of their seedlings onto her still form almost as if it was in an effort to bury her presence here on this Island

But Stacey knew nothing of this! How long she was in this position she didn't know but quite suddenly she became aware that there was a boat currently approaching the place. At first she jumped up determined that it must be Steve returning to the Island to try to find her but then as she looked out she saw that the craft approaching was one that belonged to the Marina back at the Hall. For a moment she then thought it could be Meredith Drew who had decided to come back for her and indeed she was even musing on delving her way deeper into the foliage so that he would not see her, when she realised as the boat drew closer that it was not Meredith Drew at the helm but that the person currently manipulating the craft was holding his lips taut in expression as his eyes searched the outline of the Island in an attempt to see if he could spot her.

"I thought that you might require a lift back!" It was not Steve's voice but Dick Soper who had come to her rescue. "The students told me something of what has been happening in recent days and then when I spotted the boss arriving back on his own I sort of guessed I might find you here!"

"Thanks Dick! Guess you are a sight for sore eyes!" Now she thanked the Good Lord for friends and that was something that Dick Soper had consistently proved to be. Nothing else but a good friend even if he would have liked to have been more than that. Still now was not the right time to dwell on such matters.

"You don't need to say anything about what happened. The students have already shown me some evidence, his personal pictures as a matter of fact. Come on hop on board. I daresay you will be only too pleased to get away from here and we can always talk later!"

Now nothing else seemed to matter except that she felt she needed to get away from the place and without a second thought she obeyed his command. He observed her imposed silence as they moved back towards the Marina and it was only upon their arrival that he finally broke in upon her thoughts

"Sometimes you really do have me worried Stacey!" Now there was a hint of reproach in the man's eyes.

"Not intentionally I can assure you!" She was beginning to finally regain something of her old momentum but even so perhaps at the beginning she failed to understand the inference.

"You don't seem to realise Stacey that people do care about you and we worry as to what has happened to you!"

Stacey glanced at his expression, not another one surely? A hand seemed to grip hold of her. In the past she had always regarded Dick Soper as a friend, a sort of work colleague, but nothing more. She was conscious of the fact that Meredith Drew had been able to use him on the occasion of that dinner party. "Now you can hardly claim that I was that far away Dick!" Her voice exuded far more bravado within it than she actually felt. "Naturally it was good to see you but I wasn't really in any kind of danger. All that happened was that I was merely marooned on that Island waiting for a good Samaritan who would eventually come and rescue me and in this case the good Samaritan happened to be you, for which I truly thank you!"

She disembarked upon the jetty assuming a stance of dignity but now uncertain of what to do next. If she returned to the office then Clive Warner would be bound to ask questions and that was a something she felt she could well do without at the moment, in addition she was also conscious of the fact that she was still garbed in that wet suit, somehow she had to find a place where she could change!

"Perhaps I ought to run you back home?" Maybe he could read her thoughts for Dick now looked questioningly at the wet suit she was still wearing.

"That won't be necessary I can assure you Dick. I have my clothes here with me, I can always change in the cloakroom and anyway I guess I'll have to face Clive Warner sooner or later so I suppose the sooner the better!"

As it was it appeared that Clive was pleased to see her even if it was evident that his curiosity was aroused after having seen Meredith Drew returning to the Hall sometime earlier and on his own.

"So what's the story Stacey?" He fixed her with a pair of luminous eyes that almost suggested that he knew something of the truth already and woe betide her if she decided to fabricate upon the facts.

"Merely a difference of opinion!" She didn't want to illuminate any further, all she wanted to do now was to immerse herself in her work and attempt to wipe away the questions that were even now hammering away at her own brain. "I believe you said something about the end of the month returns that require typing and faxing through to head office?"

"It isn't quite the end of the month yet Stacey. In fact we have another week left in it!" He reminded her with a tone that she found difficulty in tolerating without screaming out.

"Oh so it is!" She glanced at the date displayed on the office wall. "In that case I'd better get on with the accommodation lists for next week!"

"Are you sure you feel up to it Stacey?" He had now adopted a more serious tone as if he had already guessed that things were not all right by her initial conversation.

"Of course I'm all right. It is simply that my mind is currently circulating around several tasks that I need to complete. I'm simply allowing my thoughts to attempt to assume some order in them!"

With that Clive had to be satisfied at least for the time being, besides the man had work of his own to see to and with one last look at his charge he left the office. Not so Avril Togas however for the moment the boss disappeared into his own Holy of Holys she sidled over to where Stacey had positioned herself.

"Come on then spill the beans. We all know whom you have been with. Don't tell me that you actually repelled the man's advances?"

"Whatever happened I can't see that it is any of your business Avril!"

"Oh be like that then if you must, after all I only wanted to help! Two heads and all that sort of thing! Personally though I don't think you would know a good thing even if you fell over it. I really can't say that I understand you at all Stacey. The man has class as well as money and he obviously fancies you. Just give me half a chance ---!"

"As far as I am concerned you are welcome to a full chance Avril because quite frankly his type leave me feeling stone cold!"

"So by that I take it that you still prefer that feckless soul that half of the country is now looking for? Oh well I suppose it takes all sorts and besides your attitude in dismissing Meredith out of hand will help me with my own chances in that field! If he needs someone else to pose in a wet suit for him then he knows where to look!"

With his hiding place now rumbled and with a full two days growth upon his face as well as feeling the need for a shower and a change of clothes, Steve decided that his next move must be to try to sneak back to the boarding house before the others were up and about that morning. He already had a key to get into the place and he assumed that if he remained very quiet he would be able to complete his toilet and get away again before anybody stirred.

His plan however did not go entirely as he had predicted. For starters he had forgotten that Bob Eldon, one member of the team, was a persistently light sleeper and therefore Steve had no sooner let himself into the accommodation before he was to spy this character watching him.

"What the hell -----?" For a moment Bob did not recognise Steve but then having rectified this matter. "Where on earth have you sprung from looking like that?"

"I believe that is something I have come here to attempt to rectify!" Steve now furtively glanced around almost as if he was frightened in case his friend's initial call had woken someone else in the household. "Let me get to the bathroom first will you? We'll talk later!"

Much to his initial surprise the other man appeared willing to allow him this latitude, and Steve presumed his reasoning was possibly along the lines that if he was spotted in that condition then they would all be in danger of being evicted from their current accommodation. Even so Bob was waiting for him when Steve, duly refreshed and changed emerged from the interior and out into the cottage garden at the back of the property.

"Guess you look a little better now anyway!"

"Well in that case go on put the kettle on and we'll bring a brew outside so that we won't be disturbing anyone else!" Steve gave his orders upon seeing him yet the other man still looked a trifle reticent.

"But Mrs Adams might object to us using her kitchen facilities!"

"Hopefully if we are in luck Mrs Adams will still be in the land of the sublime providing we keep it quiet!"

Reluctantly the other moved across to where the kettle was situated now possibly realising that if he wanted to hear anything of this story from Steve then he would have to bow to the other's wishes. Whilst he was doing this Steve made to sit at the picnic table that had been placed outside of the property to cater for better days.

"Now I consider that I have finally earned my story!" Bob set the two mugs down. "Let's start by you telling me where the hell you have been to get yourself into that state?"

Steve took a sip of the hot mug of tea. "Oh I guess I've been sort of sleeping rough for the last couple of days!" He issued his limited explanation as if this was quite enough to explain everything.

"But why ----what brought that on?" Obviously the explanation was not enough for Bob.

"You should know the answer to that well enough. To put it in simple terms I have been lying low because we are being harrowed from pillar to post for those damned designs, therefore I took the responsibility on my own shoulders, remember?"

"I believe at the time you also intimated that you had somewhere to go with them if I remember correctly!"

"I thought that I had at the time. Unfortunately however things don't always work out as planned!"

"Then you could have come back here?"

"I did come back here a short time ago so that I could make myself presentable for the show. Tell me has anyone been around making enquiries during my absence?"

Bob frowned for a moment before responding. "Just one person to the best of my knowledge!"

"And no doubt that was the Police Inspector?"

Bob shook his head puzzled for a moment. "No, this was some well dressed city bloke. Guess he appeared a little frustrated with your absence especially after we told him that we didn't know where you were. He claimed something about the whole business being childish and said that all he wanted to do was to save you a great deal of trouble in having to seek out a friend of his at the air show. But then he said if it proved impossible to find you beforehand then it was imperative you should meet with this guy although he did say he wouldn't be very pleased to be disturbed when he was officiating, which again, he claimed, was the very reason why he himself was endeavouring to save everyone a great deal of trouble!"

Steve twisted his lips. "This well dressed city bloke, did he have a name then?" Perhaps he already knew instinctively the answer to that.

"Yes as a matter of fact I believe he said that his name was Drew, Meredith Drew or something like that. Anyway he left a phone number where you could contact him!"

"I believe that we have already met!" Steve's voice showed little emotion in it. "As a matter of fact the last time I saw the bloke I believe I had just floored him. I don't really feel he was any too pleased about that so I expect by this time I will have a black mark against my name!"

The conversation was interrupted when the back door opened once again and this time another member of the team, Jonathan Brownhills came out to join them. "I thought I heard voices. Is this conversation open to anyone then? Can it be true that the prodigal son has finally returned to the fold?"

"Not exactly. I actually came here to smarten myself up! Anyway considering the household seems to be stirring where is our studious friend if you two are up and about?" The newcomer guessed from his tone that Steve did not feel quite as light hearted as what he tried to portray.

"Lee quite naturally is still in the land of the sublime where I suggest we leave him but to get back to yourself by the look of you I would suggest you stayed around for a while and took some rest. At least stay and get some food inside of you!"

Steve shook his head. "I thought I had made it perfectly clear that my presence here would only serve to place the rest of you in jeopardy. Therefore it is best that I disappear before Mrs Aiken puts in an appearance for the less people who know I have been back here the better!"

"But where will you go to?"

"Not far I promise you. Don't forget we have been commissioned to complete a task this weekend at the Air Show!"

"You talk about not being spotted but surely you will be seen at that place?"

"Upon that I will have to take my chances I am afraid. Jonathan there is something else though you could possible help me out with Am I right in presuming you have some camping gear still in the boot of your car?"

The other man nodded. " Yes I never removed it after last time although I must admit one can hardly consider it to be very up beat for it is more of an emergency kit really!"

"Well I consider this to be an emergency so if you don't mind I would like to borrow it from you in order to give myself a little authenticity when I book in at a campsite I have spotted. The place is remote enough for it to still have space available even though it is the height of the season and yet it is far enough away I hope to avoid detection! Anyway I still have the car to commute in!"

The other man nodded. He knew Steve well enough not to attempt to argue with him once the man had made his mind up over an issue and without any more ado he tossed his car keys in Steve's direction. "Here then, you are welcome to help yourself although I can't say that I agree with what you are doing. I understood that we were all in this together!"

"Then I will see you on the Glebe around ten tomorrow then!" Steve stood fingering the keys. "I'll post these back to you through the letter box when I've got what I want!" He left leaving the other two looking at one another in a perplexed fashion.

"Think we are being excluded over something?"

"Maybe, although knowing Steve I guess not!"

"Then is there nothing we can do to dissuade him?"

"Such as ---? No, apart from giving him our support I guess there isn't!" He went into his pocket to reach for a cigarette.

"I thought you had given those up with all the adverse publicity about them?"

"These happen to be my excuse for being outside at this time of day. What's yours?"

"That's simple. I heard voices and so I came to investigate and found you talking to a cigarette!" He toyed with a mobile in his trouser pocket conscious now that he needed to use it. "He mentioned a campsite, which direction do you think he is heading in then?"

"Search me!" The other shook his head. "I suppose one would have to search diligently to find a campsite in the Lake District!"

"Well if we can have no influence over him then I guess I'm off. I guess I've just remembered something I have to do anyway!"

----------Stacey glanced up with a mixture of surprise and apprehension when the door opened to admit Clive

Warner. Not that it was Clive's presence that worried her but rather the one who was accompanying him at the time, and spotting the features of that detective who apparently appeared to be everywhere where he wasn't particularly wanted her heart visibly sunk. What could this man want of her now? Yet she had hardly time to dwell upon such thoughts before she also noticed that this time around the two of them were smiling and apparently behaving quite affably to all and sundry. She also noted at the time that the Inspector was carrying with him a yellow jacket, not carelessly but something he appeared to be treating with respect.

Even so it was Clive who was the one to open the conversation almost in a subdued manner as if he wished to covet a favour from her but did not know how to word his request.

"All right then Clive what's on your mind then?"

"Stacey-----!" The words finally began to emerge but not in Clive Warner's usual manner but still with a much softer approach altogether. "Stacey you may or may not be aware that Detective Inspector Forsyth happens to be a member of the Rotarians and furthermore it is their organisation that prove to be the mainstay of the Air Show to be held this weekend!" Well she knew about the Air Show of course but the policeman's membership of this august group came as quite a surprise. Somehow she had never visualised this man as having any interest outside of his policing.

"In actual fact the Inspector is here to beg a favour from us for it appears that several of the stewards from that organisation who should have been on duty over the weekend by being responsible for car parking, the selling of programmes that also serve as admission tickets to the enclosure and manning the entrance gates have tragically succumbed at the very last moment to this dreaded swine flu and consequently, even though the various groups come together for this event from all over the county they are now still short of manpower. The favour the Inspector has therefore come to ask us is whether we would consider helping out by taking their places. I have already said that I am willing to do my bit for such a good cause and several of the others are also willing to help out. Therefore the point is would you be willing to take the last jacket and join us?"

Stacey fell silent for a moment in sheer amazement. So it would appear that this law officer had a life outside of the police force after all, this was indeed something that she initially found difficult to credit. In fact the notion that this man could have any interest outside of policing had never occurred to her before. Glancing at the one who so far had remained silent perhaps there was also an element of surprise when she noted that the eyes she recognised as normally steely had now adopted an expression of deep pools of pleading in them. Perhaps it was upon noting this expression that Stacey decided that she really had no axe to grind for after all in his day job the man was only carrying out what was obviously expected of him and what he was paid for. Therefore this inkling of charitable work to her mind now seemed to place an entirely different complexion on the matter. It was then that she half nodded an agreement still more out of surprise at this turn of events than anything else, and furthermore she supposed a further bonus would be that whilst she was in the Rotarians company she guessed she would secure at least a temporary relief from the attentions of Meredith Drew.

"Thank you Stacey!" This time around it was the policeman who spoke almost suggesting that he had not dared to speak out previously, at least not until he had gauged her reaction. It was then that he handed her the jacket he was holding and she could catch a glimpse of the legitimate markings upon it that signified that this was for real after all. "I wondered if you would consider helping out to sell the programmes of admission at one of the entrances to the place. There will of course be somebody with you so you won't exactly be on your own and there will also be regular relief for you, one reason why we need a full quota of bodies in order to cover for the various duties. I myself will at the time be stationed on the Promenade at least for a session and Clive has agreed to accompany me there as my own partner had also gone down with the dreaded virus as well!"

She nodded again. After all this was a very worthy cause. Still she demanded her moment if only for devilment. "But what if it is raining? What will we do then?"

"Don't be so pessimistic Stacey!" This time around it was Clive's turn to reprove her. "Tomorrow, at least according to the weather forecasters, it is going to be a glorious day weather wise!"

"Then we will just have to hope that they have got their forecasts right for once!" Of the two the Inspector definitely sounded the more cautious. "Anyway the show opens at ten, so if everybody is say at the Hall gates for nine thirty I will have the opportunity to make folk known to one another and to introduce you to Bert, your opposite number for the day. With everyone arranging to meet up there it will be possible for us to pair off and give us all nice time to get to our respective posts!"

She picked up the jacket after the two of them had left together and then wondered on a certain ludicrous situation if Steve, whom she already knew wanted to be at this show, would have to pass by her on the gate. The thought of this amused her and she swore to herself that if the man still refused to speak to her then she vowed that she wouldn't let him in to the blasted enclosure no matter what anybody else said to the contrary.

If she did have any suspicions that she had been singled out for this task for reasons still unknown to her, such suspicions were rapidly quelled and proved to be quite unfounded when she spotted several of the other members of staff there the following morning apparently all conscripted to step into the breach at the last moment. Indeed even Avril Togas was present, and having received a duty that did not suit her purpose she was literally complaining that her car park duties would be locating her too far away from the main action for her liking.

"But every job allocated is equally as important today Avril!" The Inspector looked solemn as he eyed the agitator before finally hanging a collection bucket over her arm. "That is especially true if we want the day to run smoothly!"

"Well I'm certainly not doing car park duties again tomorrow otherwise I am not coming at all!" The girl was obviously sulking and making the most of the situation by pouting her lips a mannerism that she had perfected beautifully.

"All right we will agree on that one. I will see to it that a changeover will be available for you!" This was certainly a very different role for the Inspector to play now, for Stacey had never expected to see the man trying to act as an appeaser. "But today our positions have been set. Therefore all I can say now is the very best of luck to everyone!"

Stacey found her partner Bert, an older man possibly just short of retirement age, to be quite chatty as they made their way towards the Glebe and consequently they soon covered the distance past the shops and restaurants that despite the early hour were now showing signs of life possibly in anticipation of having a bumper day trade-wise with the expected influx of visitors to the place, and soon the two arrived at their own designated post ready for the anticipated onslaught. To start with Stacey did ponder as to whether Meredith Drew had also had his help enlisted, but one look at the official party when they arrived was soon to dispel any such notion that she might have been toying with. Amongst this party and appearing there as large as life as well as acting out the role of bon ami was the figure of this same man.

A goodly half of her wanted to shout out upon spotting him to inform this august gathering of this person's secret hobby that lay in the form of photographing young girls in the various stages of undress. Realising however that this was neither the time nor the place and still anxious less such actions would cause her to miss the arrival of Steve, she swallowed hard and decided to shelve the matter for the time being for now was neither the time nor the place to expose this man. In actual fact she decided that the Inspector must have had the same idea for despite receiving those complaints from the students he seemed ill prepared to take any form of action. At least, or so she convinced herself, that could be the only possible explanation of the situation!

Although their position had been designated as the one on Rectory Road, which had nowhere near as many folk entering than they did at the main gate, Stacey soon found that they had quite enough to cope with and their bucket was filling nicely. By this time some of the U.S small armoured personnel vehicles had arrived and their drivers were willing to stop and chat with them especially upon seeing Bert for apparently the man had been doing this job for many years. Still she supposed that this small talk certainly helped to pass the time away.

★ ★ ★ ★

Chapter Seven

In the event and despite all her good intentions to the contrary, Stacey was destined to miss Steve's own approach to the show that morning. To start with she had not reckoned on there being more than one entrance to that field, so whilst she in turn scanned the faces of folk arriving at the gate on Rectory Road she was unaware that Steve had already made his own entry by the main gate that was situated on the Glebe itself. In point of fact the man himself had arrived early, for his mission was to attempt to seek out what he considered to be a prime vantage spot for himself.

He had met his friends as he had arranged at ten that morning but after due thought he then tried to persuade them to enter the arena separately to himself for even at that time he had an uneasy feeling that someone would be on the look out for them arriving together.

"But this doesn't make good sense at all!" Bob Eldon had not been slow to voice his opinion on the matter. "We came here in good faith intending to go to this air show together to tend to this copter when it arrives ---- Even you yourself said that you would meet us here at this time and now you are suggesting that we all go in separately?"

"Perhaps Steve is right!" It was Lee the studious one of the four who decided to lend his voice. "Following on from what he has told us they are after all expecting a group of four to arrive together and therefore that would make us easy targets!"

"So then what do you suggest we do once we are inside, creep behind one another in single file?"

"Just leave me to find the man by myself first please. The rest of you go and enjoy yourselves before the copter is due to arrive. If I am successful then I will most certainly report back without delay." In truth Steve felt they had said enough for the last thing he wanted was for them to be seen bickering outside on protocol. He knew this was not the way he had initially planned things but then surely it was the case of needs must when the devil drives!

Thus now situated as he was on the undulating pastures of the Glebe that normally paid lip service to the amateur golf course, an area that had currently been neglected in the wake of this event and had suffered the removal of its flags and pins, there was indeed a wide expanse for Steve to cover if he was ever to locate his would be contact. Towards the centre of this area however, and well out of sight of the on going fair that was now making the most of their position, Steve noticed the copse of trees that would certainly provide an adequate shelter from any prying eyes that day as well as, if required, also provide an ideal spot for a meeting to take place as this copse was situated away from the crowds who gathered expectantly at the time of each programmed event. He glanced upon his arrival almost automatically at the girth of one of these trees destined to give him shelter. The markings upon it conferred its great age and he was forced to wonder what tales that tree could have told of times long passed.

He watched too as a butterfly hovered overhead signifying perhaps that the joys of summer had finally arrived. But then at that moment things were quiet and all serene, but come the early part of the afternoon when the arriving crowds had grown thick, filling those grassy spaces in the enclosure with teeming humanity that appeared high in expectation, such natural things of beauty would disappear with the advent of those noise shattering machines. Before then however there was time to sample such free delights of nature where even a rabbit sought the opportunity to spend a little time in the sunshine.

He smiled as he remembered eyeing the community bobby standing close to the arena initially with suspicion before realising that the man's main concern that day was health and safety rather than apprehending anyone. Perhaps therefore enjoying the eloquence of that unexpected sunshine Steve felt at least for a time able to relax, for the next thing he remembered was the sound of that multitude of voices as the teeming crowds sought to join him whilst in addition a voice over the intercom now endeavoured to explain the order of the afternoon's events for those unable to read the language of the programmes they had purchased. One thing however was now quite clear to him, it was time to start casting his eyes around to search for his quarry.

Steve was finally to spot his would be contact emerging from the area where most of the officials had gathered around those marquees erected to house any visiting dignitaries. The man, Steve had to admit, looked non too pleased at having been disturbed from partaking in his quota of the on-going jollies, yet he knew that this was a task that his own superior in London had set for him and one that he could no longer refuse. In his hand Tim

Greatorex scrumpled the note that one of the many helpers o the field had handed to him depicting the designation of this so called meeting place.

"Sorry but I am afraid that you will have to excuse me for a while, there is something I have to attend to!" The words he had spoken aloud to Meredith Drew had not pleased that man either, for he considered that after all the effort he had put into his endeavours of getting his hands on the designs first, he was now being contentiously dismissed and that was something that most certainly did not suit this person!

Therefore all in all Tim Greatorex' approach towards the designated place passed in something of a dour mood. "If you should consider the idea behind those damned plans he has holds any merit when you have seen them, then bloody well get them off him!" His superior had spoken, but there again perhaps the man in London was still smarting over Steve's own rapid disappearance. In the period that had followed Greatorex had to admit he had tried unsuccessfully to use his own underlings to try and wrest those plans away from the man in the hope of saving himself the trouble. But so far all such attempts appeared to have ended in abysmal failure even after he had used his so-called friend, the same person that craved his attention here today. Yet the main thing that riled him above everything else was being forced to complete the mission for himself, especially as the person in question happened to be this puffed up non-entity who apparently had shown the effrontery to suggest that he was the one who could possibly design features for a new aircraft

Finally arriving at the designated venue with lips so terse that they looked they might split at any moment, he waited whilst he almost pawed at the ground like some thwarted stallion. Where was the devil then? Why on earth wasn't the man here?

One of the model aircraft droned its way into the skies above the spectators heads at least giving them something to watch as the air ambulance had been forced through necessity to cancel its appearance at the last moment and it was under the cover of this droning that Steve finally made himself known.

"Mr Greatorex?" His approach was subservient enough, but not to Greatorex's liking.

"Well your damned plans then, where are they?" Tim Greatorex looked around in the hopes of seeing some evidence relating to their presence.

"I understood that the idea was for this to be an initial meeting so that we could arrange a venue for later!"

"What! Are you trying to tell me that you haven't even brought them with you? That I am in effect wasting my time!" Steve prayed that the explosion the man appeared to make with his words did not sound too much like a rocket being fired off.

"I considered this place to be far too open to bring them here. I thought the idea was for us to arrange a follow up meeting?" Steve's thoughts had turned onto Stacey. Of course he couldn't produce the designs at the moment for wasn't it the case that she had the actual documentation. He only trusted that she had kept them safe.

"In my opinion you take quite a great deal on yourself young man!"

"Well considering that I have already been hounded by varying sources for them over the past few weeks, that it hardly surprising. Under these circumstances I felt it rather foolhardy to bring them here with me today for you see I feel I owe my colleagues the assurance that they are being well cared for!"

"You have spunk I will give you that. Therefore where do you suggest such a meeting could take place? As I am only in this area for the duration of the air show I believe you will have to decide upon such a venue immediately!"

Steve's thoughts raced. Would he have time to contact Stacey and find out where she was keeping them? Would she in fact be in any hurry to tell him after their last meeting? Finally he took the bull by the horns; if the girl was still renting the cottage then doubtless they would be there somewhere. "Are you familiar with Ferry House at the other side of the car ferry across the Lake Mr Greatorex?"

The man pursed his lips. "One can suppose that I have heard of it why?"

"Then I will meet you there after the air show has finished for today, say six o'clock this evening. They are lodged not too far away from that place!"

"Then I suppose that will have to suffice. Not totally satisfactory I must say Mr Futton for my time is considered to be rather valuable!"

Steve did not respond, his main thoughts now rested upon finding Stacey and persuading her to return his property after behaving like an eel with her on that previous occasion. But then surely that was something she would have to explain!

It was during one of her break periods from the gate when Stacey herself had wandered onto the field that she first spotted Steve. At the time the man was no longer worried about being spotted for now his main objective had been to escape from this arena and now the business with the helicopter had passed to get far enough away from the place and over to the other side of the Lake. One person he had therefore not expected to see there was Stacey herself making her way over towards him.

From Stacey's point of view all that she desired to do was to set the record right between them and to try to rub out the occurrences of the near past, yet now the man currently facing her was to all intents and purposes behaving like some polite stranger.

"The documents I asked you to look after for me; are they still at the cottage? I presume that you are still renting the place!"

"Not for much longer I am afraid. You see my mother decided to leave yesterday. I didn't go back there last night having got myself embroiled with this affair today but it is my intention to go back tonight to clear all my things before I terminate the lease. Oh you needn't look so worried. As far as I know your pieces of paper are still intact!"

He winced at her reference to them. "They are not pieces of paper Stacey as you so haphazardly call them. They happen to be important both to me and to the group that I worked with. As a matter of fact I have someone who is coming tonight to cast his eye over them. So much the better if we can use the cottage as a venue I would say!"

"I don't really remember saying that you could!" She felt her hackles beginning to rise at his attitude towards her. This meeting was not going at all in the way she had intended it to and Steve appeared to think far more about his damned pieces of paper than he did about her. "I told you I was hoping to clear my things out tonight!"

"Then perhaps you can delay that for a while!" Of all the nerve, she now positively bristled. Steve noticed this and tried to allay what he felt must surely follow on from these words. " Still I guess I am fortunate in finding you here. How did that come about? I didn't realise that you had a penchant for model aircraft before!"

"I am here because I happen to be working!" She referred to the yellow jacket now over her arm with something of a flourish. "A group of us have come as a favour to a certain Detective Inspector who also happens to be a high ranking Rotarian but one who suddenly found himself short of staff through no fault of his own!"

"You are helping Detective Inspector Forsyth?" A note of incredulity now sounded in his voice.

"Why shouldn't I be? After all even you must admit that it is all in a very good cause!"

"Then does that mean you are allowed to go at will into the royal enclosure?"

"When I am not working on the gate, yes I suppose so, that is always providing I want to, which I can't see as being the case!"

"Lend me your jacket for five minutes will you?"

"What for? Look what exactly are you playing at Steve?"

" I would like to try to find out for myself exactly what is going on in there at this moment in time!"

"Steve –you can't do that!" He was tugging the jacket off her arm now.

"I promise I will have it back to you within five minutes. Please do this for me Stacey!"

"Steve –be careful. Meredith Drew is up there!"

His face changed and she almost saw him bristle as she said the name. "Your new lover you mean? Don't worry Stacey I promise that I won't touch him this time, you are welcome to him. All I want to do is to listen in on his conversation!"

He was gone with that jacket before she had a chance to respond to say aye or nay. Yet within the five minutes, true to his word, he was back bearing a look that was impossible to depict. He said nothing about his venture merely "What time do you finally finish here?"

"I think that the gates close around five!"

"In that case I will pick you up outside of the tourist information centre!" For a brief moment a wave of expectation crossed her heart but this was quickly dispelled with his next words. "That way I will be sure to get you back to the cottage before my friend arrives at Ferry House!" He nodded again taking her acceptance for granted for even before she could think of the words to utter he was gone, replacing the borrowed coat back over her arm before he did so.

"Stacey!" It was Bert's voice now reminding her that their break time was over and therefore she returned back to her own position still deep in thought and not knowing whether Steve had left the ground and not knowing either what his business was with Meredith Drew!

------------Driving to the ferry with a man who cared to observe a mood of silence, Stacey took the opportunity to once again look out across the lake. Her eyes took in the form of Lady-Holme. Upon it from the position she was now in, it almost looked as if some of those trees had suddenly lost their foliage almost indeed as if they had been gripped by a disaster of some magnitude.

"I will be back within the half hour!" He dropped her quite unceremoniously outside of the cottage and sped off. Still Stacey had no time to brood for now yet another surprise awaited her. It came in the form of her mother, the woman she had believed to have returned home the previous day, who upon hearing the car stop had appeared at the front door with arms folded tightly across her bosom.

"And where the hell do you think you have been, I thought that Saturday was your day off?" The woman looked none too pleased.

"But I understood you to say that you were returning home yesterday!" She made some attempt to rectify the issue.

"Well I changed my mind. I don't believe there is a law that forbids one to do that. Anyway you didn't return home last night so I was hardly in a position to tell you now was I?"

"I have been helping out as a steward at the air show today!" Stacey implanted the news as if this was an explanation that incorporated everything.

"And last night? Did your stewardship extend to the night shift as well?"

"There seemed to be little point in coming back to an empty house. Remember I thought you had left!"

"So what made you change your mind today. I believe I heard a car stopping but then it was not yours, so who brought you back tonight then?"

"As a matter of fact Steve dropped me off. He has some business to attend to over this side of the Lake!"

"So the black sheep has returned. Well I guess you had better be coming in. I expect you will want some tea?"

"Anything will do I'm not really hungry!" Her mother frowned upon these words.

"So you are expecting him to take you out for a meal tonight then?"

"No I am not. He is coming back here though. At the moment he has gone to meet a friend whom he is bringing with him to ponder some papers he left with me some time ago!"

"I see!" Stacey had the distinct impression that her mother did not see at all.

"Now what do you think you are doing?" Still the disgruntled woman had been silenced with the arrival of that car. Steve she could say little about for after all he had been Peter's friend and she had known him almost since his childhood but the newcomer she now spotted had eyes that were implanted into his head far too close for her to consider him to be a honest broker, plus the fact the man wore an air of arrogance about him. Upon reflection too Stacey decided that perhaps the woman was right in her assumptions for she later could have sworn she saw a look of avarice appear in the man's eyes when Steve had produced the papers

"So where's he come from then?" Agnes Kershaw frowned as she belied the figure of Steve heading towards the cottage with his companion. "I thought you said that it was over between you?"

"I said nothing of the kind. Steve has just brought a friend to show him some plans I have been keeping for him!"

"You've actually been keeping something for him? Honestly our Stacey I sometimes don't know what gets into you. You throw away your chances with that nice Mr Drew for the likes of this lackadaisical character--------!"

Still Agnes' surprise at seeing Steve was as nothing when compared with his own surprise at spotting Agnes there. "I thought you said that the cottage was empty, that your mother had gone home?"

It was time now for Agnes to sniff laudably although it must be appreciated that at that moment she had definitely got hold of the wrong end of the tale. "Well her mother is still here if that makes any difference to you. Anyway where are you supposed to have been these last few days? Why I should be concerned about that I really don't know except for the fact that I don't like seeing my girl upset!"

Stacey felt Steve's eyes fixed on her. "Shall we say that I've just been around, sort of here and there? By the way this is Mr Greatorex. I don't suppose you will know who he is but in actual fact he is one of the country's leading aircraft designers!"

"Then I can't for the life of me think what he is doing here. There isn't an airport for miles!"

"Please give us some space Mum!" Now it was Stacey's turn to plead. The other almost looked at the point of refusing and issuing a verbal rejection at being ordered around in her own home by those she considered to be her juniors, but there was something in Stacey's expression that finally persuaded the woman to relent.

"All right I suppose you can have the parlour. I won't be for disturbing you there if it is all that important. Not that I am interested in such things mind you!"

The silence that surrounded Tim Greatorex possibly signified that he had not experienced anything like this. Perhaps it was the sheer novelty of the situation that kept the man quiet until after Agnes had ambled off, but after that he immediately turned upon Steve ignoring Stacey.

"The papers then ----we have wasted quite enough time already!" Steve looked in her direction and for Stacey it was a simple matter now to retire to her bedroom and retrieve the package from her nightdress case without revealing where they had been kept!

Maybe after all her mother had something in that cold tone she portrayed after all for Stacey could not say that she was over impressed with this man that Steve had finally returned with. In the meantime she remembered that much to her mother's dismay she had ignored the meal the other had set before her simply order to go to check that the documentation was still well secreted within that place for the approval it would appear of this man!

"Totally inadequate as well as being completely unfeasible I am afraid!" At length the visitor straightened his back after folding the papers to give his considered opinion on the matter. "Hardly surprising really for you have not served an apprenticeship to design of any description!" Stacey now heard the man express his disgust and somehow she could not help allowing her heart to go out to Steve. Still the latter appeared now to be too intent to notice this motion.

"We had limited resources to draw up the design!" Steve was now on the defensive. "Also remember that I am an engineer and as such it is our job to monitor the behaviour of such machines that I believe to be quite unpredictable as they stand at the moment!"

"Well I can't see any advantage in these for myself, but as you yourself have just said the designs could have been better prepared using a professional hand!"

"Bearing in mind the spate of recent disasters one could ask the question as to why a professional hand has not endeavoured to try to develop a new prototype before!" Now Stacey could hardly believe that this was the Steve she knew speaking. "To put it in a nutshell if they had succeeded before this time then I might now have lost my best friend and Stacey here might still have had her brother alive!"

The man grunted yet again. "Then I will tell you what I am prepared to do. I will take these plans with me and give them to my own team and allow them to decided whether there is any merit in them!"

Much to her surprise Steve shook his head. Surely this had sounded to be a fair offer. "No I simply wanted your opinion Mr Greatorex as I was initially advised to do by our mutual contact in London. There was never any mention of you being able to serve the idea out to your own team!"

Perhaps the other was now shocked at Steve's refusal. Perhaps initially he had seen this as being a simple matter to get hold of the plans as he had been instructed to do on some feeble excuse. Perhaps even then the man who was facing him went up in his own estimation, but then Tim Greatorex was a paid servant of the establishment and they were the ones who had decided in their wisdom that these new ideas should be confined to the dustbin

"Then I am afraid that if you refuse this offer there is nothing more to say Mr Futton, and as you are unlikely to get a better offer from anyone else perhaps you ought now to try to recycle the paper that they are drafted out on!"

"I will run you back to the Ferry!" She watched as Steve grasped hold of his knuckles until they turned white. "In fact I am on the point of leaving myself so therefore a better idea is for me to drop you off back at the Old England!" Steve made to gather up his gear. He seemed determined now to leave the place without even looking in her direction. Still he did manage to pause in the doorway, more out of politeness than anything else. "Thank you for the hospitality anyway Stacey. I expect that I will see you around sometime. In the meantime I hope that things go well for you with your new attachment!"

He was gone before she could respond perhaps because his final words had completely caught her off balance. Left behind after the two men had departed though those papers still cluttered up the parlour and she guessed her mother would have something to say if she spotted them lying there. Almost automatically therefore she gathered them together and replaced them in the nightdress case. Why she did this she couldn't really have said at the time except perhaps she was a creature of habit like the woman who assailed her the moment she realised that the two men had gone.

"Well?" She now demanded as if Stacey could enlighten her into what had happened. In truth she had watched the retreating forms for herself after she had heard the front door opening from the position she had allotted herself not too far away from the main source of the action. "I suppose one could say it was short anyway!" She sniffed to show her disapproval of the situation. "I see you've tidied up those papers they left ---the rubbish men come tomorrow!"

"They could be important Mum!"

"Not all that important if they left them lying around like that. Anyway I heard the visitor say that they were useless!" Agnes immediately clapped a hand over her mouth as she realised that Stacey would now guess she had been listening in to their conversation. Not that she meant anything by it she only wanted to know if there was anything she could have done to help. Stacey however did not seem to bother at her mother's words however for she seemed to be far too wrapped up in her own thoughts and Agnes wondered whether this was a good thing or not. "Had they finished with them then?"

"They appear to have finished because they have now left!" She felt as if she was choking back a tear, a factor her mother did not miss however, or perhaps the woman was used to scrutinising her daughter's face.

"So you still think something about him, is that it?"

"I suppose that is true!"

"Well did you tell him as much?"

"How could I mother? It was a business meeting!"

"Then where is he now?"

"I don't know. I don't think he wanted me to know!"

"Stuff and nonsense girl. Look if you want him girl, although goodness only knows why you should, then get out there after him and find him. I really give up on the antics of young people nowadays! Anyway enough of that I have been thinking, do you really have to go stewarding again at that Air show tomorrow because to my mind you look as if you could do with the day off?"

"A promise is a promise Mum, you taught me that remember!" Stacey sighed almost reluctantly at the thought. For once she would have fancied having the day to herself, perhaps taking her mother out somewhere, learning the art of conversation with the older woman again and trying to forget all about Steve Futton!

"I'll tell you what Mum, why don't you come across and meet me when we finish tomorrow, by that time the crowds should have all dispersed and your noisy aircraft will all have gone away. Then we can go out together for a meal if you like?"

"How will I be able to tell when the thing finishes our Stacey? These things have a habit of going on forever!"

"Just watch for the red arrows coming over. When they have passed by, so will the rest of us! It is only a fly past tomorrow anyway for they performed their stunts for us today!"

"Well I suppose it's something to look forward to. At least I will have you to myself for an hour or so!"

Keith Forsyth pursed his lips as he listened to what his caller had to say over the telephone later that same evening. The contents of this call from a senior member of the Rotarians did not please him at all for he had promised himself a quiet evening that night after the efforts of the day and at the time he had been priding himself with the success of that venture, for the first day of the Air show appeared to have been an outstanding success despite the one or two minor hiccups that had been successfully sorted out.

"I tell you the man has failed! He walked away without those damned plans after all!"

"But ----?" The Detective Inspector paused wondering now what he was supposed to do about that. After all he had carried out his own instructions from his senior to the letter, he had involved Greatorex as ordered, so surely he could not now be expected to do more. Besides the whole matter was now getting in the way of his policing and therefore he felt now that he wanted rid of it.

"But nothing man! I want to know what you intend to do about this situation as it stands now!"

"What I intend to do?" The brusqueness in his voice obviously did not please his caller.

"Yes man, you are after all on the spot so as to speak. Therefore it now appears that I have no other choice but to depend on you!"

"Then I need time to think!" The policeman was now desperately trying to stall whilst he got his own thoughts in order.

"Time is something we can ill afford and not a commodity that I had in mind! But tell me, this would be engineer that all the fuss is about, where is he now?"

"I'm afraid that I have no idea Sir!" Perhaps he spoke without thinking if he wished to avoid the wrath of the other.

"But it is supposed to be your job to know where people are in your territory! What about the girl that is involved then?"

"As a matter of fact she is currently working for me as a temporary steward at the Air Show this weekend because I was short staffed. But I am sure that she has no idea where this Futton is either!"

"Then maybe she could be persuaded to make him reveal himself. If she did then it would safe you from a great deal of foot slogging at your end!"

"And how do you propose I do that?"

"Well you are the law around those parts aren't you? Surely it is not beyond your power to make the girl disappear for a time, long enough that is for lover boy to come out of his hidey-hole. And when he does you can guess what the price of the girl's parole will be!"

"But as far as I know the girl has done nothing wrong. Are you asking me to break my code of ethics?"

"Nonsense almost anyone can be found to have done something that is wrong, just think up something and act upon it!" With that the receiver at the other end of the line was slammed down leaving Keith Forsyth feeling both confused and inadequate. The man had always taken a pride in his police work and yet now it appeared he was being forced to abandon the ethics he had always held as sacrosanct by someone whom he had always previously regarded with a measure of respect.

He took several minutes to think out a strategy that he portended might possibly work and at the end of that period, his mind was now resolute. To the best of his knowledge the man's colleagues were still staying at that bed and breakfast accommodation close to Windermere town. That fact he had written down on record. Maybe they were the ones to be persuaded to reveal the whereabouts of their erstwhile colleague for to his mind the girl could prove to be of far more use if she was allowed to continue to wander free.

After some further deliberation he was to dial yet another number this time to a mobile that he knew the user kept about his person and which would also be switched on as the person concerned could not bear to think he was missing out on any contacts who wished to get in touch with him.

"Oh he's staying at some camp site or another as far as I know!" The response to his question came rather tentatively. In truth Bob Eldon was surprised to receive this call and perhaps in one sense it served to worry him.

"And the location of this place?"

"Sorry that is something I don't know!"

"But you are sure he is staying at a campsite?"

"As sure as I can be. At least he borrowed the camping gear off Jonathan here and said he was looking for a site well away from the mainstay of activity!"

"What about the new designs then? Oh yes I have heard of them, in fact I believe I know of someone who happens to be interested. Have you got them there with you?"

"No Steve took them off for some reason!"

"And you let him take them just like that? I understood that this new design was a joint effort, and that you had all been working on it?"

"We have, the four of us were involved!"

"Then might one ask why you have allowed one person to simply go off with them when you don't eve know where he has gone?"

Bob Eldon bit his lip. He had been uneasy with Steve's decision from the start but the others at the time had appeared willing to go along with the idea. "I understood Steve was worried in case they fell into the wrong hands!"

"That is a complete load of nonsense. I do happen to know that several different sources are now interested and would like to discuss the project with the whole group. I suppose you have never considered that Steve might possibly be out to find the highest bidder and dare I say not entirely for the group's benefit either!"

"But we know Steve, we have worked together for some time!"

"And so when the project was completed that made everything all right, did it? Are you absolutely sure it did Bob?"

The man in question now swallowed hard. He didn't mean to but a tiny question of doubt now seemed to be gathering into a thick lump in his throat. Keith Forsyth took his silence as a sign that his message was getting through. "Anyway this campsite you were on about. Do you know anything about it?"

"Only that he said it was remote!"

"There are many remote camp sites in this area, so that answer won't get us very far!" Now Keith Forsyth was beginning to lose a little of his patience.

"He did say that he was going to the Air Show to see someone there!"

"I did hear that he was at the Air Show today. The point is, what do you consider will be his next move?"

"Well there was a girl at one time who lived in this area but I was given to understand that affair was all finished and done with!"

The Inspector's thoughts turned yet again onto Stacey. Was it possible that she could have met Steve on the Glebe that afternoon after all? If that was true then there was still a chance that she would know where the man actually was. Pity though, he hadn't really wanted to have to go out again that evening for there was something he wanted to watch on the television for a change and thus he wondered whether he dared leave the matter until the following day when she would be back on duty again for the Rotarians. If he skilfully changed the jobs around and persuaded her to work with him on the Promenade selling programmes then he might possibly be able to catch her off guard, and that way he would probably learn far more than he would in visiting the cottage at this time. That was it, he decided, that was exactly what he would do!

"All right then Bob. But if you do hear from him at all or find out by some means where he is actually staying then contact me will you?" He replaced his receiver thoughtfully. Now he supposed he would have to think of a way to approach Stacey Kershaw without raising any alarm on her part!

From her point of view Stacey was surprised when Keith Forsyth signalled her out the next day. At the time she had already found Bert, who was quite looking forward to the girl's company again and the two of them had started of on their way to the Glebe when with another girl accompanying him he caught them up.

"Stacey I did previously mention that we would be changing around today. It will of course help to pacify certain people like Avril Togas who claims she has been deliberately been sited too far away for her to be comfortable in the role. With that in mind I would like to ask you to work with me today selling programmes on the promenade. Clive has already volunteered to do car park duties and Amy here will take over your old role with Bert. "Guess you must be being promoted lass to be requested to go on the Promenade!" Bert grinned at the news in a good-natured fashion. He was sorry for his own part that Stacey was going to work elsewhere because he had enjoyed working with the girl but as he supposed they were all working for the same cause, such issues should be ignored!

The crowds seemed to be in no way as great as they had been on the opening day, possibly due to the weather for the early hours had been subjected to a heavy shower, not that the swans, ducks or geese were grumbling for they had simply moved further off the shingle and more onto the promenade, an act that consequently placed them in a better position to search out tasty morsels for themselves that these humans were possibly carrying for after all they all seemed to be carrying plastic bags around with them and what else did one keep in plastic bags?

"I have heard that you plan to stay on at the cottage after all?" She supposed that the Inspector was only making polite conversation although how he had managed to get to know about her change of plans in such a short time and almost before she had known herself, she had no idea. But there again she supposed one ought to consider that it was the man's job!

"Yes, my mother has apparently changed her mind about going back home yet!" She spoke as if it was the woman's prerogative to be able to change her mind.

"I also heard that your friend Steven Futton was here at the Air Show yesterday. Did you happen to see him Stacey?"

At the time she didn't know whether to reply yea or nay. Yea in case she had been spotted speaking to Steve, or nay because she felt no inclination to draw attention to the fact. In the event she decided to play it safe and to say neither. "I did know that it was always his intention to attend the show along with his friends but he certainly didn't enter by the gate that I was on!"

"So you haven't seen him since?" That was a difficult one not to lie to yet instinctively she knew that she had to do her best to try to protect the man she still loved even if he, for his part, appeared to have finished with her.

"I think I already said Inspector that my mother is staying on at the cottage. She really had enough to say about me being out all day yesterday as well as not returning to the cottage on the previous evening because I presumed the cottage to be empty, than to further her annoyance by entertaining any company last night!"

He grimaced but seemed to accept her explanation. Still she supposed there must be some other reason why he wanted her to work close by him now on the Promenade and more in the public view today. Could this be in case Steve or any of his mates could see her and possibly make themselves known? It was this thought that served to make what would have been an acceptable day, a time of tension instead!

★ ★ ★ ★

Chapter Eight

"But that man is a policeman our Stacey!" True to her word Agnes Kershaw had arrived to meet her daughter promptly at five on the appropriate evening, only to find her in the company of this officer, who may not have been in uniform that day but who was nevertheless still an officer of the law. One look at her mother's face moreover was quite enough to inform the girl that the older woman now found this situation to be quite intolerable!

"Mother have you ever considered that perhaps the man happens to have another life outside of policing!" Stacey now responded with something of a sigh to her mother's almost belligerent attitude, for Agnes Kershaw always had to view any matter in terms of black and white and to this woman's mind she still could not comprehend what this man was doing out of his uniform, whether he was working or not, never mind collecting money for some cause here on the Promenade. For that, she solemnly decided could have little to do with policing.

"Oh well, I know some people might possibly condone this business but to my mind that is not how a policeman should behave our Stacey! Now you did tell me to be here at five o'clock and I am here promptly but you don't appear to be ready!" Realising that her initial argument had fallen upon deaf ears, a matter that did not please her very much at all, Agnes Kershaw now endeavoured to change the subject.

"We are just about to finish!" Stacey cast her mother something of a winsome smile knowing full that the other was merely biding her time as well as her tongue whilst she waited for her. The day she had to admit had passed pleasantly enough with the Inspector as her companion but in truth she was glad that it was now drawing to a close for being with him that day had most certainly placed Stacey on edge. Noticing now that her mother was still not totally convinced by her words she made a gesture by taking off the yellow jacket she wore and then handing it back, rather pointedly, to the Inspector.

"I think that I can now beg to be excused Keith. You see I promised to take my mother out for a meal." Then turning to her mother without giving that man any chance to reply. "Actually the Ship Inn looks rather promising, if you have no objections Mum for I believe that today they have stretched a point and kept it open on a Sunday because of this air show. We might possibly manage to get a lakeside view which will probably suit you best Mum!"

Her mother shrugged her shoulders. In truth she couldn't have cared less about the venue for it was the opportunity to share time with her daughter that she coveted the most!

For his part the Inspector nodded in agreement, not that he could have offered any form of objection at the time and therefore he decided that perhaps the point of least resistance would be the best way especially when confronted with these two women! Thus after taking their leave of him, the two of them began to drift off in the direction of the place that Stacey had previously mentioned. "Keith is it now then?" The woman was still determined to have her say for she really did not comprehend policemen who chose not to wear their uniform but preferred instead to wear someone else's yellow coat, and Stacey sighed. In truth, was her mother now looking for things again and noticing matters that did not exist? At the time however Stacey felt that she had too much on her mind to provoke an argument!

Still she had to admit that the meal they were served was pleasant enough and Agnes for her part now appeared to acquiesce and enjoy sitting out overlooking the quayside walk. In all truth so in fact did Stacey for her eyes were transfixed upon the duck waddling along the quayside even if to her mind the duck had now only one duckling following on behind and she could not help wondering what had happened to the rest. All of this was however until her eyes happened to come to rest upon a certain figure. There were not many folk walking along that part of the lakefront at this time but there was no mistaking the figure of Bob Eldon who was at the time talking rather earnestly to someone who had just disembarked from one of the yachts that were currently moored there. She knew Bob Eldon by sight, she remembered the photograph that Steve had once shown to her but he was in fact the only one of the group apart that was from Steve that she could recognise from that photograph of the gang of four. The other two faces had been blurred and to her eyes rather indistinguishable. It was then that Stacey strained her eyes to get a better view of his companion but the shadows were now falling fast in the place at this time of the day. It was actually her mother who had followed her gaze and who recognised the stance of this new person practically straight away.

"Look there is that nice Mr Drew!" Even as Stacey refocused her eyes to take note of this supposed gem of wisdom issuing forth from her mother's lips, the other person, now in turn having spotted them, started to wave and having apparently finished his conversation with the young engineer, the man, horror of horrors, began to wend his way towards where they were currently sitting wearing a beaming smile to grace his features.

That was the point when Stacey begged to be excused claiming that she needed the ladies room. In truth she felt there was no way she was going to be entertained by the likes of this one! Her mother on the other hand appeared to have no such compunction and even went so far as to welcome the man's presence.

"Now don't tell me Mrs Kershaw that you of all people have been interested in the Air Show, especially after all you have previously said about it?"

"Me? Never! A load of nasty noise that's what it is. No I came here to meet up with our Stacey----Now where has that girl gone to?" She looked around but Stacey had by this time completely disappeared from sight.

Meredith Drew shrugged his shoulders almost too good-naturedly for it to be a natural expression although it might have appeared that way to the uninitiated. "Actually it was you I wanted to speak to Mrs Kershaw. I actually believed that I had missed my opportunity when I heard that you had returned to Caton and then lo and behold I spotted you sitting here!"

"I changed my mind about going back just yet but you intrigue me for you said that you wished to speak with me?" The woman was pleasantly delighted with his words and decided that this must be a moment to be savoured for after all it wasn't very often that eligible young men sought to have a conversation with her.

"Well yes. You may consider this to be a confounded cheek on my part and I won't be offended if you should refuse. But perhaps you have already heard that one of my interests lies in the field of photography. Well ever since I first saw you, there appeared something about your eyes that I wanted to capture on film. A certain expression, perhaps it is even your own whimsical remembrances of the past. That I cannot say but I would very much like the opportunity to attempt to capture it on film!"

"You would?" Flattered Agnes managed to blush rather prettily. In actual fact she was quite unused to such comments nowadays since she had been left a widow and quite frankly especially after such a long period she quite enjoyed it.

"I would, with your agreement of course!"

"Then have you brought your camera with you?" Agnes looked around almost expectantly hoping to see such equipment of which he spoke and when she could not spot it he smiled at her by now puzzled expression.

"The equipment is not something that I usually carry around with me when I have no way of knowing whether or not I will spot such an interesting subject matter as yourself. But if indeed you are willing to allow me to photograph your likeness then perhaps we could arrange a meeting. Indeed if it is convenient I could come to the cottage some afternoon?"

Agnes may have been flattered but her mind still worked quickly. Of course she knew full well that Stacey would object to her having any association with this man, but then if Stacey just happened to be at work at the time---

--! "Then perhaps you could make it one afternoon just after lunch. That way I cannot conceive that we will be disturbed!"

"Splendid, and after I have taken the photographs perhaps you will then allow me to take you out somewhere?"

Agnes blushed for she had lost the habit of being flattered by a man, especially one as good looking and as eligible as Meredith was. Stacey must really be a damned fool to shun this man's advances. But she supposed that with a little encouragement on her own part the girl could be persuaded to change her mind. "What day did you have in mind then Mr Drew?"

"The name is Meredith please, as I believe I have told you before. I am Meredith to all my friends and the title Mr appears to be so formal in such circumstances. How about Tuesday this week then?"

"Tuesday I consider will be perfect!" Agnes cast a fluttering smile now in his direction.

"Then I will be at the cottage early in the afternoon as you requested. There is also another matter, I would in fact be much obliged if you and your daughter attended a forthcoming function at the Hall. You see being in charge of such a venture obliges me to hold these little tea parties from time to time and I would value your companionship at one of these events that just so happens to be coming up in the near future. But no doubt we can speak further about this when next we meet. But now I am afraid that I must crave to excuse myself, for it so happens that as one of the invited dignitaries to the Air Show I have still a function to attend!"

"But you will miss Stacey!" Agnes almost gave a pathetic wail for she really did feel she could have kicked the girl for not being present even as she wondered where on earth she had got to after all this time!

"That I am afraid is a great pity but I am afraid that I do have to go now. But no doubt you will be able to fill her in with the content of our conversation but as I said I must now take my leave of you Agnes!"

She bristled with a sense of pride when he used her Christian name but almost at the same time she decided there that Stacey must learn nothing about the arrangement they had made for she had the distinct impression that Stacey would be ready to move heaven and earth to stop it. Besides, after all one could consider that it was none of that girl's business anyway and if she related what had happened she realised that this would more than likely invite a mouthful of objections from her daughter. Besides which, the girl would be at work when Meredith came round to the cottage therefore the way Agnes viewed the matter was that the arrangement that had been made was entirely between herself and Meredith.

"Well has he gone, what did he want anyway?" Agnes supposed she still must have been dreaming when Stacey after seeing that the coast was clear decided to return.

"Yes he has gone. As a matter of fact he merely came across to present his compliments and pass the niceties of the day, something that doesn't appear to happen much in today's society. Speaking of which I must say Stacey that I thought it was very rude of you to dash away in the manner you did!"

"I told you that I needed the ladies room Mum and anyway you know full well that I cannot stick that man!"

"Now that I consider is not very nice of you at all Stacey. In fact I consider it to be the art of bad manners! Meredith has never done you any wrong!" Agnes' face now appeared to be almost critical of her daughter. Stacey had no doubt that the woman meant what she said for she had noticed that her mother's back had stiffened in the manner it did when she felt justifiably annoyed!

Stacey swallowed hard upon hearing her mother's words. She had not revealed to the other what had happened on Lady-Holme, nor had she any intention of doing so for to even mention the occasion she seemed in her own eyes to be degrading herself. "Well I'm sorry but I can't help my instincts Mum. But it appears to have grown quite chilly sitting here now. Perhaps it is time for us to make a move. Anyway I believe that your favourite programme is on the box tonight!"

"Is it? Oh yes so it is, I remember now!" In truth Agnes had quite forgotten all about any such programme with the events of the last ten minutes stirring her blood.

"The question is, do you still want to go back and watch it or shall we think of moving on somewhere else for awhile?" Stacey was still puzzling as to exactly what Meredith Drew had been doing talking to Bob Eldon and where on earth that individual had subsequently disappeared to. Could it be that he was now with Steve?

"Oh I do believe that as there is something decent on the box tonight, which I have to admit makes a welcome change, we will go back there then. Oh and before you jump down my throat any further Meredith has invited us to some tea party he is holding at the Hall in the near future. Details are to follow!"

"Mother you know perfectly well that I cannot stick the man so why on earth have you got us involved in one of his exploits -----?" She broke off suddenly as she remembered previously spotting him with Bob Eldon. Perhaps after all that was something she ought to try to find out about if only for Steve's sake. "Oh well we'll see what comes of it then!" Even so, she reminded herself, if she did discover something that was not exactly kosher, then how on earth was she going to be able to convey the facts to Steve?

In truth the problem she toyed with was to raise its head above the parapet sooner than she had imagined. Glancing out across the lake as she returned home from work the next day it was to spot a small boat out on that aqueous mass with two men on board who did not at the time appear to be in any hurry to go anywhere, whether this was to head for the shore or to continue with their voyage up the lake. In truth the boat had at first been almost obscure from public view and Stacey herself spotted the vessel from Ferry Nab as she was waiting for the ferry to take her across with her car. The conversation that appeared to be continuing on that vessel seemed to all intents and purposes to be something of a deep nature and to the apparent exclusion of anything else at the time. Yet on the other hand one could not claim that the same appeared to be antagonistic in its content.

Close by to where she was standing a family of four were also biding their time as they waited for the boat to return from the other side with those draw ropes that made a hasping noise as the vessel grounded against the receiving slope. Waiting patiently for the return of the vessel from Ferry House they had left their car in order to join her on the slade and the dog that they had in tow was now obviously objecting most strongly to the fact that it was presently tethered and thus could not dip its paws into the tempting aqueous mass and consequently the animal vented its feelings upon the matter by barking with some gusto in an attempt to get its point across to what it considered were its oblivious owners.

Not however that the noise it made disturbed the two still deep in their conversation. Straining her eyes in an attempt to catch a better look at them Stacey noticed with something of a surprise that she could just about make out the features of one of the two, a factor that made her crane even further to see whether she was right in her assumptions. This time she felt sure that she was correct for one of the men in the boat was Steve. At first she was so surprised at seeing him there that she believed she was not acquainted with his companion, that was however with until a sudden flashback she remembered the man who had been speaking with Meredith Drew on the day she had been having tea with her mother overlooking that quayside walk.

The conversation was now obviously over for it was at that moment she saw Steve start up the engine to the craft. At least the point that today he was not attempting to row the vessel brought a momentary smile to her lips. But now the ferryboat had arrived, and it was as she finally boarded that she was convinced she saw them moving towards the confines of the Marina and by the time the man had been around to collect his fare from his passengers and she had managed to leave the car they had completely disappeared!

She suddenly remembered the fax she had received earlier that day. To be honest she had initially taken it upon herself to make the first move to try to find out whether the firm B.A.E. would be interested in viewing Steve's new design. Perhaps she had exceeded her brief in doing this but at the time she had only been aware that his initial plans or the design had come to nothing. In fact it had been Dick Soper who had first drawn her attention to the advert in that scientific magazine, one which the man appeared to enjoy collecting. Why he had drawn her attention to it, Stacey had no idea, unless it was pure coincidence, for as far as she knew he was completely ignorant of what had happened previously, unless she herself had inadvertently let something slip about it, but she thought not! The rest of the action had been Stacey's own doing, although whether Steve would deem to accept anything from her hands anymore still remained a slightly different matter. Still Dick Soper had proved yet again what a good friend he really was, sometimes she mused, without even realising it! Even so whether Steve himself would ever accept anything that she did or said anymore was a different matter!

The metal restrainers on the deck were finally lifted and the time was now opportune when she had to follow the long procession of vehicles off the boat and up the steep hill that awaited them, that in its turn led to Sawrey and Hawkshead. Her own destination at the time was of course the cottage, where she was to find her mother employed in making the best of the mild weather conditions presently occurring to hang out some small items she had washed in the back garden.

Today however the woman was most charming in her greeting: The mild mannered smile she cast in Stacey's direction when she arrived back there certainly had the girl puzzled and she wondered what on earth was on the woman's mind to cause her to behave in this manner. Of course Stacey had no way of knowing that Meredith Drew had visited that same afternoon and maybe the woman, upon seeing her daughter, was now suffering something like the pangs of a guilt complex. Even so Agnes still felt that there was something she needed to impart to her daughter, even if she already knew what the girl's reaction to this would be before she opened her lips.

"Mr Drew came around earlier on today about that do he has invited us to back at the Hall!" She mentioned nothing about the camera or the man's sudden claim to have brought the wrong lens with him and would therefore need to come again on another afternoon. "He is considering next Saturday as a matter of fact. Apparently it is the Boat Regatta on that day and therefore that in itself will attract visitors to the town. In addition he is also hoping to have something of an attraction for himself stationed in the grounds of the Hall!"

"Then if he is setting up something in the grounds of the Hall I guess I will have already been witness to it and therefore I cannot see what good my coming to this function will accomplish!" She attempted to prevaricate but Agnes was determined she was having none of it and after what had happened in recent days Stacey decided that it was pointless at the time to pursue the argument any further. Not of course that she had any intention of attending. Perhaps it was therefore unfortunate that she allowed her mind over the forthcoming days to dwell upon other matters such as spotting Steve and Bob Eldon in that craft together and why she had previously seen Bob Eldon speaking to Meredith Drew on the evening of the Air Show. At the time she had no satisfactory answers that came to mind, plus in addition she was also still puzzled as to how she could get the context of that fax through to Steve when he now seemed to be deliberately avoiding her and she, for her part, had no idea where he was staying.

In point of fact she knew that the other three had been staying in bed and breakfast accommodation for the duration of the show, but even after she had traced the whereabouts of this place, hoping that Steve's so-called friends could help, it was to find that they had already packed up and left.

"Guess they only booked in until the end of the Show!" Their former landlady greeted her almost as if she had posed a daft question. "Well that was what they came here for in the first place and now I have other guests to attend to! Not that one of them seemed to spend much time here I admit, but then the rent had been paid so I suppose that was no skin off my nose!"

Turning away Stacey had still been left puzzled with her sighting of Bob Eldon first of all on the Quayside Walk even though she supposed his presence at that time could have been excusable whether his contact was or not, but she was even more puzzled over the timing of spotting the two together in a certain boat more especially after their landlady had intimated that they all must definitely have left town by that time.

Therefore with her thoughts so engrossed in far away pastures she found herself accompanying her mother to the Hall on the following Saturday. It was much to her surprise however, when still disgruntled with the thought of having to attend but after offering the point of least resistance when Agnes had persisted with this invitation because she could no longer think up any legitimate excuse as to why she should stop away, Stacey was to discover that this so-called tea party was being held in recognition of the Shelter Box, an enterprise set up by the Rotarians. What Meredith Drew held in common with these people remained a subject of conjecture although she noted that Keith Forsyth also appeared to have his name on the guest list!

Upon spotting the policeman Stacey had to admit that the other could easily have been mistaken as being grumpy in his attitude. It most certainly did not appear to be to the man's liking that he had been included on that guest list anyway and Stacey could not help but wonder if he like herself had received his instructions to attend willing or not for she had already gathered that the policeman had little time for the likes of Meredith Drew!

For his part Keith Forsyth had been musing at the time whether this invitation had been made as some sort of gesture to persuade him to forget about other issues, like the one he had currently been persuaded to shelve for lack of independent evidence concerning the case that the students at the centre had first brought to his attention. With further proof there was little doubt that this man would already have taken some form of action for he himself was convinced that Meredith Drew had some case to answer. But that man was not without influential friends and moreover it appeared that the man himself did not fully comprehend any dilemma in this matter. Moreover Meredith had himself been aware that the Rotarians were currently sponsoring this so-called tent they had named Shelter Box, which he supposed could be termed as being in aid of a good cause and therefore Meredith Drew had been determined to carve himself a piece of the action, no doubt in the expectation of receiving praise and attention emanating in his direction!

It was Meredith however who was the first to make a beeline towards the two women when they first made their appearance. Maybe at that time Stacey would still have found some excuse to escape from this situation, but possible realising what was currently at the forefront of her daughter's mind, Agnes Kershaw had laid a firm hand upon her arm.

"I am so glad that the two of you were able to come!" Meredith now gushed upon his words as he applied each syllable quite succinctly. Yet in all truth it was Stacey's expression that he sought most of all. "Our friends from around these parts have erected one of these Shelter tents out in the grounds for us to view, so do come and take a look around the place and then you can give me your considered opinion!"

Somehow it appeared that by the time they had reached the outside of the building Meredith had nevertheless managed to get between her mother and herself as they had moved through those doors obligingly. The entrance to this tent affair appeared to offer access through a long porch like structure and it was as she turned to see whether her mother was following her that Stacey was to find herself now facing this man at very close quarters.

"You appear to be a little on edge my dear. Dare one pose the question as to why you should feel that way even if it does make you look even more attractive? Oh I know that we have had our disagreements in the past but surely we can put those behind us and forget all about them now!"

She shook her head showing her determination to get back to her mother on the other side of him. At least she believed that would offer her some form of security against this man. But Meredith was not for moving and realising her intent a sickly smile began to creep across his lips curving them into what could be described as a sardonic smile. To her mind she believed that he was now on the point of grabbing hold of her and putting off listening to any objections she wanted to raise about the matter until a later stage. From her own position of course Agnes could not see what was going on between them. In fact it was only when she heard a voice call out from behind her that she grabbed hold of her handbag a little tighter and brought the object across her bosom for its protection.

"Apparently there is a telephone call for you Meredith!" The man in question was obviously now angry at this interruption as he turned to meet the Inspector's forthright gaze. "It's something to do with the land for a timber lodge I believe, at least that is what I think the caller was referring to!" Surprisingly enough the Inspector imparted the feeling that he was glad to have been able to bring this message. Not that his recipient seemed in the same frame of mind to receive it, for this one's face now bore signs of positive fury as he made to push past Agnes in order to make his way back into the Hall.

"I'm afraid that I can't really say that the men you appear to chose as your companions do much for me at all Miss Kershaw!" Stacey now wondered whether she was glad or sorry that the Inspector had now reverted back to form.

"But Mr Drew has been most kind to us in many ways Inspector!" It was Agnes who, after deciding it was time her voice should be heard, decided to put in her own two pennyworth. "I must say in all my dealings with Mr Drew I have only ever seen him as being a very honest and worthy gentleman and what is more I consider it to be a great pity that there are not many others like the man in the world today!"

At least the woman now appeared so prohibitive that even the Detective Inspector felt forced to hold his tongue. "Thanks Keith anyway for your timely rescue, I guess I owe you one for this!" Stacey nevertheless had the grace to murmur her thanks to the man as they gratefully left the place. "Let's go home Mum, this place gives me the creeps!" Now she was almost begging but it was not to be.

"Nonsense girl, anyway we haven't had our refreshments yet!" Agnes fished in her purse before tipping a pound coin in a strategically placed collection box and in return had the pleasure of hearing the Detective Inspector murmuring his thanks. "Well I consider that it is a very worthy cause even if I doubt whether those young people it is intended to help will appreciate it. Anyway in the first place they ought to have more sense than to go traipsing around on those fells in all sorts of weather. Mind you during the time I have been here I have become more than convinced that half the population in these parts are as nutty as fruitcakes.

She followed the woman back into the banqueting hall where the buffet had been laid out almost like a lost child or some evacuee from the blitz. Somehow she no longer felt in control of her own destiny. The Inspector had also followed and was now reviewing this scene with something that resembled a streak of humour, which was something she had never expected to see in Detective Inspector Forsyth.

"These meat patties are good!" Her mother of course felt the necessity to sample even before they reached the small table where they were sitting. "But Stacey, you haven't got anything to eat on your plate yet!"

"I don't really feel hungry Mum!" All Stacey wanted to do at that time was to leave this place, and if she had felt any tenet of hunger before she had arrived here then the company present had been responsible for taking it away.

"That is a load of nonsense. Of course you are hungry. You haven't eaten for ages. Now go and get yourself something and no arguments!"

Realising it was the better of two evils Stacey helped herself to a small cake, toying with it on the plate as she took it back with her.

"Is that all that you are having girl?"

"I'll get us some tea!" This was her means to escape but it was upon her return that she realised that any means of escape was not going to be possible for Meredith Drew having taken his phone call was now heading in their direction. Not but what Agnes did not look pleased to see him.

"Meredith has promised to take me to Helm Crag this next week. I want to see this lion and the lamb they are supposed to have there!"

"We will be viewing it only from off the road of that I can assure you!" Perhaps Meredith suspected that Stacey believed he was about to have her mother fell walking.

"I'm afraid my mother has been watching television again. She's got herself rather hooked on the Wainwright Walks programmes that seem to be running at the moment!" Well she supposed she had to say something and that appeared to be innocuous enough.

"I am capable of reading about them for myself our Stacey!" This time Agnes was toying with her trifle.

"Well Grasmere is a charming place anyway and the surrounding scenery is beautiful to say the least so I think you can excuse your mother's enthusiasm Stacey!" She wondered if this was a slight on her because she had not taken Agnes to this place for herself. Still where on earth Meredith found all this spare time from when he always complained that he was busy she didn't know! Neither come to that did she know why a man like him wanted to be hindered with the older woman so frequently. Perhaps

Agnes realised something of the girl's current thoughts for she suddenly became pre-occupied with the food again.

"Everything is lovely Meredith and so appetising, who did the catering for you then?"

"A small local firm. Indeed I like to lend my support to local firms!" The man was obviously charmed that someone had noticed and bothered to pass comment.

"This girl doesn't know what she is missing claiming that she is not hungry, see if you can persuade her to eat a little more Meredith!"

"I am honestly telling the truth when I say that I am not hungry. I appear to have a lot on my mind at the moment!"

"Well they do say that a problem that is shared is halved Stacey! But surely you are still not worrying about your boy friend are you? I understood that it was all finished between you. By the way what did happen to him after he left the Island with the policeman giving chase? Did Keith manage to catch up with him?" The eyes were on her again almost as if he was daring her to say something about his own role but knowing all the time that he would not succeed in embarrassing her in front of her mother.

"I really have no idea!" Well this was partially true at any rate for she had no idea where Steve was at the current time. She only wished that she did for there was the matter of the contents of that fax she had received but had been unable to pass on to him.

"But didn't he bring that man to the cottage after the Air Show?" Agnes posed the question in all innocence as she wiped the cream off her fingers. "Didn't he bring the man to show him something that you were keeping for him?"

Stacey swore under her breath as she noted the hardness now creeping into the other man's eyes. This situation demanded some quick thought. "Guess I had forgotten.

You see they didn't stay for very long. They went into the parlour and I don't think I even had a chance to say anything to them. Then they were both gone and as far as I know Steve took the papers with him at that time. I haven't seen anything of him since although I know the four have left the bed and breakfast accommodation where they were staying, something I believe that had to do with their work. But I know they initially came because of the Air Show but now that they have gone I think it highly unlikely that I will find anything else out!"

She wondered if there was a chance that Meredith Drew had swallowed her story but one look at his face informed her that he had not! Still ever the actor he now portended something of a performance over something that may well have deceived her mother but nevertheless did not serve to deceive him and Stacey knew that she would need to be on her guard in the near future!

"Well did you manage to get the message through?" It was Dick Soper that portrayed his curiosity once she was back again on the work front. Sadly she shook her head, Dick was the one who had first suggested this so she supposed he had a right to know.

"They all appear to have left the area and without leaving a forwarding address either!"

"One of them hasn't. I'm right aren't I in saying that Bob Eldon was a member of the group?" She nodded. "Well I have news for you for that one is still around in this area. As a matter of fact I saw him in the Albert the other night. Quite a decent bloke he seems too. Anyway if I see him again I'll get him to contact you if you like. Perhaps he will have some idea of his friend's whereabouts!"

Stacey remembered witnessing the scene out on the Lake! Bob Eldon had most certainly not been by himself on that day! " Thanks anyway. I guess it would take quite a bit of onus away from me if you managed to do that Dick!"

"Anything I can do to help a friend!" Stacey was struck with how pleasant this man was. There was no mistake Dick Soper was becoming a real friend to her. "By the way how did you go on at the tea and bun fight?"

"That!" She now pulled a wry face. "For me personally it meant that I was haunted by a certain person I would rather forget about but appear to find the same character at every turn!"

"By that I suppose you mean that Drew is up to his old tricks again. Don't worry there are plenty around these parts who share your abomination of that fellow. In fact I was talking to Tom Smethurst the other day and I gathered from his sentiments that the man has already over stayed his welcome!" The moment passed and Stacey had pushed the incident to the back of her mind when Dick, true to his word sought her out yet again.

"Thought you might be interested but I spotted a friend of mine last night. Apparently Bob Eldon is currently staying at some campsite in the Grasmere Region. Hope that is of some help to you anyway!"

"Thanks Dick, you really are a friend!" Stacey however was deep in thought as she wended her way home after work that evening.

"They really are very good!" Agnes Kershaw bristled with pride as Meredith Drew placed the snaps he had taken of her down on the dining table. In truth the woman was flattered, indeed who of her age wouldn't have been to be asked to pose as a photographer's model. The man in question however wore a more doleful expression as he shook his head.

"Sorry Agnes but these are really not good enough. Certainly not to enter into any photographic competition I am afraid!"

Agnes Kershaw swallowed back her obvious disappointment. To be thus informed that she had not succeeded in making a suitable subject for him caused a wave of remorse to pass over her for now she decided that it must be like everything else in her life, her age was against her! Meredith obviously needed someone who was younger and more vibrant to pose for him. Yet when she falteringly ventured upon the matter the man, much to her surprise shook his head yet again.

"That is nonsense Agnes. My goal was to be able to express the maturity of the years in my photograph. I will leave it to others I consider to be less capable to characterise the features of the young, but I am afraid that they will be unable to find a subject with the same depth of character that is so naturally born as what I can see in you!"

"But you have just said that the photos are not good enough?" Now she was definitely puzzled.

"In that case my dear maybe you will bear with me whilst I take some more!" He was twisting the opening to his camera case even as he spoke and Agnes herself immediately made a beeline for the mirror in order to straighten her hair. He paused for a moment before he spoke. "I was wondering if this time around it might be possibly for me to get a more meaningful shot, for example, do you happen to have a dressing gown that you could slip over your clothes?"

Agnes regarded him in a rather puzzled manner but nevertheless disappeared into the bedroom to return about thirty seconds later wearing the same. "Will this do?" Her voice was hesitant as she posed the question for in actuality she felt something like a prat dressed up like this. Meredith however studied her rather critically before responding.

"I wonder, maybe this sounds rather silly to you but do you have something like a cuddly toy you could hold almost as if you were reminiscing over something in the past. That way maybe I will be able to capture the wisdom of the years that I am searching for in the shot. I'm positive that if I can succeed in doing that then the result will surely be a winner!"

"You mean something like this?" Haphazardly Agnes picked up the object that was closest to where she stood. This so happened to be a fruit bowl that had been left standing on the table.

"Well not exactly. How can one possibly get a modern day fruit bowl to evoke the lifetime of anybody's memory?"

"Well I suppose it could if it was old enough!" Still he preferred to ignore her comment. Instead some sort of inspiration seemed to strike him upon her words.

"That's it! I did mention a cuddly toy before and we need something that when you hold it would be bound to evoke some sort of memory from a bygone era?"

"Nothing as far as I know!" Agnes thought for a moment. She supposed a photograph would be rather trite considering that Meredith wanted this to be something different. Besides as far as she knew she had no ancient photographs with her at the time. But then she supposed there was always---------!"

"Wait a moment I have just had a thought!" Meredith had little idea that his patience on another matter was about to be rewarded when she quickly returned carrying that nightdress case, although his first words hardly led one to assume this.

"What on earth is that thing? I can see that it is some relic but I never realised that you were into space invaders!"

"It's a nightdress case. Stacey's as a matter of fact. We initially bought it for her when she was a child in an effort to try to teach the girl to be tidy, but then she actually took a shine to it and wouldn't be parted from it!"

"Well I suppose one could concede that it does have some merit. You will have the memories there I suppose. O.K. we'll try it, at least I suppose there are memories that are associated with it?"

"Oh yes----!" Agnes had started to fiddle with the catch that opened it up. "Now what on earth has the girl got inside of it, this hardly feels like her pyjamas?" Her hand now inside of the case touched upon a sheaf of papers. "What on earth is she doing keeping these in here. I told you that girl has never learnt. She has never been tidy in her life!" She missed the sudden look of avarice in Meredith's eyes as she began to withdraw them out of that case in order to see what they were. "You will never believe this. It is all that rubbish that was left lying about the other night after those fellows had been round. I told her to get rid of them then!"

His eyes now positively gloating Meredith made an effort to pass over the waste paper bin but by this time Agnes had decided to stuff the papers back inside the case thus ignoring his offer. "Just wait till I see her, I will have a thing or two to say about this. Until then they can damned well stay where they are because I positively refuse to tidy up for her anymore, not at twenty-five years of age! What is more I do believe that is her car I can hear now!"

Chapter Nine

Stacey's brain seared into activity as she viewed the scene that awaited her upon entering the cottage: She was so surprised in fact that for a moment she even forgot to query the presence of Meredith Drew for her entire being became set not upon the fact that her mother was now clothed in a dressing gown but upon that pyjama case she was currently hanging onto, and her mind was caught up in the methodology of how she could possible rescue it and more importantly its contents away from the grasping hands of Meredith Drew.

"I thought you knew Mum that Fred doesn't like to be disturbed from the place where I left him?" The admonishment was childish and yet the tone in her voice left everyone in the state of some surprise and that included Stacey herself as she stretched out her hands in some vague attempt to grasp hold of her talisman.

"Stacey, for goodness sake act your age, talking as if this is some sort of a toy! Besides from what I can see this pyjama case hasn't got your pyjamas in it at all. In fact is crammed full of rubbish!" Agnes' response was definitely on the defensive. She felt that now she had little alternative but to sound in this manner for she immediately sensed her daughter's fury that they had possessed the nerve to remove the object from off her bed. "In actual fact we only wanted to use it for a photograph!" She added the latter phrase almost as an afterthought for up until this moment Stacey had never queried what Meredith was doing there posed with a camera in his hands.

"What do you mean, a photograph?" At least it appeared that Agnes' words had startled the newcomer back into some sense of reality.

"Meredith here has asked me to pose for a photograph, the subject of which he decided would be that of a mature person, and the photograph he wants to take is one that he wishes to enter for a competition!" At least Agnes felt that she could still hold her head up high in pride considering that she had been the one who had been chosen to pose for this!

"He wants to take a photograph of a nightdress case?" Incredulity echoed from the girl's lips as she attempted to catch a glimpse of the man in question's face. Not that she appeared to have much success in this but had she succeeded she might well have become aware of the look of damned annoyance that was now portrayed in this creature's face

"With me on it as well of course! Still I'm afraid that the idea to include the nightdress case in order to make the image appear more meaningful was my own! But if you feel so strongly about it then here, you can take the thing!" Meredith now positively cringed as the woman tossed the case back in her daughter's direction even before he had managed to get his hands on it and moreover the recipient of this article grabbed hold of it quite tightly almost as if she was determined that no one would dare to wrest it away from her. "Meredith simply wanted me to be posed looking at something that evoked memories from the past. It was that look in my eye that he wanted to capture on film!"

"If he wants a photograph of you then what is wrong with these he has apparently already taken?" Stacey nodded to where the discarded shots had previously been discarded on the table.

"Because in his opinion they lacked a certain quality that he believed was necessary for him to portray in the competition if he was to stand any chance of success!"

Stacey began to wonder if the man had a voice left to speak for himself after all until Meredith came out with the expression. "Maybe I should go!" The man, she had to admit, now looked decidedly uncomfortable almost as if he decried the notion that his actions should be worthy of scrutiny. "In actual fact we didn't expect that you would be home so early today!"

"That to my mind appears to be perfectly obvious!" Stacey still clutched hold of her precious icon as she allowed her eyes to dart furiously in the other's direction.

"But you did say that you would take me out after we had taken those shots Meredith?" Now it was Agnes' turn to show her agitation.

"Perhaps it would no longer be a good idea for today especially now that Stacey is home. But I do remember that I did promise to take you to Grasmere and so if it is all right with you I will call for you early tomorrow?"

"Tomorrow it so happens that I have the day off myself!" Stacey deliberately lied. She realised of course that she would have to make this all right with Clive but on the other hand her work was up to date. Anything she could do to spoil this little tete a tete then she most certainly would act upon it!

"Well in that case why don't you come as well Stacey?" It was the voice of Agnes again and that individual lady most certainly did not want to forgo any opportunity of a trip out with Meredith whether her daughter had the day off or not!

"I consider that to be quite a good idea Agnes!" She hated the familiarity with which he addressed her mother but then Meredith had currently only one thing now on his mind and that was in planning just how he could devise some scheme to get those papers from off the girl and without arousing her mother's suspicions in the process!

"Oh I don't really know whether it is for me!" Stacey hated even the thought of such an expedition but not half as much as she hated the thought of him becoming any wiser than what she was herself and now that he had found out about those papers and where they were currently hidden she supposed it surely could only be a question of time before he managed to persuade her mother -----!

"Take no notice of her Meredith. Of course the girl knows! In fact now that Stacey isn't working tomorrow I think it is an excellent idea. I know full well she will enjoy the day there because she herself has been telling me all about the place. Following on from what she told me I have taken the opportunity to read up a little about the place as well. Did you know that St Oswald's Church in that village was the place where the Wordsworth family regularly attended? Not only that but it has also three entrance gates to the place because it originally served three parishes each with its own separate entrance; a lych gate for Grasmere, a wrought iron arch for Rydal and Ambleside and a smaller gate for Langdale! Then after the church at Rydal was completed Wordsworth himself served as a Church Warden for a time. There is also a lot more that I have read about the place too, I bet neither of you have heard of the Coffin Route from Rydal to Nab Scar that was initially used to carry the deceased from Rydal and Ambleside for burial in Grasmere Church?" The woman sank back rather breathless after her preamble and appeared now to be a little flushed but nevertheless she was pleased to have been able to expound her newly acquired knowledge, and Stacey gazing at her by now flustered expression was forced to smile in spite of her initial concern.

"Well at this rate we won't be needing a guide book Agnes!" At least Meredith managed a smile. "So in view of your mother's recently acquired knowledge on the place surely you are not going to disappoint her Stacey?"

She looked from one to the other before making up her mind. Of course her first challenge would have to be somewhere where she could secrete those papers again where no one for any trumped up reason could get their hands on them, but maybe it would be all to the good if she kept a wary eye on the antics of Meredith and her mother as well anyway. "All right then Mum. I suppose that if it means so much to you I could stretch a point and come with you after all!"

It was therefore still bearing some reluctance at what she considered to be an imposed chore that Stacey allowed herself to be persuaded into Meredith's car on the following morning. At the time she was indeed so reluctant that in fact once the day had dawned she had initially contemplated volunteering to go there by travelling in her own car and merely follow on behind them. After contemplating such an action however she decided that to be caught following their car could indeed be deemed to be childish in manner and she reminded herself of the second of the two reasons. The first of these reasons was straightforward enough, for after catching her mother and Meredith together the previous evening she was wondering what it was that existed between the two of them. Secondly she knew full well that Meredith whether by foul means or fair, was more than a little anxious to get his paws on that nightdress case and reveal its contents. Also in mind was the news that Dick Soper had confided in her that consisted of Bob Eldon being spotted at a campsite situated close to this vicinity.

Naturally she had not forgotten that one of the last times she had seen him Bob Eldon had been speaking with Meredith Drew on the quayside walk after the Air show, but on the other hand she had also spotted him after that on the boat talking with Steve Futton when she had been in the process of crossing the lake. What that had been all about she still did not know apart from the fact that the discord had appeared to be quite tense. Yet Bob Eldon must be the one if any of them where who could give her the opportunity of tracking her ex-lover and demanding his attention! Once that was established surely she would be able to get rid of these designs once and for all as well as being able to inform him of a certain fax and the interest in them that was now obviously being shown by B.A.E. systems, for although she had been charged to look after this documentation it was no longer a viable solution and therefore the man must in all fairness take them away, whatever he happened to think about her at this time!

In truth she had been so worried now about leaving them in any place that before she had actually got into the car she had managed to hitch the papers in a sort of pouch around her middle, hoping against hope that the weather would not prove so unkind as to persuade her to remove her coat otherwise she could imagine her mother's passing remarks about the fact that she appeared to be putting on weight. She most definitely had to find some way now of returning these to their rightful owner! Whether she had actually expected to see Steve in Grasmere if it was the case that Bob Eldon was reputedly there was an entirely different matter but at least she supposed she could always wish that would happen.

Therefore Stacey bit her lip during the journey as she sweated in her outer garment and only wished she had some earplugs with her to block out the sound of that man's grating tones as he cruised the car through the outskirts of Ambleside. She had no doubt that Meredith was actually enjoying this situation. Somehow it appeared to give the man a feeling of power over her and upon this notion he was positively gloating!

The rain in the early hours of the day had now seemingly added a depth to the colouration of the surrounding greenery and it almost appeared that such growth had lifted its lips anxiously in order to catch the very last drops of the life giving substance. Moreover even at this time the mist was still nestling on and apparently showing reluctance to leave those mountaintops thus giving the whole of the scene an appearance like a veil of secrecy that had been sent to surround and enclose the valley. Indeed even the white cottages situated by the roadside appeared like sign posts bearing directions to another land.

"It will lift of course!" Meredith spoke the words reassuringly in Agnes' direction for the woman was still determined to spot her Helm Crag and the current elements had made this feat rather difficult. Stacey glanced at the person who had made such a profound statement critically. Could it be true that this man was able to portend the weather because he was blessed as some saint, or was it in truth some devil? Quite naturally she quickly decided on the latter explanation!

Perhaps however there was some consolation for her when Stacey spotted the sign by the roadside advertising the forthcoming Grasmere Lakeland Sports Show, which appeared to be including every event imaginable and even though she had no reason to do so at the time she committed the date to memory! Meanwhile having parked his car in a position where everybody could spot it, Meredith made to lead the way along the riverside path and over the Millennium Bridge towards the village. His excuse for this act was he said because he wanted Agnes to spot the access road that eventually led one up to Helm Crag and she supposed that it was true that one got a good vision of the lion and the lamb from off this track, where the sheep in the field, now wearing their summer attire appeared to take an interest in their words!

"But what about the church with the three gates, I thought you said that we were going there?" Maybe Agnes had assumed that they were not heading towards the village after all, for the path they were following twisted and wound almost in a teasing manner and often caused one to get the impression that they were about to arrive at the place before quite suddenly the path would dart away once again thus allowing the River to act as the separator between the individual and his goal! Along the path that they had followed the once trickle of water had first of all developed into a dashing stream covered in fern to keep its secret and had now turned itself into a torrent and finally the torrent itself became a river that would feed itself ultimately into the Lake.

Meredith smiled almost benevolently at her concern before pointing his umbrella to the point where the track joined onto a road that ran by the church of St Oswald itself. It was whilst they were there and Agnes was examining the commemorative stones in Wordsworth's daffodil garden, searching to see if anyone she knew had been there and paid such a tribute, that Stacey seized the opportunity to wander away from the two of them. After all her own excuse for coming here had not so much been rooted in the past but in expectation of being able to make contact with the living!

Even though it was still quite early in the day other pilgrims had now begun to gather in the centre of the place and therefore Stacey felt some sense of relief that there were now enough folk round about for her own action to be questioned. Yet it was by the sign that advertised a forthcoming beer festival to be held in the following month that Stacey finally spotted the figure that she considered to be a likeness of Bob Eldon. Not that personally she had ever met the fellow but nevertheless her two previous sightings gave her enough confidence to now approach this stranger.

"Bob Eldon?" She spoke hesitantly for even at this time she was still wondering whether she was doing the right thing. After all she had first spotted the man when he was talking to Meredith Drew and that could mean that he was no friend of Steve's after all. But under the circumstances she had to face facts, if she wanted to find Steve then she had to take a chance and if possible without divulging too much from her own past at this stage.

The man turned upon the mention of his name, curiosity showing in his eyes, wondering whom it was who had called out his name. And as there were other folk about his eyes did not immediately take on the form of Stacey leaving the girl to muse on the fact that the clouds that had been white and fluffy upon their arrival and seemingly promising a better day to come, had now grown thick, dark and even sinister in their appearance.

"I believe that is what they call me!" His eyes had now at last become fixed on Stacey but his look admonished her for the fact that she should have made this effort to disturb him.

"We haven't met before but if I say my name is Stacey Kershaw perhaps that may hold some meaning to you?"

He shook his head. "Why, should it or something?"

"I believe that you are a colleague of Steve Futton. Am I right on that one?"

"And you consider that matters?"

"It matters to me. You see I need to get in touch with the man rather urgently and as it happens you just happen to be my best and indeed my only hope now of tracing him!"

"Then I am afraid that I am sorry but I cannot help you!"

Possibly it was her expression at these words that conveyed her present emotions yet his eyes had now moved past where she was stood and had rested on the figure of Meredith Drew who along with Agnes in tow had just emerged from the church gardens and were now currently looking where Stacey herself had wandered off to. "You came here with that man?" She found it difficult to establish whether it was condolence or scorn Bob Eldon was handing out.

"Mr Drew do you mean? I suppose one could say that I travelled here in the same car as that person mainly because that happens to be my mother he is currently with, but I most certainly did not come with him voluntarily. Why, do you happen to know Mr Drew then?"

It was a shot in the dark. She knew damned well that this fellow knew him for hadn't she seen them together with her own eyes? And as if to give some justification to her claim it was at that moment that Meredith spotted them, and recognising Bob he shouted out in greeting.

"I never thought to see you here Bob. I thought you would have long since left this area?"

"There is another show coming up here shortly!" The other man mumbled his words almost as if he was issuing them reluctantly and Stacey remembered the sign she had spotted on the main road before they had venture into this village. "For want of a better word I happen to have got myself involved in it!" Did that mean that Steve would also be involved in this? Her heart now began to race a little at the thought. Well at least she considered that it offered her another avenue of approach.

Meredith Drew nodded and Stacey was left to wonder why this man had not posed more questions in the man's direction, but by this time Agnes herself had arrived upon the scene muttering about not having seen the Coffin Trail yet. Although Stacey knew full well that this lane was situated closer to Rydal she was not for saying anything for to her mind at least if the two of them disappeared looking for the place then there was a chance she might learn more from Bob Eldon. Still obviously Meredith Drew had other things on his mind.

"But I really think that those delightful tea rooms overlooking the river would make a far better option my dear!"

Her mother was tempted, that Stacey knew only too well but then Agnes, true to form whilst she was still so determined shook her head. "We can leave that until later I think because I know that once I sit down then I'll swear that I will never get up again, which would be a great pity for then I would miss half of what I have come here to see!"

"In that case are you coming as well Stacey?" Meredith shrugged his shoulders in resignation. At the same time however Stacey got the impression from the way he spoke that he most certainly did not want to leave her behind especially if she was talking to Bob Eldon.

"All right ----but I do believe there are some Lakeland shops around and I have it in mind to purchase one of those fluffy white lambs that they are famous for here. I was reminded of it when we passed by the sheep in that field on the way here!"

"Oh take no notice of the girl!" Agnes had caught Meredith's incredulous look that a grown woman would crave to want something like that. "You see I am afraid that our Stacey has always been the one for collecting peculiar items!"

The other grunted for he was obviously not persuaded by the woman's argument but Agnes had still more on her mind that she wished to impart in his ear lobe. "Let's go down as far as the Lake now for I want to see Heron Island where the red deer have been known to swim across to!"

"Sorry wrong lake Mum I'm afraid, you are now talking about Rydal Water!" This time Stacey could not help but correct her mother in her assumption but this did nothing to stop the smirk that was in danger of developing on Meredith's face.

"Now is that a fact. But then of course one tends to forget your own superior knowledge of the Lakeland sights of special interest. Still never mind we can always console ourselves by buying some gingerbread instead!"

She watched for a moment as the two apparently turned their backs on her quite deliberately leaving her still feeling more than a little irritated, to cross over to this place and perhaps she was more than a little surprised when she heard Bob Eldon who was still within earshot almost murmur the words to her

"The show holds a promise to be very good Miss. If I were you then I wouldn't miss it!"

She had been unable to learn anymore from Bob Eldon for the man had disappeared like a will 'o' the wisp and therefore it was Clive Warner whom she finally decided to approach in an effort to find out what else she could glean about this forthcoming show, claiming as her excuse that several guests staying on the site had been enquiring about it.

"I only know what it says in the events guide book about it!" Clive pursed his lips thoughtfully displaying a look that assumed in the very least and especially in his position he ought to know! "Although having said that there is quite a lot that appears to be happening there this year! In fact quite a lot is happening in that area over the next couple of weeks. I believe it starts off this week with the Rydal Valley Sheep and Hounds trials. But the Lakeland show itself is not totally based on agriculture or so I am led to believe, for instance bands have already been employed as well as displays and trade stalls so I expect it will prove to be quite an attraction!"

"Thanks anyway Clive!" She was now puzzling as to what she could do with those designs of Steve's in the interim period, after all she could hardly walk around the office appearing as if she was pregnant and now aware she dare not take them back to the cottage under the circumstances she had no idea whom she could entrust them to in the meantime or even what place she could safely leave them and discard them off her person.

Her answer came in the unlikely form of one of those timber lodges that had not up to the present time been sold. Indeed at the moment there had not been any enquiries about the place probably due to the credit crunch and people being unwilling to spend in the current economic climate, and Stacey conceded that even if there were enquiries during the short time before this Lakeland event, then she did have the access to a key for the place and therefore she could remove them again very quickly and without causing any suspicion!

"Thinking of buying this one are you Miss?" It was Tom Smethurst who met her as she left the place after depositing the goods well out of sight in the building.

"I only wish that I could Tom, but there again I could hardly afford it on my salary!" She managed to turn the matter into something of a joke. Tom knew full well that she had access to any unsold property on site and so he didn't find it unusual to see the girl coming from the place, even if his presence had given the girl quite a shock. But then the man's main interest had been in those rabbits that appeared to be far more prevalent this year and Tom was partial to a bit of rabbit stew, never mind all the damned folklore that surrounded them.

With the documents now out of the way Stacey found that at least she could now relax a little bit more! The forthcoming event, being on a Sunday, when most of the office staff had the day off from their toils, she also found that quite a contingent of them were also planning to attend this event. Well she supposed she must consider that there was safety in numbers. That was of course until she heard the nature of some of these events and that there was even one in which the office staff were considering competing in. Moreover, once she had expressed an interest in attending, she also found that her name had been included with the rest of the group.

"You are entering us for a tug of war competition?" Now she was incredulous at the very thought.

"Why not. It is after all the Lakeland Sports isn't it? It's of Viking origin and therefore anything goes. All right we admit that we might not pass the post first but just think of the fun we will have competing!"

This idea of fun didn't really suit Stacey's ideas at all for how on earth could she have entered if she had happened to have those plans wrapped up around her like a support belt. After all she could hardly have taken part wearing her outer gear and neither could she have got stripped off like the others. Perhaps it was just as well that she had found another place to deposit them in the nick of time! Yet now it was Agnes who proved to be yet another thorn in her side.

"You mean that you are actually competing in this our Stacey, then I insist that I come along to watch you!"

This was most certainly not the idea at all. From her own point of view she had organised herself to see Steve if he should be there!

Nevertheless at the time and wanting to forget about any such thing as a forthcoming tug of war, whether she was with her work colleagues or not, she deliberately made to concentrate her efforts on her mother's own day out, knowing full well that once she embarked upon that subject she would be forgetting all others. "I never asked you but did you enjoy the day we spent at Grasmere Mum?" She never elaborated on the fact that she herself had breathed a sigh of relief once she had spotted the door of the cottage again for the rest of that day had passed by almost like an impasse and moreover she had felt decidedly uncomfortable in Meredith's continued presence. Spotting Bob in Grasmere as she had done had also evoked those same thoughts as to his connection with Meredith or whether this was indeed a fabrication made up in her own mind and she should therefore have trusted the man with her news.

"Well there is one thing I have to say about it, there seemed to be a lot that I missed out on!" The woman now held the expression that somehow she had been deliberately deprived. "Although I suppose I must admit that Meredith made a charming host. What is more I think the man has got his eyes on you too our Stacey; perhaps you in return ought to try to be a little pleasanter to him in return!"

"Where was it that you wanted to go then that you haven't yet seen?" Stacey sighed realising she needed to change the subject yet again if she was to keep her mother away from dwelling on herself!

"Why I wanted to go to those places you mentioned. At the time you said that they were on that other Lake, the one closer to Ambleside. I admit I did think that Meredith might have suggested us going but on the other hand you seemed to be in such a hurry to get back and I didn't get a chance to persuade him!"

"In that case if you feel that you have missed out then I will take you Mum!" Well she supposed that was the lesser of two evils although considering that Agnes had her own car and was not exactly decrepit she didn't really see why on earth the woman couldn't have taken herself off to these places whilst she herself was working.

"But when will you be able to take me then, I thought you said that you had to work?"

"I suppose that I could ask Clive for some leave that is due to me. Not that he is really in favour of us taking time off in the busy season and I have already badgered one day out of him this week!"

"When will you be able to arrange it for then? After all you are doing him a favour being in that competition in your own time aren't you?" Agnes certainly showed no sympathy on Stacey's current dilemma.

"Well I suppose a Thursday will be as good a day as any. I guess there isn't as much coming and going from the camp on that day!" She had forgotten of course that the coming Thursday was the day of the Sheep Dog Trials and therefore the roads were likely to be busy on that day as well as the car parks teeming with folk!

"Then we will go this coming Thursday!" Agnes announced deeming that the matter was now settled. "Anyway if you are taking me then it means I will have no need to drag Meredith away from what he has to do again. After all the man has already been more than kind to me. That's another thing, what happened to those papers you had to make all that fuss about when he was taking my photograph? You made me feel quite ashamed at the time!"

"Oh you needn't worry anymore about them now. I've dispatched them!" Stacey crossed her fingers behind her back and hoped yet again that the documentation was safe.

"Well I have far more to worry about than you and your pesky papers even if you are still untidy our Stacey. Now when we go to Rydal this Thursday I would like to see Wordsworth's seat, the Coffin Trail of course, Heron Island and the church where Wordsworth was church warden at one time!" She rhymed off the imaginary list counting the number on her fingers as if to reinforce her determination, and with something of a sigh Stacey decided to let her be!

Clive may have appeared surprised when she approached him but in fact he eventually went along with the idea for he realised that Agnes could be a demanding character when she had set her mind on doing something. Fortunately the day that they had chosen dawned bright with the sun shining from the early morning and therefore Stacey was now condemned to listen to her mother going on in raptures over everything she saw, even if in truth she did voice some objection to the mud on the path she had to walk along in order to visit one item on her itinerary, that of Wordsworth's seat! Stacey herself had her own eyes fixed on the road as the traffic was beginning to build up because of those Sheep Dog Trails. Curiosity finally getting the better of the girl she eventually left her mother to rest for a while in Dora's field, for Agnes now claimed that her feet were killing her with all the walking Stacey had made her do, and having deposited her mother and told her she would be back in a few minutes time, she herself wandered back along the road to have a look at what all the fuss seemed to be about.

There was not a great distance between Rydal and Ambleside and the field where she had earlier spotted as being the place where these Trials were to be held was situated just on the periphery of both of these townships. Earlier when they had passed by in the car she had spotted some tents being erected but this time however she was to see something that almost served to stop her dead in her tracks, for now in this field before her she caught a glimpse of Steve and Bob together obviously now in the process of erecting some fences and gates to cater for the competition.

Yet even as she still toyed in her mind that she surely must be wrong in her assumption that Steve would be employed in this manner and even as she sought to convince herself that the man was after all a person who was on the run and possibly now seeking some form of employment and therefore in all truth it could be them after all, both men appeared to simply disappear from the scene leaving Stacey to wonder exactly how much of this sighting had been aroused from out of her imagination!

Perhaps in all truth it was Clive who was the one instrumental in her finally tracking Steve down even though he himself did not appreciate his efforts in this. Working in isolation at the camp Stacey had never thought of the place as being part of a larger conglomeration of half a dozen or more sites. Not that was until Clive found he needed to contact someone at the Troutbeck site and for some reason he was unable to contact anybody there by the telephone.

"Guess they are not for answering!" He frowned and then as his eyes fixed themselves upon Stacey. "You don't feel like doing me a favour do you?" The eyes now attached to her form almost had a pleading expression within them. "I mean I know that you have got your car here with you and therefore you could if you are willing, run this package up to Troutbeck for me. It contains some supplies that they are currently shouting out for and I have tried unsuccessfully to contact them by phone to tell them to come down here to collect them but I think it might have proved far easier for me to have contacted someone on the other side of the world rather than a place barely four miles away! Anyway for want of a better explanation, so far I have had no response from them!"

Stacey glanced out through the doors of the office. Well at least she supposed it was another fine day and the opportunity of a change of scenery in such weather wouldn't do her any harm. This, she concluded was especially true when she caught the envious look from Avril Togas that she was the one who had been asked to do this task. But then of course that girl didn't have a car at her disposal, not even an old banger like the one that Stacey possessed!

"All right then I will take them for you!" It was no skin off her nose for Clive had been good allowing her the time off previously but she still deliberately smiled rather sweetly in the man's direction if only to infuriate Avril Togas a little more. "I suppose you will want me to leave the package at the office there?"

"That will do fine! Thanks Stacey I owe you one for this!"

She wondered how many times she had heard that expression in recent days still she had to admit that it was good to get away from the camp for a while. Troutbeck may not have been far in distance but at least going to this place served to take her away from the main hub of thronging masses that patrolled the side of the Lake not to mention their metal death traps, and head up into the hills, past the historic solid stone and slate built house and into a completely different type of scenery where the beautiful valley lay hidden away in the lea of Kirkstone itself. Even the air seemed to have a fresher feel to it here now that she was away from the Lake and thus she felt content to be able to linger there for a time so that she could really savour the taste by taking deep breaths of the surrounding fresh air.

Maybe if she had not been tempted to linger after she had delivered the package to the office there she would never have spotted them. Yet the truth of this situation was now almost enough to make her laugh for amongst its other facilities Troutbeck had a campsite for tents and touring vans as well. The fact was that this place also close to where she was at the time, but she almost rubbed her eyes in wonder when as they were walking along the path in the act of returning to their tent from the wash room she spotted them and that was when she started to run over the bridge across the stream there like a woman who could have been said to be demented.

"Steve!" She wailed the name in pathetic tones simply hoping that the man was within earshot and would acknowledge her. Still he had obviously caught the sound of her voice in the air that was so fresh that it obligingly carried the sound further than she had first anticipated for he turned as it wondering who it was who was seeking him out. Now noticing her presence for the first time he appeared at first surprised and then perplexed. Even so after saying something to his companion he moved forward towards her. But as he drew closer she could see no welcoming expression in those brown eyes.

"Steve I need to see you!" Her opening phrase was trite; she knew that full well especially considering that she was now standing alongside of him.

"Well then, what is it that appears to be troubling you?" His lips were set in an unfathomable expression.

"First of all I have received a fax that I believe you might just be interested in and secondly it is now imperative that you take those papers from my keeping. For I now believe that Meredith Drew is on their track and short of carrying them around on my person in a form of a body belt I am now afraid of leaving them anywhere!"

"In that case I presume you have them with you now?"

"Please have a heart Steve. I came here on an errand, not really expecting to see you, that indeed was the surprise!"

"Then if you have been so concerned about them why didn't you mention the matter to Bob Eldon. I believe that the two of you met in Grasmere the other day?"

So her message had got back to him after all, and yet he had never acted upon it! "The answer to that is simple. You see I don't know who I can trust anymore for the last time I spotted Bob he appeared to be having an earnest conversation with Meredith Drew!"

"And you therefore took objection to him speaking to your boy friend, is that it? Did you think that by speaking to Drew Bob was taking the focus of attention away from you then?"

"No I did not! In all honesty I have so far done my very best for you and if that has not in itself been sufficient then the next person who asks me for those papers can have them with my blessing!"

"I'll meet you on the car park when you finish work!" Now at long last he appeared to be taking her words seriously yet he still showed no outward signs of affection towards her. "You mentioned a fax I believe?"

"Oh that was only from B.A.E systems expressing an interest in your work but I don't suppose that is of any consequence to you now!" Stacey was annoyed by this time and so she turned away leaving the man to gaze rather ponderously after her. Her intentions now were to try to rid her mind of such vexations and with this in mind she decided that she would go back to Townend to clear her mind and relax her enough before she returned to her work.

Still he was on the car park promptly that same evening when she strolled through those gates after leaving her vehicle where it was already parked outside of the centre there. Even so he took the package from her without uttering a word so that she presumed this was all the thanks she was likely to get for her efforts. In all fairness she did think at one time he was on the point of saying something to her but at the time the spectre of Meredith Drew could be seen approaching and this vision was certainly enough to make Steve change his mind about saying anything but simply to walk away leaving her to gaze after him in some perplexion!

"Tell me then, did my eyes deceive me or was that really Steve Futton you were just speaking to?" Now it was the turn of the other man to demand some knowledge as to what had been going on. But by this time Steve had disappeared back into the centre of that car park that was full at the time and where he felt he could lose himself. She sensed the anger sounding in Drew's voice as he almost spluttered the words from his lips almost as if he was suggesting she had exceeded her brief. "I saw you pass something on to the man!" The voice had changed its tones to accuse her and she felt compelled to attempt to extradite herself from this torrid situation.

"No, you are quite wrong Meredith. As a matter of fact it was a gentleman who is currently staying on site who left some articles back in reception and consequently I chased after him to find him and return the same! We get enough articles left in lost property!"

For his part Meredith snorted for he obviously did not believe her tale and for a moment she actually thought that he was going to chase after Steve. Then he obviously changed his mind and eyed her with a look of contempt.

Indeed the look he currently gave her should have sounded warning bells to Stacey!

⋆ ⋆ ⋆ ⋆

Chapter Ten

Perhaps Stacey was so caught up in that compelling look that she failed to observe that a second figure was now approaching. For his own part Keith Forsyth had covered the distance required of him with a determined tread. Once again it appeared that this man had been charged by his so called superiors to undertake a mission, and moreover this time he had been reminded that after his abysmal attempts upon a previous occasion that failure was not now an option for him.

Nevertheless he was undoubtedly surprised to see the subject of his quest on the car park. His orders had been quite simple and they were to remove this nuisance factor from out of the equation. He had not questioned the reasoning that lay behind this dictum for he had felt at the time that his own position was still in some jeopardy yet what appeared in his eyes to be more to the point was that he held the means to carry out this order already within his possession for he still was holding those photographs passed to him when the students had complained over the fellow.

Consequently whilst his eyes now rested upon this subject now present in his thoughts they did not immediately focus upon Stacey Kershaw as the girl still stood in some obvious distress in that place but rather they were to rest upon the person whose stance now appeared to loom threateningly over the girl. And yet the one whose eyes still portrayed a sardonic gleam in them never once belied the by now stern expression of the Inspector.

"I believe that I have reason to have a word with you Mr Drew!" The policeman now adopted the tone of his profession.

"Inspector ----this is indeed an unexpected pleasure!" The showman had rapidly regained some of his charisma for by this time his attention had switched off the girl and onto the policeman.

"In private, if you don't mind!" Keith Forsyth clicked his tongue to give his tone even more effect and whilst Meredith himself might well have been surprised at the temerity in the other man's voice he knew better than to argue with this officer of the law especially when he happened to be in the public gaze.

"Then my office is at your disposal Inspector!" Meredith made something of an elaborate gesture but for his part the other man barely acknowledged him as he strode forward purposefully towards the gates leading to the Hall leaving Meredith to follow on behind like some itinerant schoolboy now compelled to follow the headmaster.

In truth Stacey appeared now to be ignored altogether and thus the girl, still feeling somewhat shaken by Drew's earlier appearance, stood silently by and watched as the two of them disappeared. She was in fact still occupying the same position when her form caught the attention of Dick Soper who was currently leaving the place for his evening nuptials.

"Thought I spotted your car on the staff car park Stacey. You are late leaving tonight----?" Then perhaps for the first time noting the girl's expression he hastened to add "Is something wrong, you seem a trifle distraught if I might be forgiven for saying so?"

"No, I'm just on the way to collect my car, I had a job to do for Clive!" Realising that his eyes were now fixed upon her Stacey hastily assumed a different mannerism. Whatever had just passed was after all a private matter and not one she felt willing to share with anyone even if this newcomer did appear to look slightly pleased with himself although why that was she did not know. Still he did not appear to be totally convinced with her argument and she supposed his next sentence was uttered in an attempt to discover more.

"If you are not in a hurry maybe we should go somewhere and talk, at least retire to La Costa for a coffee?"

"Sorry I need to get back to the cottage otherwise I will have my mother fuming because of my protracted absence!" She now adopted something of a fixed smile, not that she felt very much like smiling at the time but nevertheless found it necessary to give a lie to any message she may have given to the contrary.

"Pity about that. Another time then?" The man accepted her decision although Stacey had the distinct impression it was not at all to his liking and consequently the girl made haste to make a get away. The fact that when Dick Soper himself also moved away he was still wearing a smile across his features escaped her notice for her sole intention at the time was to rapidly gain access to her vehicle.

Crossing the ferry she noticed the ripples on the water as she viewed those signs denoting the six M.P.H. speed limit in the close proximity of the Bay. Yet it was no in coming tide that had caused those signs of the speed limit to now almost disappear from view, but rather it was the stiff breeze that had suddenly sprung up following those earlier showers of heavy rain that had caused the wave of ripples that now also lapped against the sides of the ferry boat even though its progress across the lake was slow and sedate. Moreover as if that was not enough to cement this feeling of unease the once blue waters had seemingly turned into an ominous black. Stacey shuddered as she started up the car again as the ferry ground to a stop. The sooner she was back at the cottage that day the better!

Not that today the cottage was destined to bring her mind much relief for when she arrived back she was to find Agnes herself in a state of agitation.

"I think that perhaps after all it is time I thought of returning home to Caton our Stacey!" The girl knew that the tenancy of the cottage was due to expire at the end of the month and that the owners were planning on returning from the States but nevertheless her mother's words brought her up sharp.

"Perhaps I ought to consider coming home with you!" The mood she was currently feeling had finally found a voice.

"Don't be silly, your work is here!" Agnes immediately raised her objections, puzzled as she was by her daughter's newfound attitude. "Finding alternative employment that would suit you would not be very easy at this time our Stacey especially with the on going credit crunch and the unemployment queues now growing in length. Besides you can hardly claim that I will be moving a million miles away and sometimes I think you are forgetting that you have your own flat in Windermere!"

"Sometimes it has felt decidedly peaceful to be able to get away to this side of the lake!" Stacey omitted to state how she had felt on other occasions but then in all truth she had to admit that over the weeks she had grown quite fond of this cottage and so although she knew it was a necessity parting with it, the idea acted as an additional blow in her thoughts!

"Strange that you should come out with a statement like that!" Agnes studied her daughter carefully. "I was under the distinct impression that coming to this place was a chore to you. But the fact of the matter is that we now have no alternative but to give the cottage back if the owners are returning! Still I have a feeling that there is more to it than what you say. I know my own daughter and my guess is that something has happened, well what is it Stacey?"

"Nothing, precisely nothing!" Now she found it easy to lie in order to keep her innermost thoughts secret for she did not want to discuss them not even with her mother. "I guess I keep thinking about these sports I seem to have got myself involved in this coming weekend!"

"Ah yes, your tug of war team! Meredith was on about it the last time he was round!"

"Excuse me Mum I think I need to change out of these clothes into something more relaxing!" She made her excuses in haste now that man's name had been mentioned yet again for in truth she was sick and tired of hearing the name spoken. Perhaps the good thing about it was that if they left the cottage he would have no further excuse for coming round here and coaxing her mother into revealing her own activities. Not that there seemed to be very much to reveal at the moment for she had finally managed to part with that documentation and now Steve could please himself what he did with it as well as the fax she had also passed onto him. And yet despite all of this and despite the fact that Steve had expressed no interest in seeing her again she still felt the threat of Meredith Drew and thinking again about that person quite unwillingly she wondered why Keith Forsyth had suddenly appeared on the scene in such a manner.

Perhaps she was to find this out sooner than she anticipated. Initially she supposed she should have noticed that something seemed amiss when she saw him driving his car from the Hall the next morning, the speed of his vehicle well exceeding the parks five miles per hour speed limit for moving traffic, and bearing a look that resembled a livid rage upon his face as he waited for the barrier gates to open for him. At the time she would not have been surprised if he had driven right through them, but then after giving him a cursory glance she had decided that if he had got up on the wrong side of his bed then it was really none of her business anyway and after all she simple just wasn't interested in that man's antics or indeed anything else about that satanic creation that had crossed her life!

It was Clive however that broke the news sometime later and when he did so Stacey could not help but feel that her boss held a lighter tone to his voice as he spoke. "I believe that Meredith Drew has left the Hall!" Light as the tones were he held an almost confidential tenet in his words. "I gather there has been a spot of trouble up there, Keith Forsyth was round with him last night, it was something or so I am led to believe about some photographs that have been taken unlawfully and the matter has reported to the police by the students there!"

The word photographs made Stacey take notice although Clive obviously did not see her back stiffen. "Anyway to cut a long story short the man has now left under something of a cloud and what is more I have also heard that Dick Soper is to be appointed to take his place!"

Stacey remembered being on the car park and seeing Dick Soper emerge wearing what could now be taken to be a guarded smile across his face. So that was what it had all been about? Well if that was the case she most definitely was not sorry to see Meredith Drew depart, although the thought of his expression of intent against her before he had returned to the camp with Keith Forsyth still served to give her the shivers.

"Then perhaps we ought to get a card or something to congratulate Dick!" Another voice had chipped in and Stacey now looked at the speaker of these words in incredulity. Was it a fact that Avril Togas never gave up with her manhunts?

"You are probably right Avril. Anyway if you get something then we can all chip in I am sure!" Stacey sighed, now as far as she was concerned they could all do what they wanted.

"I wonder though how this will affect our own position!" The novelty of having imparted the story now beginning to wear off, Clive Warner was no doubt considering the additional timber lodge they had already ordered. "Maybe Dick will go along with it if we are nice and try to accommodate him. But I suppose we will have to wait and see upon that score!"

The others had little idea what the boss was speaking about although Avril never at a loss for something to say especially if such words proved to enhance her own position. "In that case I will have to exert my magical powers of persuasion over him!" The girl smiled sweetly but by this time Stacey had lost all interest in who had said what and when for she still held an uneasy feeling in her bones regarding Meredith Drew whether he had been ousted from his palace or not. She supposed to call the man a pervert could appear to be a slight exaggeration but to her mind he most certainly had possessed a demeaning effect upon the feminine sex.

"Anyway to change the subject, how is our team shaping up for the sports this weekend?" For his own part Clive was now trying to push the incident to one side.

"If you are referring to that tug of was we have entered into well I suppose all right, always providing of course that we are drawn against a team with weak muscle power!" In all truth Stacey was not interested for the talk of Meredith Drew had reminded her yet again of Steve's own attitude towards her when they had met on the car park the previous evening

They were in fact just about to close the office that night however when much to her surprise Stacey was to spot Bob Eldon heading through the gates towards the Hall.

"I just popped by to congratulate the new boss of the Management team up at the Hall as I just happened to be passing by the place!" She wondered why the man felt he had a need to explain his actions, after all what went on up at the Hall was no concern of theirs. Yet she also had to admit that there was something about the man that told her that he wanted to make conversation with her and therefore she looked questioningly in his direction in an attempt to elicit what he wanted to say. "I thought that perhaps you might be interested to learn that I now believe we have the chance of finding some new employment which I believe is rather due to your own and Dick's efforts. It will of course most probably mean us moving from this area. But then I thought that you and Steve ------?"

Stacey bristled for she had no intention of discussing any such relationship she might or might not have with Steve with a person she hardly knew. Besides there were also certain answers that she needed from this man. Well folk often said that she had a habit of shooting her mouth off and she supposed that this was one time that she lived up to their expectations.

"You did say that you had initially come here to congratulate Dick. But I understood that Meredith Drew was an acquaintance of yours?" She faced him as she uttered the words and deliberately ignoring his own question about her relationship with Steve.

"Meredith Drew?" The young man with the fob of fair hair that persisted in drooping down over his eyes paused for a moment as he brushed it back and then immediately started to laugh. "You can forget that notion. Dick Soper is the one who is a mate of mine. We were at Uni together!"

"But I spotted you with Drew ---You looked like a couple of conspirators!" She refused to give up on the idea but preferred instead to now shake it rather like a dog with a bone in order to try to establish the truth.

"And so I believe you did! In fact if I remember correctly it was on the Quayside Walk and you were with your mother in that café at the time. It was on the second day of the Air Show, am I right?" So he had noticed them sitting there. But her real surprise was still to come for sensing that the girl had no intention of loosening her grip he grinned. "As a matter of fact I was trying to get some information out of him for Steve's benefit!"

"And did you succeed?"

"Not really. Anyway I guess I didn't care for the man at all!" Bob suddenly began to wonder why he was the one making the confession. "But what of yourself? Steve led me to believe that you were rather friendly with that individual yourself!"

"Over my dead body I was!"

"So then what went wrong between you and Steve? The man has been acting like a bear with a sore head lately!"

"This job you said that you had a chance of getting?" Again she refused to yield and become more forthcoming. "I believe you said that you might possibly have to move away from the area?"

"Only as far as Lancashire I hope. Still the firm seem to be very interested in the new design and are prepared to undertake making a prototype. All of which I am glad to say ought to be enough to plaster egg on certain people's faces. But why not hang on until I have had a word with Dick and then come back to the camp with me and let Steve tell you all about it for himself?"

Stacey shook her head. Much as she would have loved to have gone with him, nothing would persuade her to go where she felt she was unwanted for Steve had already shown that he had no inclination towards wanting to see her quite the reverse in fact. "No I really do have to get back to the Cottage. Mum is supposed to be leaving this weekend for I believe the owners now want the place back again. So I am afraid we have a fair amount of packing to do. Besides I know for a fact that Steve has no wish to see me, he made that abundantly clear the last time we met!"

The other man shuffled his feet over a patch of gravel in the paving as if he wanted to stay and say more. But by this time Stacey had decided that as all had now been said that was required, it was high time she headed back to Sawrey. "I really must go Bob honestly but when you see him will you congratulate Dick from me again? He's a nice guy and I couldn't feel more pleased that he got the job up at the

Hall!" And with that Stacey left without even looking back as she got into her car ready to drive off. She didn't look back because for one thing her eyes were now full of tears and that was something she wanted no one to witness.

Still she had time to rinse her face and repair the damage when she got back to the cottage for when she arrived there it was to find that her mother was not in this place! For just a moment Stacey tended to panic for the spectre of Meredith Drew had suddenly risen in front of her eyes. Surely it could not be true that this sadist had inflicted himself upon Agnes again? She admitted that the two of them had certainly appeared to be friendly enough and there was no doubt in her mind that her mother could have been persuaded to fall in with that man's plans, which would no doubt, at the same be revolving around designing a pay back time. Restlessly she moved from one room to the next picking up various articles on her travels and looking at the same time to establish whether a note had been left for her and expecting to find one. After all to her mind it was almost inconceivable that her mother should have gone off in this manner without letting her know or leaving a message.

The minutes ticked by on the clock and finally when she was almost at desperation point Stacey wondered whom she could phone up about this. Her thoughts first of all latched onto Keith Forsyth but then she rapidly dismissed that idea. After all she could hardly report a grown woman, especially one in possession of all her faculties, to have gone missing for a couple of hours! Again Steve's name also came to mind, but that was one idea that she quickly dismissed. To start with she had no intention of craving any such help from that man, and what was even more to the point she had no idea anyway of his current phone number. Yet for her own peace of mind she still craved the companionship of someone at the time and that was when she reached out to phone Dick Soper.

"O.K. I'll come round!" He sounded pleasantly surprised to hear her voice but then Dick had been a good friend to her in the past and what was more the man kept his word, arriving at the cottage in under half an hour.

"Look I'm sure that you are worrying unduly Stacey!" He had listened to her story in silence but at the same time exuding some measure of sympathy.

"I know that in all probability I am over reacting but it feels good to have someone here I can talk to and possibly shake me out of my current moribund state of mind!" He had sat himself down upon the sofa as she was speaking almost as if this action was something that came as second nature to him.

"Well perhaps you have had quite a lot on your plate recently and this just happens to be the final straw that has caused the castle to start to crumble! You did right by contacting me Stacey for after all that is what friends are for and you must have realised by this time that I have always dreamt of being far more than a friend to you! -----All right, don't worry I have no intentions of pressing my suit whilst you are so worried. It would be caddish of me to even think about it. But to return to your mother, can you remember if she spoke of any event she was interested in? After all we do appear to have our fair quota of events coming up at the moment in this neck of the woods. Perhaps it was some event that because of the amount of traffic currently on the roads could possibly have delayed her return?"

Stacey shook her head. "I don't think so. As a matter of fact we were in the process of getting her and her belongings back again to Caton before the end of the month when the lease on the cottage expires!"

"In that case perhaps I would suggest that she definitely decided she needed a break from all the mundane activity going on around here."

Stacey nodded. She supposed that Dick's words made good sense even if she was now not quite au fait with his own reasons for coming here if what he had already said was true. "Anyway how are you liking your new position? I suppose this is the first opportunity I have had to congratulate you!" She made an effort to change the subject onto safer ground.

"Not exactly a new position. Indeed most of the work that this position entails I was already doing before his majesty decided to pay us a visit and then decided to stay on!" Now for the first time in her life Stacey sensed the tinge of bitterness that had crept into the other man's voice. "The fact of the matter is I could now well do with you to come along to the Hall as my girl Friday although I don't suppose Clive would agree with me at all on that idea!"

"What exactly happened with Drew then?" She had heard the rumours of course but this was her first opportunity to speak to Dick. Besides by posing a question back at him she sought to avoid answering his own.

"He received a warning concerning certain photographs and was told he had to immediately to leave the area before a more serious charge was brought against him. But we don't really have to discuss that villain do we?"

"I didn't realise until earlier on today that Bob Eldon was a friend of yours?" Now it was Stacey's turn to deliberately move to change the tenet of the conversation by asking still more questions. She certainly did not want to discuss her own role or to be involved with anything else at the moment in that place. Her idea had been to get away and return to Caton with her mother and up until now she considered that was the best solution all the way round. Not of course that her mother had agreed to any of it!

"Well yes, we have been mates since our University days!" Stacey swallowed hard, a pang now shooting through her as she remembered back to Steve and her brother Pete when they had both been at University together, and the way in which Pete had brought Steve home and ultimately the way the two of them had first been thrown together. Dick glanced at her expression. "I guess it is still Steve then Stacey and no one else stands a chance?"

"That is all finished with now. He left me in little doubt about that the last time I saw him!"

"Don't be so sure about that Stacey. Anyway to change the subject, whilst I am here maybe you will allow me to ask for your advice on the Triathlon I have been requested to organise?"

"A Triathlon?" Stacey looked puzzled. This was the first she had heard about it.

"Yes it's a project that has been initiated under the auspices of 'Take to the Streets', a national activity programme designed to fight spiralling inactivity and also raise large amounts of money for charity in the process! No doubt you have heard of the Great North Swim coming up in September and also the Ride and Stride that involves bikes and walking. Well I suppose you could class this as a combination of the two. It is supposed to be a fun event and entries will be based on teams of couples although both participants will be expected to complete all the events on the course. The route hasn't yet been finalised and I'm actually looking for your approval. In my own mind I considered a cycle ride into Bowness from Ings, swimming then around one of the Islands in the Lake and then legging it back on foot to the finishing line at Ings. Well what do you think?"

"Have you considered the traffic on the main road heading into Windermere? It can get rather busy especially around lunch time!" She was dubious and showed her doubts by wrinkling up her nose, an endearing feature to those who witnessed it but one which she was herself completely unaware of.

"Well we will of course have to get agreement from the Highways to halt the traffic along that stretch for a limited period, but that doesn't have to coincide with the peak periods and moreover it shouldn't be for very long as it will be only at the start of the contest and when the competitors wish to return to the finishing line at Ings there is a way across country to do that! Also if we leave the event until late September the main season will be largely over and most of the other activities including the Ambleside Marathon will have been completed. This year the whole idea is still in its embryonic stage but if we are successful then it could become a yearly event. I can also persuade the students from off the Management course to participate in it although if we do get sufficient entries this year they can act as Marshals for the event. In fact the only drawback I can visualise is that wet suits will be obligatory for the swim part as the water temperature is bound to be below 15C at that time of the year. But we have already got permission to utilise a specially designed I.T. tracking system!"

"To my mind you already appear to be well organised so what would you require me to do then?" Curiosity about the event had finally overcome her.

"Get involved if you would and then you will be able to offer advice on issues as they arise. Bob said that he was sure that you would co-operate if I asked you nicely!"

"You are saying that Bob Eldon said that?"

"Yes, initially it was his idea! Apparently he had previously approached Drew with the idea but he got rather short shift on the idea from that man!"

So that was the reason he had been speaking to Meredith Drew the day of the Air Show. "There is one thing however you ought to know Dick before I commit myself and that is I can't swim, I never have been able to!"

He looked a little surprised but nevertheless glossed over her statement quickly. "Well I am not exactly asking you to go into the water Stacey. After all it is your assistance in the organisation of such a course that I require not viewing you in a wet suit!"

She wondered if he was now referring to the previous episode and found her face flushing a little. "In that case you can count me in then Dick for I reckon it is for a good cause!" She paused as she suddenly heard a key being turned in the front door lock. "Anyway there is one thing you have certainly helped me over the time lapse Dick and I believe you were right in the first instance for Agnes is finally back!"

She was right of course for the woman under question entered the cottage rather like some Grand Duchess of a bygone era about to embark upon her duty of eyeing her subjects. Even so she stopped short when she spied Dick and could not avoid the look of surprise that spread to her eyes.

"This is Dick from the Hall Mum, but where have you been until this time? Indeed if it hadn't been for Dick's influence I would have phoned the police ages ago about your so called disappearance!"

"Don't talk so silly girl. As a matter of fact I availed myself of the opportunity to visit Kendal in order to witness the Minifest currently being held there, for if I am about to return home I need to make the most of the time I have left here!"

"But you never let me know. You didn't leave a note for me!"

"Didn't I? In that case I must have forgotten all about it. Forgetfulness comes with age or so they tell me. But in truth I fully intended to be back before this time; that however was before I found the whole day so fascinating. So you say this is Dick from the Hall?" Now the woman looked a little more critically at her daughter's companion, so much so that she had the other person feeling rather uneasy at the time.

"Yes it is and what is more Dick is a very good friend of mine. But before we go any further what about the packing? I understood that was our priority!"

"Oh no doubt we will see to it child, so do stop fretting over small things. But there is one thing, I must see this tug of war that you have got yourself roped into before I leave. Are you involved in this activity as well Mr –er Dick?"

"No Ma'am that is for the office staff to compete in so the activity excludes me. Anyway now that your mother had returned no doubt you will feel more settled Stacey so perhaps I ought to be thinking of making tracks!"

Stacey nodded. Perhaps she understood only too well that the man had little inclination to be saddled with further questions from her Mother, which inevitably started immediately he had left the premises.

"Well and who was that then our Stacey?" Her respondent sighed. Please, she begged, don't tell me that my mother is at it again.

"I thought I had already explained. His name is Dick Soper and what is more he happens to be a very good friend of mine especially when I feel that I need one. Other than that please do not start getting any ideas. By the way Dick has now taken over the Management Team up at the Hall after Meredith did a speedy exit from the place!"

"Ah yes—poor Meredith. I feel sure that people acted a little harshly in condemning that charming gentleman. What do you think about it our Stacey?"

"I think it is high time we put such opinions to the back of our minds and concentrated on starting to sort your things out. If you are determined now not to go back until after the Show then it will no doubt place us in the midst of the Bank Holiday traffic because in truth we have to be out of this place by the end of the month when the lease expires!"

"In that case the problem is easily solved. I will come back with you to your flat over the other side of the lake until the Bank Holiday rush is over!"

Stacey grimaced but gritted her teeth to stop her thought from exploding. It appeared that her mother could provide an answer to everything!

"So I have heard that the new broom has decided to make a clean sweep!" It was Clive who gently chided her to get her thoughts to return to the present as they were preparing to get ready on the morning of the show. Nevertheless Dick's idea concerning the Triathlon appeared to have been well received although she herself was to find that she was still being ribbed for the role she had apparently played in it.

"I suppose that is one way of putting it!" She placed the remainder of the tackle she needed in her rucksack and fastened it up.

"So what has he exactly got in mind for you then?"

"At the moment it has been suggested that I make myself available at Ings to first of all check in the competitors and then at a later stage monitor their return."

"So have you had many entries yet?"

"Give us a chance please. As far as I can gather we have so far got about a dozen names from folk who would like to take part in this event, but it is after all early days yet and in any case with it being a new venture Dick doesn't really expect the field will be over subscribed to this year, not in its inaugural year anyway!"

Clive grunted. In truth he had only been making conversation with her. He certainly liked the new man up at the Hall for he had been quite affable in the timber lodge deal that his predecessor had initiated. Yet across the room it was now Avril Togas who was adept at catching his attention. Avril was already moaning about her hands and the damage this tug of war would do to her recently acquire talons and that was even before she saw any rope that needed pulling and she was now bleating a lament about how long it had taken her to grow her nails and shape them in the form of the brightly red painted talons.

Still Stacey decided that they had one thing in their favour for at least the weather had started out in portraying the elements of it being a nice day ahead for them and this in some measure helped to allay the presence of the older woman who persisted in following her around the stalls and repeatedly asking her when the tug of war would take place and at the same time voicing her strong opinion over the Cumbrian Wrestling that was currently taking place.

"Those two men could hurt themselves carrying on like that!" Agnes nodded abruptly in their direction showing full commitment to the words she had uttered. "Couldn't they have found something better to do with themselves rather than behave in that fashion?"

"But it is a traditional Lakeland sport Mum!" Stacey attempted to adopt an air of patience whilst at the same time it did cross her mind as to what her mother would have said had she been present at the annual Guming Championships at Egremont. Yet now perhaps because Agnes was still looking around to find out what was going on, found something else to focus her attention on.

"That girl from your office Stacey. She now appears to have found herself a new friend. Why, bless my soul, isn't that the man you used to see, the friend of Pete's who used to come home with him in their vacations!" Totally unaware of what effect these words were now having upon Stacey, Agnes had risen from her seat to strain her eyes to establish whether she was right. Stacey followed her gaze with some trepidation and felt her heart sink as she realised that her mother was indeed right, for currently at the far end of the field and now dancing around this man in what can only be described as some tribal war dance, Avril Togas held a look of triumph in her gaze. Stacey bit her lip telling herself that this just didn't matter to her at all for whatever had existed between the two of them was well and truly over! And as if matters were not bad enough it was Clive Warner's apparent turn to drift across and comment on the situation.

"Seems as though our Avril has now found herself a new attraction!" The tone the man adopted was dry enough for Clive was already well aware of the string of beaus Avril had the habit of collecting to faun around her. "Anyway I guess I am now in the process of rounding everybody together for your first heat will be due at any time!"

The first heat passed off well enough, possibly because Stacey herself leant renewed vigour into her own efforts. It did little of course to help her emotive state but quite possibly it did help to relieve some of the tension she was feeling.

"Well done!" At least Clive appeared pleased with their success. "There's one thing anyway, we won't be leaving here with the booby prize! It's the men's heat coming up next."

Scarcely interested Stacey nevertheless now felt duty bound to look in the direction of the on going contest and for a moment wondered what Steve was doing taking part in it. Not she admitted that there was anything in the rules to stop him for the contest had been thrown open to anybody who was willing to participate in the sport. It was then that she noticed Avril jumping up and down at the side of the track and the sight sickened her.

"I think I'll go and get a tea for us Mum!" She didn't want to witness this performance any more and consequently she bided her time around the tea tent until after that particular bout was finished before she returned to base.

"Well you took your time I must say. By the way your fellow's side won!" Agnes appeared to be completely enjoying herself by this time and Stacey swallowed back the retort that Steve was most certainly not her fellow with some gall. "Tell me something that is puzzling me though. If the women are competing against each other and the men are doing likewise, what is going to happen when there are only two teams left? Surely the winning women won't have to compete with the men?"

"I shouldn't think so Mum. Anyway I doubt very much whether that will concern us because I'm sure that we will be knocked out long before then!" She stopped as she noticed that Avril Togas was back across the field again busily congratulating Steve whilst Bob Eldon looked on behaving like something of a spare part. "You're not finding it draughty in this part of the field are you Mum because we could move if you like?"

"No, I'm not ready to move because here I have a splendid view of all the events as they come up as well as all the folk entering and leaving. Look, I do believe ---Isn't that Meredith who is coming through the gate now?"

Stacey followed her mother's pointing finger. Surely Agnes must be mistaken. Meredith Drew would hardly dare to show his face here after all the trouble he had caused. Anyway he had been told to leave the area. But then she swallowed hard, it was indeed Meredith Drew and what was more he had begun to head in their direction. Mesmerised as she watched the approach of this spectre Stacey failed to notice the eyes of a third person that were now piercing in her direction, eyes that were indeed bearing condemnation!

★ ★ ★ ★

Chapter Eleven

"Meredith, this is a surprise! We certainly didn't expect to see you here. Indeed we thought that you had already left the area!" It was her mother who extended the welcome as Stacey cringed in the background wondering what on earth the rest of the team must now be thinking. A band had started to play on the far side of the field and the melody that floated across to reach her ears did little to placate her current mood of melancholia.

"But surely you did not think I would go and miss the Sports Agnes for I am after all one of its supporters and we do raise quite a substantial amount for charitable causes!" Even as the words issued out of his mouth Stacey felt his eyes raking her figure almost as if they were undressing her on the spot.

"I think Clive is waiting for us to get ready for our second heat!" She almost choked knowing that the sadist was enjoying her discomfort. Actually she couldn't have cared less whether Clive was ready for them or not for she knew he would have to wrest Avril away from her new toy before that time. All she needed was the excuse to get away from this person.

"I see that we have visitors?" Clive had obviously noticed his arrival. His tone was positively dry in its execution leaving one in no doubt as to what he felt about this unexpected arrival.

"Unwelcome ones at that I would say!" The words she managed to utter now almost choked her.

"But then your mother doesn't appear to agree with you!" Clive nodded across in the couple's direction where the two appeared to be deep in conversation.

"Please will you get the team together ready to line up for the next event ----please Clive? Then will you occupy us with something whilst we are waiting please?"

"I don't suppose that Avril will like that!"

"I don't give a damn what Avril likes or dislikes!"

Clive cocked his head to one side as he realised her fervour. "Well be careful just how you handle this situation Stacey, please!"

Much as she would have been happy if they had failed in their second heat and then they would have been eliminated and would have had some excuse to return back to Bowness, this however was not to be for they pulled the other team over the line on the first two occasions and therefore much against her mood they now qualified to take part in the quarter finals. After the heat however Stacey still did not choose to return to the place where she had left her mother with Meredith. Instead she was still hanging around the main tents when Bob Eldon spotted her.

"I've just heard you have made the quarter finals, well done. Not like me because I was knocked out in the first round. Steve is still doing well though!"

"Then you weren't competing in the same team?"

"No we sort of volunteered our services at the last moment to make up numbers and consequently Steve was drafted into one team whilst I was put into another. Anyway it looks as if Steve has inherited a group of heavy weights in his team. I see they have just got through again!"

"I also notice that his current fan club is now wending her way across to him!" Her words sounded bitter and Bob gazed at her searchingly.

"Look why don't you go across to him? Get there before her and sort things out between the two of you!" Realising even before he spoke his idea was likely to be rebuffed, Bob nevertheless felt duty bound to make the suggestion.

"No way!" The response was adamant and Stacey revealed nothing of the feelings currently building up inside of her. Bob shrugged rather reluctantly at her words.

"Are you here on your own then?" Now he was attempting to make conversation out of politeness.

"No, as a matter of fact I have my mother here with me as well as the rest of the team. At the present moment however it appears that she is entertaining!" She glanced across to where she had previously left the two of them and noticed much to her relief that the unwelcome visitor now appeared to have left. Well at least that was something, she sighed almost to herself. But something still rankled her mind, was it indeed all right?

Anxious to catch a glimpse of something else in the show before her next event she left Bob with a faint smile and moved towards where the stalls were situated, possibly at the farthest point in the field from the main road. It was a few moments before she realised that she was being followed.

Deciding that this phenomenon must be a figment of her imagination she turned with every intention of giving a friendly greeting to whomever it was who had chosen to take the same path as herself. Yet upon turning she was to suddenly freeze in her tracks for the person who was now advancing upon her bearing an evil leer across his features was none other than Meredith Drew. Then even before she could cry out in her horror the man had grabbed her wrist and was practically forcing her back into a copse of trees and out of sight of the main gathering.

"So you were seeking to avoid me?" The voice that echoed sounded cruel and twisted as his face now leered closer to her own so that she could stench the sweat that had amassed upon his brow from hurrying after her.

"No ---as a matter of fact I need to prepare for the next heat!!" Stuttering she put voice to the first thing that came to mind.

"Then perhaps I ought to assist you in your preparation with something like this!" She knew even before he acted that he intended to force those evil lips upon her own and now her valiant struggles appeared to make the man all the more determined. Forcing her back against a tree his hands now obviously were searching for more yet he drew breath in order to spit out still more insults in her direction. "I think that I deserve a little something in the way of a reward from you and this time you are going to give it to me my dear!"

"Then take that!" She had already closed her eyes waiting for the inevitable her throat now parched and unable to call out when she heard this second voice. Mesmerised she opened her eyes in time to see Steve fell the intruder with a blow to the jaw. But the man who had come to her rescue still looked glaringly in her direction.

"Steve!" She managed to say his name in little more than a whisper.

"It's time you got back for your quarter final." The tone he applied to his voice was expressionless and there was no emotion now emitting from his eyes. He walked with her to the edge of the clearing and then watched as she returned to the team without giving her any words of encouragement and then quite suddenly as she turned round to look for him he had gone!

----------The fact that the team managed to get through first the quarterfinals and then the semi finals appeared to ride over her almost as if she was in some hazy mist. But after that it was the finals themselves, the time when the winning ladies team had to face the winning team from the opposite sex. And as if that was not enough Steve himself after getting through the semi finals was with this burly group, his eyes still quite fathomless but his muscles flexed as if he was determined to let nothing stand in his way. Meantime Avril Togas was currently protesting loud and clear that the whole scenario was not fair, only to be informed in response that this was after all a tradition and not something that had been imported to accommodate the whims of the feminine sex.

Of course it was always anticipated that the men would win this bout of friendly rivalry but the idea was that having succeeded these masculine specimens would treat the ladies they had beaten afterwards. But whilst most of the men in the team appeared to be jovial and good natured about the whole episode Steve was someone who didn't lose his steely look of determination. Moreover this time around after all that had happened Stacey herself did not feel able to support the team in their efforts at all and as she lay sprawled across the ground, having been pulled over the line with unnecessary force she was also to witness his look of satisfaction as he moved away from the scene.

"That wasn't fair at all. The whole thing was a travesty!" Now Avril Togas was pouting. "And what was more Stacey you made no attempt at all to resist them by pulling on that rope, which literally meant that we were without a quarter of our team in the final analysis!"

"Oh for goodness sake go and get yourself a drink Avril. You were never intended to win anyway, that is all part of the game!" It was Clive who finally came to her rescue and helped her back onto her feet. "Are you all right Stacey? Look, don't take this thing so much to heart, it was meant to finish on a high note anyway!"

"I'm all right, I guess I simply slipped in the final analysis and no doubt I will have bruises as a memento from it by tomorrow. But if you don't mind I think I will skip the refreshments you were on about for I really need to get back to my mother!"

Clive accepted her decision somewhat reluctantly and consequently Stacey prepared herself for yet more verbiage when she finally reached her mother's side.

"Did you hurt yourself when you slipped like that our Stacey?"

"No Mum, I fell on grass anyway and it broke my fall!"

"I still can't agree with having women competing against men in that fashion. It's hardly fair for starters!"

"It's traditional Mum!"

"Maybe it is but that doesn't make it right, does it? Anyway Meredith was most disappointed at not having the chance to speak with you for the man is going away you know!"

"And the sooner the better!" She mumbled the words under her breath. She didn't want to have to explain what had happened.

"Sorry, what did you say? I didn't hear what you said!"

"Oh I just said that it was a shame. Anyway perhaps it is time for us to be making tracks as well!"

The woman looked disappointed. She had obviously been enjoying her afternoon but nevertheless on Stacey's command she began to gather her things together. "Wasn't that friend of Pete's in the team that beat you Stacey?"

"You mean Steve, yes he was!"

"Then he can't think much about you if he can do a trick like that on a girl. Well that's what I think anyway!"

"Perhaps you are right in that Mum!" Stacey thought of that hard expression on his face as he had regarded her whilst she was on the floor as she deliberately bent to pick up her mother's things.

"Meredith was telling me about the photographs he has been taking, did you know that he ahs entered some in a national competition?"

"I can only hope that he has entered the right ones!" Stacey let out a snort.

"What do you mean by that our Stacey?"

"Nothing mother, just leave it please. I just meant the ones he took that were suitable for such a contest!"

"Oh I am sure Meredith has an eye for a good photograph. I remember he wasn't satisfied with the first photographs he took of me at the cottage. No Meredith is a bit of a perfectionist!"

"I'm sure you are right for the man obviously knows what he wants!" She thought of the photographs he had taken of the students and shivered at the grotesque thought. "Well are you ready to go now then? The roads are bound to be crowded when this affair is finished so if we leave straight away we ought to be able to miss a lot of it!"

--------"If you ask my opinion then I consider you are a bloody idiot!" Bob Eldon faced his friend who apparently now appeared to be gathering his things together, with a look of puzzlement on his face. "The girl quite obviously thinks something about you and in return all you can do is walk around like a bear with a sore head!"

"Do I need to remind you that a new job awaits us and what is more instead of dwelling on the past I consider it is now high time we got ourselves installed in the area?" Still the man whom he addressed chose to ignore his comments.

"So now I suppose your idea is to go without saying a word to her?"

"If you must know Stacey now has other interests I'm afraid. Anyway she will probably be better off without me being around to remind her of the past!"

"And who says that the girl has other interests apart that is from you?"

"Put it this way, I am not prepared to take on Meredith Drew or anybody else as a rival for her affections!"

"And yet I can honestly swear to you that the girl hates the ground the devil stands on. And if you don't believe me then go and ask another mate of mine Dick Soper! The only surprise to me is that someone else has not snapped her up with your damned protracted absence! In fact if you weren't my mate then I would seriously think of sporting my own charms in her direction!"

"I am not in the habit of asking anyone to make an attempt to deny what I have witnessed with my own eyes!"

"Well if that is the case I think it's about time you visited an optician because you are obviously in need of glasses. Surely you yourself was witness to her expression when you finally banjoed the fellow on the sports ground!"

"Shall we change the subject if you don't mind. What are you doing now anyway?" Steve endeavoured to backtrack a little. "What's in the letter anyway?"

"As a matter of fact the chap I spoke of, Dick Soper, is planning a sort of Triathlon. All in aid of charity of course. He has asked me if we are interested in taking part because as it is its inaugural year he will probably need all the entries he can get. Hence I'm currently filling in a form to enter it!"

"So how come this Dick Soper and his proposed activities have managed to involve you? We don't even live in the area now!"

"Because he happens to be a friend of mine and I value his friendship. Friends usually try to help each other out if you've not noticed! Dick and I were at Uni together so anything I can do within my power to help him out I will. Besides which, all the sponsorship money that is raised is in a good cause, for the local hospice I believe!"

Steve frowned as he suddenly remember Pete and the friendship they had shared and he supposed that if the boot had been on the other foot he would have acted the same. "Fair enough if that is what you want to do but please don't involve me for I have had enough of that place!"

"Sorry but I have already involved you. You see one requires a partner for this Triathlon!"

"I've already said it's high time we moved on, the new job, remember? The firm seem to be very interested in the designs!"

"And that precludes us from taking part in this sponsorship event that is to be held one weekend? Come off it Steve. Are you sure you are not adopting this stance because you are frightened of facing reality?"

Steve Futton frowned. In truth Bob's words had managed to seek out a fertile breeding ground in his mind even if he did try to ignore this feeling for Steve was most certainly not a person who found it easy to admit he had been totally wrong in his initial premise. Still it was with something that resembled a bad grace that he finally took hold of the paper Bob was now holding out to him. He supposed that on this occasion he must concede that Bob was right. They did have a duty to support the local charitable cause as much as was within their power!

After politely enquiring how they had got on that day, Dick Soper ignored the fact that the ladies still considered it unfair that they had to finally compete against the men and instead appeared to lose interest for his thoughts at that time were focussing upon his own venture into the world of charitable causes. In this he had chosen the local hospice for that was a cause that everyone in the neighbourhood seemed to have an interest in and for their part the officials from this place had certainly no objections to his attempts to raise extra cash in their name, for after all every penny raised would go into providing extra comforts for all of their patients.

Initially Dick had to admit though that he was more than a little surprised by the reception he received. He had initially expected there to be few takers in this inaugural year especially considering all the other events scattered around the county at this time. Yet this event appeared to titillate the palates of the general populace of the area and consequently he found himself inundated with requests for entry forms. And the forms were subsequently returned, along with the required entry fee necessary to provide police support and the hire of the bicycles and other items needed, like a constant flood tide!

Consequently Stacey, having initially promised to help out, soon found that her spare time was rapidly filled both tabulating and entering the competitors names on the official list and then placing the competitors in pairs ready for the event. Perhaps Dick had after all listened to the complaints from the Sports day by the girls of having to compete against the men but his choice at pairing male and female together for these events puzzled her until he explained the philosophy behind it.

"For the last thing I want is some irate female complaining that the competition is unfair!"

Two of the forms that were returned however Dick sought out personally and then placed them to one side without mentioning the fact to Stacey, but what she didn't know was that Bob Eldon had not been slow in speaking to his friend once he had got Steve to agree to take part in the event. Consequently it was only on the evening prior to the appointed day that Dick made his grand declaration to his assistant.

"Sorry about this Stacey, but it now appears that we have one male too many in our pairing and consequently going spare. This person has paid his dues and therefore I am going to have to ask you if you will partner him?"

"That's ridiculous Dick, for at the last count we had one female competitor that was surplus to requirements!"

"Ah but then that was before I received a couple of late entries from two male competitors. One of them can obviously partner your spare girl but the other male still needs a companion I am afraid Stacey!"

"But I thought you said my task was to be at the start and finish of the contest and I was to be stationed at Ings?"

"Well with a little bit of persuasion I have managed to find someone who is willing to take that role over for you Stacey, which in turn will then leave you free to join in with the fun! Let's face it after all the hard work you have put into the organisation voluntarily you deserve to see something of the festivities which you would hardly see if you stayed at Ings!"

"But I thought I told you before Dick, contrary to your expectations I can't swim!" Now a tone of perplexion had entered into her voice

"For what the swimming part amounts to you can always use one of these!" He reached for one of the new foam swimming aids that the beginners generally used. "This will certainly help to keep you afloat and I'm sure that your partner, once he realises your limitations, will help to tow you over the stretch required. After all you are not in the event to win merely just to take part!"

"But will my so called partner feel the same way about things? Perhaps he will have other ideas. Maybe he will want to try to win!"

"Oh don't worry I will have a word with him. On the other hand I know your cycling is quite proficient and that you are already an avid walker on the fells when you get half a chance----!"

"In that case when will I meet this mysterious partner then?" Perhaps at the time she was nursing some idea of confronting the man with the truth even before it was time for them to set off.

"Oh you'll meet him on the day. He comes from out of town. I have already posted his number to him so all you have to do is to look out for someone wearing the number 839 which is the same number you have here for yourself!" He handed her the official registration number. "And for goodness sake stop worrying about it, after all it is all in a good cause. So all that you have to do is to try and enjoy yourself tomorrow!"

"But I haven't got a wet suit!" Again she raised her objections.

"Then you can take your pick. There are dozens that have been left at the Hall. You ought to know that for if I remember correctly you wore one before!"

Stacey's face seared a bright red in its colouration. This was perhaps because remembrance of that previous occasion came back to mind. And perhaps because of this she questioned no further. All she hoped for was that Dick had paired her with someone who was pretty tolerant.

Still her mind was taken away from such matters when that same night she received a phone call from her mother.

"Just ringing to see how you are our Stacey!"

"I'm absolutely fine Mum!" Now she wondered what else her mother had to impart for she knew full well that the woman had not phoned simply to enquire about her health without having some other ulterior motive. Fortunately she did not have to wait long before she received an answer to this.

"You'll never guess our Stacey, but that photograph that Meredith took of me, you know the one at the cottage when he had me posing in my dressing gown, the one he felt satisfied with; well I have just received a letter to say that it has won a competition. I never entered it in fact I knew nothing about it at all, so it appears that Meredith must have entered it in my name! I knew that you were being grossly unfair with what you said about the man's motives at the time, and this proves I was right. I always had faith in him and my faith appears to have paid off!"

Stacey almost choked at the other end of the line. "Look Mum, just how do you know all this?"

"Because I have the picture here in a newspaper in front of me saying that this photograph won the competition. Apparently he called it 'Serenity!' and according to the write up he has received a prize for it as well. I think the man has been very misjudged by a lot of people!"

"Please I beg you Mum, please have nothing to do with him again whatever excuse he makes!"

"Why shouldn't I? Anyway I don't suppose I will get the chance. He did tell me that he is planning on going to the States in the near future!"

"The question I would pose is whether the States is a big enough place for him to get lost in!"

"Now that is not very nice at all our Stacey. Sometimes I completely fail to understand you. So you said that the man was fined for taking pictures of those girls? Well I am sure that he meant them no harm for after all photography is his hobby and I didn't mind him taking photographs of me!"

By the time she replaced the receiver Stacey felt exhausted. There was certainly no arguing with her mother when she was in one of her moods. But the matter had helped to take her mind off the following day she supposed, if only to reveal afresh the shadowy nature of Meredith Drew and that was one matter that she felt she definitely wanted to leave in the past.

Neither could it be said that her state of apathy was lifted when she set eyes upon her companion for the Triathlon the following day. The first thing she had noticed was the number he was wearing on his tee shirt and that was even before she took a look at his face

Thus wearing her own badge of office she made her way to introduce herself.

"Hi, I'm Stacey Kershaw!" She had set off by trying to appear friendly but this was a look that simply froze upon her face when the man turned round to face her.

"I know full well who you are, you needn't worry about the niceties!" The voice that greeted her was clipped in its tones almost as if the speaker had found great difficulty in responding at all.

"What on earth are you doing here?"

"I could ask you the same but as for me I was badgered into taking part in this charade by someone I considered to be my friend!"

"Well I happen to be here because I just happened to help in the organisation of the event Mr Futton. Not that anyone cared to inform me that the spare man I was asked to leave my desk to accompany was you! Indeed if I had been informed that was the case then I am sure that my answer to the request for my services would have been totally different!"

At least her words seemed to have made some impression upon him for now he turned fully to face her speaking a trifle more ruefully in her direction almost indeed as if he now regretted his initial outburst. "Then if I might be permitted, can I ask how your cycling is?"

"My cycling is absolutely fine Mr Futton. As a matter of fact how is your own?"

"O.K. Stacey I guess you have made your point. But as we have both found ourselves in this fix I suppose we just might as well get on with it and try to bury our differences for the time being!" He started to walk towards where the bicycles were parked waiting now for her to pick up her own so that they could proceed to the checkpoint and

Stacey was left to marvel at the man's tenacity in wanting to carry on under the circumstances!

The ride down to Bowness she nevertheless found invigorating. Maybe it was the case that each push she made on those pedals appeared to relieve the tension she had felt and she became aware of his silent approval at her prowess as they arrived at the Marina. It was at this stage that she flashed a smile in his direction and then noting his expression. " You needn't get hold of the wrong idea, that was for Dick! I would hate the thought of him to be watching us and having a laugh at any obvious antagonism!"

Her expression nevertheless caused Steve to laugh, his earlier antagonism towards her seemingly to have dissipated. Still in all truth up until that moment in time Stacey had forgotten about the second part of the Triathlon that involved the swimming. Somewhat nervously she reached for her foam swim aid even though the new rapport she had now built up with Steve had wiped away her initial fear of this part of the competition.

"But what is that?" Now he definitely looked puzzled.

"Sorry, but you see I can't swim!" She looked at him through wide-open eyes as if she was pleading innocence to some hideous crime he believed that she must have committed.

"What do you mean, you can't swim? I saw you for myself on that Island remember. At the time I believe I am right in saying that you were half in and half out of a wet suit and if my memory serves me right the suit was wet at the time!"

"I have already told you, I can't swim Steve and I am afraid that I have always been the same. I have been told in the past that it is something to do with my sense of balance.

And the time you spotted me on the Island in that gear was immediately after I had been set up for a photo shoot!"

"Well I have to admit that I did notice that there was a camera involved!"

"And naturally you immediately jumped to the wrong conclusions!"

"You can hardly deny what I actually witnessed with my own eyes!"

"And if I said that I had been conned into the situation that day would you believe me? And if I also told you that I absolutely revile the one who was operating the camera at the time -------? Still what's the use? You obviously have made your own mind up to prejudge the situation and you don't believe me so I guess I am wasting my time in trying to protest my innocence!"

"Perhaps you need to take hold of your swim aid for I believe it is time we were in that Lake!" He picked up the aid and handed it back to her and she still gleaned nothing from his expression. "I suppose the only idea is for me to attempt to tow you round the Island then?"

Stacey nodded. No way was she now going to confess that even the thought of going into the Lake now made her shudder. Maybe however Steve did notice that her eyes were tightly shut when they finally ventured out into its depths for his tone towards her suddenly changed yet again.

"There's no way you will sink if you hang onto that foam thing and if you feel it helps then keep your eyes closed and leave the rest to me. I promise that I won't let anything happen to you. That is of course if you can bring yourself to trust me again?"

If she could trust him; that was a laugh! Hadn't she always trusted him even with her life? She felt his strong arms now around her gently guiding her through the water and just for a moment all her fears and doubts seemed to have disappeared! Feeling totally wrapped in protection Stacey felt now content to remain in this cocoon like shell and in truth wished with all of her heart that these moments could last forever.

Yet the change came quite suddenly. It came as she sensed that Steve was stopping in the water even before she was witness to his outburst.

"I just don't believe it!" Yet now even as he spoke his tone towards her had changed for there was a note of compassion in it. "Do you think you could possibly hang onto this float thing of yours just for a few minutes Stacey?"

She nodded as she opened her eyes and began to focus upon his line of vision. Ahead of them on the lake itself was a rowing boat. Although to spot a rowing boat on the lake could hardly be considered to be unusual this craft was transporting one certain person the sight of whom made her flesh begin to run cold. She was forced to watch now as Steve headed towards the back of the craft, not that she could have moved even if she had been able to swim, not at the sight of that person in such close proximity. In fact it hardly registered with her at the time that this creature had a camera in his hand. Yet she had little time to dwell upon the identity of this trespasser before Steve was glancing back in her direction. "Well, shall I?" He mouthed the words even as his hands moved towards the stern of the vessel still unobserved by the occupant of the craft. Realising his intention and ignoring the fact that such an action would result in her putting her nose in the water Stacey nodded her agreement gladly.

As such one rowing boat proved to be little match for the silent attacker who had by this time appeared to gain enough strength to tip the vessel onto its side. Yet it was the sight of Meredith Drew floundering and spluttering in the Lake that promoted Stacey to start to laugh, which, as it happened, proved to be a most unfortunate act on her part for the girl had momentarily forgotten all about the water she was in and the very act of laughing caused her to imbibe more of the aqueous fluid than was possibly good for her! And that possibly naturally enough under the circumstances was the last thing that Stacey remembered.

Stacey had no recollection of what happened next nor did she see the camera gently slide into the water and thence to the bottom of the Lake. Neither was she aware of Steve's desperate efforts to get her to the Island, or of his attempts at artificial respiration, for the next thing she knew was that she was on the shore and Steve was bending over her his face full of concern.

"Thank goodness!" Stacey could have sworn she heard his sigh of relief when she finally opened her eyes, wondering how on earth she had managed to get into this position. Not that she particularly minded for Steve was currently so close to her that she could stretch out her arms to touch him. It was as if all that had transpired in the past had now been totally swept away. "Do you realise woman you had me scared to death out there?" Yet he took hold of the hand she had stretched out and placed his lips upon it. "I should never have left you out there on your own for one minute. I should have known better. Damn it when I saw what condition you were in, when I realised that you had swallowed all that water and had passed out I died a thousand deaths thinking that I had lost you!"

Now a faint recall came to her mind as to what had happened. She tried to lift her head to look in the direction of the Lake and his arm immediately went around her shoulders to support her. From her position she could just make out the man who was still in the water and now clutching to the overturned boat. “Behold the walrus! He said that he wanted to go to the States well now he can start to swim there!” His voice sounded passionate as Steve took in the scene and Stacey soothed him her hand grasping his own. She glanced around her for a moment trying to depict where she actually was.

“You are on the Island!” He guessed what she was puzzling over and squeezed her hand reassuringly. “I brought you here in order to get some of that filthy water out of your system!” He didn’t add how desperate he had been at the time in case something irreparable had happened to her but now to Stacey the knowledge that she was back on the Island with him seemed to be almost like a fairy story. It was more than that for the look that emanated from her eyes now persuaded his lips to move even closer to her own. Closer that was until a fresh sound broke the silence, the sound of the warden’s boat heading in their direction. It was enough to make them both sit upright!

“Please don’t tell me –not again!” It was Steve who was the first to mouth the words as he spied the second figure in that craft. It was Keith Forsyth who was currently accompanying the warden on that vessel. “And they say that lightning doesn’t strike twice in the same place!” Now his words sounded more like a moan.

This time however the Inspector showed little interest of anyone on that Island for he had eyes only for the struggling Drew as the warden made some attempt to help the man onto his boat. “I thought that I had made it explicitly clear after the last time that I did not expect to see you in this neighbourhood again and furthermore if I did and more especially with a camera what the consequences were likely to be?" The Inspector had now drawn himself up to his full height and was currently behaving very much the policeman. "Well where is it then, hand the thing over!"

Perhaps Drew realised for the first time that he no longer had the camera with him and he gazed almost expectantly into the water almost as if he expected this mass to give back what it had already claimed. "I haven't got it!" His response was little more than a pathetic wail.

"You haven't got it. Well where is it then?"

"Down there!" The man motioned at the lapping wave that now almost appeared to be enjoying the situation. "Anyway I'm on my way to the States I'm not interested in photography anymore!" The words emerged through a girth of watery gurgles.

"You were on your way to the States in the middle of Lake Windermere in a rowing boat?" The response came with a total air of disbelief as to what the man was currently hearing. In actual fact it is perhaps fair to state that Keith Forsyth was completely flabbergasted. As a member of the police force the man had heard some tales but never one of this magnitude! It had actually been reported to him that Meredith Drew had been spotted in the neighbourhood with a camera, why that was the reason he had come here for himself to grab the man instead of leaving the matter to one of his juniors

"I –err--!" For once it appeared that Meredith Drew had nothing to say.

"I think that perhaps you had better come along with us to the police station and then maybe we will be able to point you in the right direction!" The Inspector still never gave the Island a second thought for he had now got the man that had been reported to be interfering in the running of the Triathlon. Now he merely waited until Meredith was firmly installed in the warden's craft before the engines were subsequently started and the craft and its three occupants made for the shore and out of view.

"Well what did you think of all that then?"

Steve eyed the girl seriously. In truth he had better things to think of now than Meredith Drew. "I think it might be a good idea if we got out of these wet suits so that they can dry off a little!" He was already unfastening his own and motioned her to do the same.

"But what about the Triathlon. They will be missing us, wondering where we have got to?"

"Then shall we let them continue wondering? Personally I don't give a damn about the competition for I know for certain that the best prize any man could hope to win is now facing me right here on this Island!" He was pulling her closer to him as he spoke whilst at the same time they moved towards the shelter of the trees that even now appeared to sport their finest bloom to mark their presence. "Never forget Stacey we have already made this our very own Island. This is a place with memories of the past and also a place that affords us hope for the future!"

The rest was silence as his lips met her own with the promise that they would be parted no more and Stacey simply sighed contentedly! After all there was little more to say and besides even if she had wanted to she doubted very much that she would get the opportunity. Not now!

★ ★ ★ ★

MY LOVE

With feeling
Tempo: 80

Words and Music by
J Steele 01253 591905

My Love

C G F G
Now you're here my love I wont let you go, un- til you prom- ise to be,
Bb G F Bb F
the on- ly love in my life Dear- est, the on- ly love for me.

OTHER NOVELS BY KATHLEEN STEELE

MARINA BAIXA ---------- Romance and Intrigue leads from the security of the Lake District to uncertainty in Spain!

ARMS OF GOLD --------- Following September 11th, what connection does the Lake at Windermere have with the Mediterranean around Majorca?

RADIANT VIBES----------- Pollution in the Irish Sea leads to strange findings and unusual relationships!

OASIS IN TIME --------- The location of those illusive weapons of mass destruction provides surprises!

PUT AND TAKE ---------- Casinos on the Fylde Coast? Would you like to take a chance?

THE UPPER CUT --------- Scurrilous behaviour on those Upper Reaches serves to create ripples that stir those once still waters!

THE PINK ROSE -------- The Border Folk's response to the proposed Regional Assemblies brings mayhem!

TWO FACED --------- Buying a computer should require a Government Health Warning!

ROUND AND ROUND --- Wind and Tide can make uneasy bedfellows in the struggle to find a new Power Source!

NEXT STOP PARADISE – Love and intrigue are stimulated on life's merry-go-round!

CHECK OUT -------- The development of the provincial Airport, heralds the development in human relationships

HIDE AND SEEK ------Hidden treasures require attention to detail, or else----!

LOST AND FOUND ------Where there's a will, there's a way!

FOOTLOOSE ----------When a positive charge meets a positive charge, then ------!

IN THE SHADOW OF THE STORM ------ Do the fish always behave like that or is this the calm before the storm?

DISTRACTION ---------- A hidden cell in the Lake District leads to a tempest of ferocity which contrasts sharply with the peace and tranquillity that place is noted for!

A LIGHTER SHADE OF PINK ----- A sequel as requested to THE PINK ROSE. Meet the various characters again as this time our friends attempt to extend their franchise into Cumbria!

THE HEART'S REFRAIN ------- The mists around those magical Islands reflect the mist that obscures Anton's vision.

THE TURN OF THE WHEEL -------Romance and fortune can be linked!

VENGEFUL RETURN----------------Two men and yet there can only ever be one boat! A sequel to MARINA BAIXA and NEXTSTOP PARADISE

NOT HERE--------------What is the connection between that house fire and those windmills out at sea?

THE RUN OF THE RABBIT-----Could the government really be conspiring to move that Nuclear Power Plant into the midst of the Langdale Valley?

STAR OF THE DAWN-------Can the star of early morning point the way to life's fulfilment?

SKETCH ME LOVE ---------The shrouding mist of those tranquil Islands serves to disguise a more sinister scheme to involve them in man's game!

SPLIT WIDE OPEN ---------Mischievous Pranks or mysterious happenings disturb the peace in the hamlet of FellBeck!

POWERFUL CIRCLES------- What is the connection between those ancient customs and the future?

BISPHAM BROOK ------- Could this be the case where such water comes to create mayhem or is there something more sinister behind the apparently innocent flow?

CRAB ISLAND --------The Atlantic Isles offer peace, tranquillity and dramatic scenery to the innocent holidaymaker yet one cannot but speculate that there is something more!

SHAP--------- The fells of North West England may provide a refuge but other things also transpire in a community that proves that they are not quite so isolated!

INNER TURMOIL----- Recovering from a trauma in her life Krisha is soon to find that the past often has a habit of catching up on one!

CRISP LIES THE TRACK -------Will the ashes of the past support the love of today?

THE VIPER'S BITE ----- Beware of reptiles with warm blood in their veins!

SOFTLY THE NIGHT ----- Rags to riches ------ perhaps?

VEIL OF SECRETS---------Can love survive the tide of deception?

If you have difficulty in obtaining any of the above copies contact 01253 591905